I0613144

William Caffyn

Seventy-One Not Out

William Caffyn

Seventy-One Not Out

ISBN/EAN: 9783741127434

Manufactured in Europe, USA, Canada, Australia, Japa

Cover: Foto ©Andreas Hilbeck / pixelio.de

Manufactured and distributed by brebook publishing software (www.brebook.com)

William Caffyn

Seventy-One Not Out

SEVENTY-ONE NOT OUT

THE

REMINISCENCES OF WILLIAM CAFFYN

MEMBER OF THE ALL ENGLAND AND UNITED ELEVENS,
OF THE SURREY COUNTY ELEVEN,
OF THE ANGLO-AMERICAN TEAM OF 1859,
AND OF THE ANGLO-AUSTRALIAN
TEAMS OF 1861 AND 1863

EDITED BY

"MID-ON"

WILLIAM BLACKWOOD AND SONS
EDINBURGH AND LONDON
MDCCCXCIX

All Rights reserved

TO

GENERAL SIR FREDERICK MARSHALL,

K.C.M.G.,

AN ARDENT AND GENEROUS SUPPORTER

OF THE NOBLE GAME OF

CRICKET.

PREFACE.

I HAVE lived to the age of seventy-one (hence the title of this work), and until some six months ago the writing of my reminiscences never occurred to me. Indeed had it not been for the fact of my meeting with an old friend—almost accidentally— the ensuing pages would never have been written. Like most cricketers, I have unfortunately kept comparatively few records of my long career. Luckily I am possessed of an excellent memory, and with this and the aid of many an old volume kindly lent to me by various gentlemen I have been able to complete my somewhat difficult task. I have given a short sketch of the state of the national game at the time of my birth; how I learnt both batting and bowling when a boy; have described my connection with Clarke's old All England Eleven, and afterwards with the United;

my visit with the first team to America in 1859;
with Stephenson's team to Australia in 1861, and
with Parr's more famous one in 1863; have given
an account of my seven years' residence in the
Antipodes, and the close of my career after my
return to England in 1871. That this record of
my career may prove interesting to lovers of our
grand old English game is my sincere hope and
desire.

W. CAFFYN.

April 1899.

THE Editor wishes to express his sincere thanks to those who have been kind enough to assist him in the compiling of this Work by the loan of pictures and other matters— Mr A. J. Gaston, Brighton; Messrs Cobbetts' Cricket Bat Co., London; Mr George Anderson, Aiskew, Yorkshire; Mr R. Daft, Radcliffe-on-Trent, &c.

CONTENTS.

ILLUSTRATIONS.

SEVENTY-ONE NOT OUT.

CHAPTER I.

CRICKET AT THE TIME OF MY BIRTH.

BETWEEN the year in which I was born (1828) and the one in which I first took part in first-class cricket (1849) our great national game underwent many changes and improvements. Not only did some mighty names arise in the cricket world during this period of twenty-one years, but the game received the assistance of an ally who sprang up at this time, and who has done more to popularise it than even any one who actually took part in it—the Locomotive. What a change in the history of cricket has been brought about by the railways! What a countless number of matches have they been responsible for! The increase in the popularity of our great game naturally dates from the time of the introduction of the locomotive. In 1828 there was

A

nothing of this kind. Matches were indeed few and far between. It was not only difficult for spectators to get from their homes to the scene of action, but difficult for players as well. We find many records in the old books of "absent o" being placed to the name of a player, owing to his not arriving in time to bat. I myself have had to walk many a mile before a day's cricket in my early years. At the time I was born cricket may be said to have flourished principally in the south of England, with the exception of a circle in the middle of the country comprising Leicester, Nottingham, and Sheffield. In the South, Kent and Sussex were the two most powerful counties, and the matches played between them created a vast amount of interest. Hampshire (the cradle of cricket) did not at this period possess such a monopoly of fine players as in former years, still they had a few first-rate men in their ranks notwithstanding.

When one considers the difficulties of travelling from place to place in those days, it will readily be seen that the arranging of an attractive season's programme in the few leading centres of cricket was no easy matter. When one county could not meet another on equal terms they played one or more "given men" from another county. This custom was kept up till a much later period. Another way of equalising two elevens was to "bar" a celebrated batsman or bowler. Up at Lord's an eleven of

LORD'S CRICKET-GROUND (1833).

From the Collection of Mr A. J. Gaston, Brighton.

right-handed players would oppose an eleven of left-handed ones. A team whose name all began with B on several occasions played the rest of England by way of variety.

The Sheffield *v.* Nottingham matches were very keenly contested, sometimes one side gaining a victory and sometimes another. One of the Nottingham players, it is said, used to ride on horseback to Sheffield before playing in this match, rising at an unearthly hour to do so. The Sheffield scorebook describes one of these contests as "a most disgraceful match," as the Nottingham umpire kept calling "No ball" whenever a straight one was bowled! — and it goes on to say that the Sheffielders were foolish to continue the game when they perceived such an unfair advantage was taken. It is needless to add that Nottingham won this match. Both of these famous towns possessed at this time some noted players. Old Clarke was the "General" of the Nottingham team, and was ably supported by such men as Tom Barker, George Jarvis, and Tom Heath. The most famous player amongst the Sheffielders was Tom Marsden, a left-handed bat with tremendous hitting powers. When playing for Sheffield against Nottingham and Leicester combined in 1826, he knocked up the huge total of 227. This would have been, indeed, a wonderful feat in those days against almost any side, but the fact that the score was obtained against Clarke and Barker's bowling renders it still more meritorious. In the year of which I write he made another large score against Nottingham — viz., 125. Tom represented England on several occasions, and also appeared for the left-handed against the right. His feats with bat and ball have been celebrated in poetry as well as in prose. He was a noted single-wicket player, and met many opponents, most of whom he defeated. Fuller Pilch, however, twice succeeded in lowering his colours. It must be remembered that although round-arm bowling had to a certain extent superseded underhand, the new fashion had many opponents, who would persist in describing it as "throwing," and declared that it had been the ruin of all scientific batting. At this time the bowler's hand had to be lower than his elbow when he delivered the ball, which must have been a cause of great trouble to the umpires. When a fast bowler was on, it must have been very difficult to detect what was fair and what unfair in this respect. No such things as batting-gloves or pads were used, and accidents to batsmen were naturally common enough. Bats made all in a piece were in vogue, cane handles scarcely being known, if at all. These unspliced bats I used myself many times in local cricket when a boy; and, strange to say, some of them drove very well. There were few enclosed grounds in England in those days where gate - money could be charged. Even at Nottingham the matches were played on a piece of ground called the "Forest," around which the old race-course ran, and which was free to all spectators.

The M.C.C. occupied the same position then as now in the cricket world, the numbers of the members and ground staff being of course small as compared with the present time. Sussex and Kent were very strong, as I have said before, although Pilch had not yet become qualified for the county of his adoption, nor had "glorious Alfred Mynn" yet appeared on the scene. Felix first appeared at Lord's in this year, but it was some years before his name figured in the Kent Eleven. Kent's palmy days were still in the future. Only one man is found in the ranks of the hop county in 1828 who in after-years was a member of "the grand old Kent Eleven" of Mynn's time—namely, E. G. Wenman. I refrain from giving a description of this and other great cricketers in this place, preferring to do so when I come to write of the time of my own introduction into first-class cricket.

Matches were played until very late in the season at this time. Some we find recorded as having taken place after the middle of October! Betting on matches was very common, and for years after I first came out the newspapers often quoted the betting at different stages of the game. It is needless for me to go over old ground and say how rough the wickets were at the time of which I write. Indeed, when we bear in mind that the wickets in most cases were prepared with a view of benefiting the bowlers rather than the batsmen and that there were no boundaries, we need not be surprised at the comparatively small scores which were made. Tall hats were the correct thing to wear when participating in a great match, although I believe that velvet caps, knee-breeches, and silk stockings were still sported by some. I have an old book giving the score of one match between Leicester and Sheffield which has a footnote quoted from 'Bell's Life' as follows: "It would be much better if H. Davis would appear in a cricketing dress instead of that of a sailor."

Playing a match for a large sum of money was very common, and single-wicket matches for sums of £10, £20, or even £50 were of frequent occurrence. As far as cricket in some of our remote villages goes, the contrast between 1828 and 1898 is not particularly striking. There were rough wickets then, and they are rough enough in all conscience now in many small places. Seventy years has not been long enough to impress the rustic mind with the fact that in order to play cricket correctly we must first take the trouble to have at least a fairly decent pitch to play on. We had plenty of cross-hitting and slogging in country matches years ago, and so we shall continue to have as long as we have bumpy unplayable

THE OLD TREE (Foreground), CASTLE FIELD GROUND, REIGATE, AGAINST
WHICH W. CAFFYN PLAYED CRICKET WHEN A BOY.

Photo. by Dann & Son, Red Hill.

wickets in our villages. If the members of some
of our village clubs would devote an evening or
two a week to the rolling and improving of their
wickets, instead of always wanting to practise their
batting and bowling, they would, I am quite sure,
find their cricket soon begin to improve. I myself
like to see a good innings played by a batsman on a
difficult wicket; but there is a vast difference between
a " *bad-good* " wicket (if I may use such an expression)
and one which has never received any preparation
whatever, and on which the veriest yokel is more
likely to slog up 20 runs than one of the leading
players of a county.

CHAPTER II.

MY CRICKET AS A BOY.

I WAS born at Reigate, where my father carried on, in conjunction with his younger brother Walter Caffyn, the business of a hairdresser. Besides this, both he and my uncle were musicians, and gave lessons on various instruments. My father played the violin and used to compose a little. He was bandmaster to the Reigate band, and when he died, while I was in Australia, representatives of no fewer than seven bands, from the Reigate district, attended his funeral. My uncle played on several instruments, including the violoncello and piccolo. My father was a fair all-round cricketer, but never attained to anything like first-class form. My uncle was a much better player. He was a good bat and excellent wicket-keeper.

They had a first-rate club at Reigate in the old days, and had some very good players as members, including R. Killick, an excellent medium - pace bowler and good bat, and Hentley, a fine all-round man and noted as a great thrower. Lanaway was another of our crack players, and old Tom Kent, an under-hand bowler, whom Fuller Pilch in his great innings played at Reigate for Town Malling, hit over a high tree, about which poor Tom was chaffed till his dying day. Pilch made 160 in the match. In his innings he hit one 6 (over the tree) and made also the following : 9 4's = 36, 12 3's = 36, and 18 2's = 36—rather a curious concidence. Lambert, the famous old-time Surrey player, played with Reigate before my day, but I remember his son playing with us. I knew the famous old cricketer, however. He used to work at the fuller's earth pits at Nutfield, and often came to my father's shop to be shaved. He used to tell me how, when a young man, he was wont to walk from Red Hill to London to play on Kennington Common. Alfred Mynn came to Reigate when I was a little boy to play for the Camberwell Clarence Club. I was taken to see the match, but can recollect little about it.

I was educated at the Reigate Grammar-School, and when about twelve years of age became passionately fond of cricket. We boys used at that time to chalk out three stumps on the trunk of a tree on the Castle Field cricket - ground and use that for a wicket. The tree is still standing at the present day. When I became a few years older, I played with the Reigate Club; and later still,

Mr Henry Lang used to engage Tom Lockyer, Sherman, and myself to play for Croydon against such clubs as the Islington Albion. It is to these matches that I am indebted for being brought into public notice. In 1848, when twenty years of age, I played for Mitcham against Brighton, and had the good fortune to get the great John Wisden's wicket in both innings, and did the same again once in the return at Brighton.

My uncle Walter only appeared at Lord's once, on which occasion he kept wicket for Surrey (who had the help of Fuller Pilch) against the M.C.C. William Clarke, the great slow bowler, came to stay at Reigate for a few months one year. Richard Killick told the great veteran that they had a very promising boy player in the town (meaning myself), and that he should like him to see me bat, so I had to go up to the cricket-ground and bat before the critical inspection of Old Clarke. What he thought of me then I never heard. Perhaps he expressed no opinion at the time to any one. During Clarke's stay at Reigate he called a committee meeting there of his newly formed All-England Eleven.

I distinctly remember a tall man coming into my father's shop one day, and asking if " W. Caffyn " was in. I replied that *I* was " W. Caffyn." The tall gentleman, who, it appeared, wanted to see my uncle Walter, replied, " Ah ! you're not big enough, my boy ! " Later in the day I found out

WILLIAM LAMBERT.

From the Collection of Mr A. J. Gaston, Brighton.

that the tall gentleman was no other than Fuller Pilch. I was brought up to the business of hair-dressing, as was also the case with my only brother, who stuck to business and never went in for cricket. My uncle left Reigate while I was a young man, and settled down in the same line at Dorking. Like my father and other members of my family, I was very fond of music, and learnt to play well on the cornet, and fairly so on the harp. My father was much averse to my taking up cricket as a profession, and when I was selected to play for the Players *v.* the Gentlemen of Surrey at the Oval, he refused point-blank to supply me with any money to get there. I managed to borrow half-a-crown, however, and received 10s. and my expenses for playing in the match, so I felt quite rich when I returned home. In 1849 I was engaged by Captain Alexander of the "Auberies" in Suffolk to play in all his matches. He was a very keen cricketer, and had a ground in the park at his house. Wisden had been engaged there the previous year, and had, I believe, spoken a good word for me to Captain Alexander. A number of capital matches were played at the Auberies, and very pleasant they were. The M.C.C. and the Zingari both visited us while I was there; and I thus had to encounter such players as F. W. Lillywhite, W. C. Morse, the Hon. Robert Grimston (who sometimes played with us as well as against us), the Hon. F. Ponsonby, and others.

Often while the gentlemen were at dinner in the evening I used to sit in the park and give them a solo on the cornet. While I was engaged at the Auberies I played with 18 of Suffolk against the famous All - England Eleven at Bury St Edmund's; and in this, to me, most important match, I had the misfortune to make a pair-of-spectacles! I was consoled somewhat with what I did with the ball, and obtained 5 wickets for 39 runs in the second innings of England. The wickets I took were those of Messrs A. Mynn, Guy, Pilch, Box, and Hillyer. Martingell, I remember, was missing from his hotel one evening, and Old Clarke for a joke sent the crier round Bury to call out, "Lost, a Martingell!" I was so proud of being seen with the All-England Eleven that, although I was not on their side, I rode to London with them on the coach when they went away, for no other purpose than to be in their society.

I never saw Captain Alexander from the time I left the Auberies, at the end of 1849, until I returned from Australia in 1871, when he came up and spoke to me at the Oval.

CHAPTER III.

My first appearance in first-class cricket was for the Players of Surrey *v.* the Gentlemen of Surrey, on June 4 and 5, 1849, at the Oval, this being the match before alluded to, when my father so strongly objected to my playing. The Gentlemen scored 79 and 94, and the Players 166 and 9 for no wickets, thus winning by 10 wickets. I made the top score of the match (46), Julius Cæsar being next with 30. I also took 2 wickets in the first innings and 1 in the second. Cæsar actually bowled 11 wides in this match! I next appeared for Surrey *v.* Sussex at the Oval a few weeks later. As this was my first inter-county match, I was, as will be understood, rather nervous. Surrey and Sussex had not met for nineteen years, and the present contest excited a great deal of interest. It turned out to be a very evenly fought game, Surrey being victorious by 15 runs. On this occasion I was unsuccessful with the bat, mak-

ing 1 in the first innings and a "duck" in the
second. I managed, however, to secure a couple
of wickets. I was not selected for the return
match, but played for Eleven Players of Surrey
v. Twenty Gentlemen of the County later in the
season. In this match I took 6 wickets in the
two innings, but only scored 1 run in my two attempts with the willow.

I did not take part in the Middlesex and Surrey
match at Lord's in the following year (which was
noticeable for the first appearance of Tom Lockyer
and Julius Cæsar on that classic ground), but represented my county in the return at the Oval,
and with considerable success, obtaining 7 not out
and 44 not out. This was the second or third
occasion on which I played against the famous
ex - Sussex bowler, William Lillywhite, who was
at this time residing in London, hence his appearance for Middlesex. The celebrated "Nonpareil,"
as he was called, had had a wonderful career, he
being at this time fifty-eight years old. He was
born in Sussex in 1792, and is best remembered
for his connection with that county. During part
of his career he kept an inn and owned a cricket-
ground at Brighton, on which many good matches
were played. Lillywhite is famous for being one
of the first of the round-arm bowlers, and was more
noted for a great number of years than any other
bowler for his accuracy of pitch. His pace at his

SURREY CRICKET-GROUND (1848).

FROM AN ENGRAVING BY C. ROSENBERG.

From the Collection of Mr A. J. Gaston, Brighton.

best was slow-medium, but at the time of which
I write he was considerably slower. His bowling
was not difficult if one played the game correctly,
but was most destructive to a batsman who tried
to take liberties with it. Lillywhite was a little
stout man with a most kindly expression of face.
The portrait of him in the old picture of " Sussex
v. Kent " is a wonderfully good one. He always
played in the regulation tall hat and never dis-
carded braces. His delivery was one of the easiest
I ever saw, and he never seemed to tire. He did
not appear at Lord's till he was thirty-five, but
contrived to play in first-class cricket for more
than a quarter of a century after that event.

My next great match was for Players of Surrey
v. Gentlemen of Surrey at the Oval (11 a side),
when I scored 40 and 15, and made my first appearance at Lord's shortly afterwards. I played for the
M.C.C. on that occasion in their match against
Sussex. I had very short notice given to me about
playing in this match, on the morning of which I
received a letter from Mr Dark (then the owner of
Lord's ground) asking me to become a member of
the staff there; and if I agreed to do so, I was to
let him know at once and then I could play in the
match M.C.C. v. Sussex on that day. I went at
once to see Mr Dark, and told him I could not
engage myself permanently to the M.C.C., but would
be pleased to play in the Sussex match which was

about to come off; and to this he agreed. My first achievement at "headquarters" was nothing wonderful. I made 17 and 8 runs and took no wickets. Sussex defeated us by 7 wickets, Wisden's bowling being very destructive.

I next opposed Sussex in their match *v*. Surrey at. the Oval, and succeeded in making the top score (73 run out). This innings was the means of making my place in first-class cricket secure. In the first innings of Sussex, George Picknell, going in late, made 9 not out, and on his side having to follow their innings, he was put in first, one of the Sussex gentlemen jokingly telling him that if he succeeded in carrying his bat *this* time he would give him a five-pound note. The result was that Picknell *did* carry his bat again for 27, being nearly half the total number of runs scored! I took part in a North and South match this year, which was one of the most remarkable I ever played in, made so by the fact of Wisden *bowling* all our wickets down in the second innings for 76 runs, of which I was top scorer with 24. Wisden's performance was indeed a remarkable one when one considers that it was a first-class match. Of course he was helped a good deal by the wicket, which was generally all in favour of the bowler at Lord's in those days. I may add that in our *first* innings we were all disposed of for 36 (W. Clarke taking 6 wickets), and here again I was the top scorer with 9 runs!

W. F. LILLYWHITE.

From a Painting by George Earp, in the Collection of Mr A. J. Gaston, Brighton.

The reason of Wisden's playing for the North was owing to his owning (in conjunction with George Parr) a cricket-ground at Leamington.

After this match I was engaged by William Clarke (always known as "Old Clarke") to play for his All-England Eleven at Cranbrook. A great and noble figure in the annals of our national game is this Old Clarke! a name to be honoured by all cricketers for all time. What an extraordinary and interesting career was his! We trace him playing for his native town of Nottingham as far back as the year 1816, getting many wickets in that district, and yet not appearing at Lord's till 1836, and not being chosen to represent the Players against the Gentlemen till he was forty-seven years of age! We hear of his opening the world-famous Trent Bridge ground at Nottingham in 1838, and originating the celebrated All-England Eleven eight years later. We trace him through a most successful ten years as manager of this organisation, obtaining a wicket with the last ball he ever bowled, and dying at the age of fifty-seven a few months afterwards. Whatever may have been the slight failings as a man of this truly great cricketer (and I am bound to confess that he and myself did not get on too smoothly together), on looking back across a space of nearly half a century one is lost in admiration of this glorious veteran, who did perhaps more than any one else ever has done to popularise our great national

B

game throughout the length and breadth of this country.

Clarke's bowling has been described by many writers. Who has not heard of his wonderful varieties of pitch and pace? of how he could make some balls get up from the pitch almost as if he had been bowling over-hand? or of his extraordinary skill in setting out his field? For the "reckoning up" of a batsman's weak play, and his bowling and setting out the field to take advantage of it, I firmly believe he excelled any bowler I ever saw. It has been suggested that Clarke owed a great deal of his success to the fact of his appearing in public late in life, at a time when round-arm bowling had become the fashion, and nearly all the great batsmen who had figured against under-hand had retired. There may be something in this, but it does not at all detract from the merit of Clarke as a bowler, for we find him, even at the close of his career, getting out regularly good batsmen who had opposed him on many occasions, and who must have become used to all his peculiarities. From what I have read of the old Hambledon Club bowlers I should be inclined to think that Clarke was an exact coun-terpart of some of them. He was more than an ordinary under-hand bowler, as under-hand bowling was understood both in my time and at the present. He was by no means a bad bat, being a hard and clean hitter; but he was greatly handicapped in this

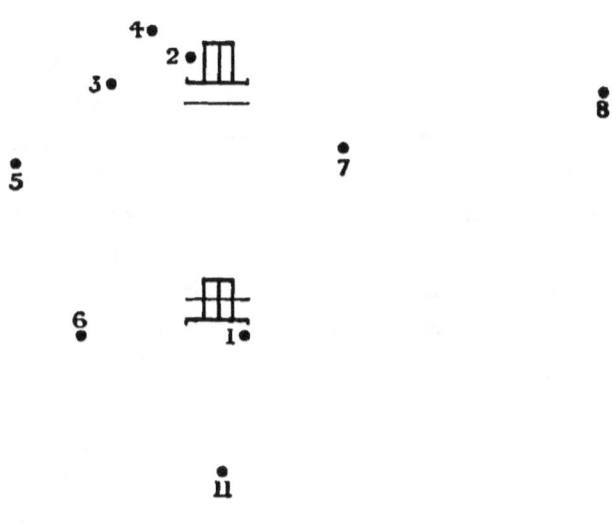

1. Bowler.
2. Wicket-keeper.
3. Point.
4. Short-slip.
5. Cover-point.
6. Mid-off.
7. Short-leg.
8. Long-leg.
9. Long-off.
10. Long-on.
11. Fielder placed for half-hit

department through having had the sight of his right eye destroyed at fives, at which game he excelled almost as much as at cricket. He would play this game for hours together, and made such hard work of it that when he leaned exhausted against the wall of the fives-court he often left a sort of silhouette of himself in perspiration on the wall! Clarke was above medium height and inclining to stoutness. He had a kind of half-grim, half-smiling expression, especially when he was getting wickets easily. The picture of him in the 'Cricket-Field' is an excellent one. He was always eager to get the best end of a wicket to bowl on. "I'll have this end, and you can have which you like!" he would say to his fellow-bowler. This remark has been lately attributed to Alfred Shaw, but Clarke was certainly the originator of it.

I have been told that when Clarke opened the Trent Bridge, and the chief matches at Nottingham were transferred there from the Forest, which was free of payment, the public were not at all pleased at having to part with their sixpences to witness a game, and that on the occasion of Clarke going in to bat in the opening match he was roundly hooted. The veteran had not been in long before he played a ball back to the bowler which grounded. The crowd, thinking he was out, cheered lustily. Clarke determined to play a joke on them, walked part of the way towards the pavilion, whereupon they cheered and hooted all the more; but the laugh was turned against them when the batsman quietly returned to the wicket and resumed his innings.

My first match as a member of the All-England Eleven was at Cranbrook, on July 18, 19, and 20, 1850, against Kent, on which occasion I scored 9 and 12. This match was unfinished owing to rain. The following week saw me at Lord's first representing the Players *v.* the Gentlemen, whom we defeated at an innings. George Parr made the top score of the match, playing a very fine innings of 65. The Gentlemen scored 42 and 58, there being only one double-figure score in each of their innings —viz., Mr Felix 22, and in their second venture Mr A. Mynn 12. Clarke and Wisden were responsible for all the wickets, and bowled unchanged throughout the match. Two famous bowlers played for the Gentlemen—Sir F. Bathurst and Mr Harvey Fellows. Sir Frederick was a big powerfully built man of 6 feet or more, and had for years been noted for his fast bowling, being for some years a tower of strength to the Gentlemen in this department of the game. He bowled very straight as a rule, and had a remarkably low delivery. As a bat he belonged to the slogging order. Mr Fellows was without doubt the fastest bowler the Gentlemen ever possessed, in my opinion. He was a fairly tall man, weighing over 15 stone, and carried himself erect as a dart. He too had a very low delivery, which was puzzling to a batsman. His pace was terrific, and many were afraid to stand up to him: of course the wickets of those days greatly assisted him. With so low a delivery it would be impossible for a bowler to give much variety to his balls, which would be played with greater ease by a batsman in full practice on present "billiard-table" wickets.

My next match was *against* the All-England for fourteen of Surrey at the Oval, which was unfinished owing to rain.

The next week I journeyed down to Newark with the All-England to play twenty-two of Newark, who beat us by one wicket. Parr played a fine innings of 56 here out of a total of 92, there not being another double figure made. Here I first encountered the Tinleys—Frank and Cris. Each of them got a fair number of wickets against us. Cris at this period had not taken to lobs, but bowled fast—very fast— round-arm. This match was a most enjoyable one, as we were most hospitably entertained. We went from Newark to Derby, where we had another un- finished game, and where I was top scorer with 28. The following three days we had a North and South match at Leamington, and here I first saw that accomplished player Joe Guy make a large score, —viz., 98 (unfortunately run out). Guy possessed a beautiful style, and was chiefly distinguished for his strong defence. He was a fine bat against fast bowling, but was rather too fast-footed to do justice

to slow.   His style of play was forward, like that of
Pilch.   Guy was a straight, well-proportioned man,
slightly over medium height.   He filled the post
of long-stop very cleverly about the time of which
I write.

My next match was England *v.* Kent at Canterbury.   This was a close match, England obtaining
the victory by 15 runs.   For Kent the two top
scorers in both innings were Fuller Pilch and E.
G. Wenman.   I had often seen these two famous
batsmen play before, but never saw them to better
advantage than on this occasion, although they were
now both getting towards the end of their career.
There have been few, in my opinion, to surpass
Pilch as a batsman with style and effect combined.
His attitude at the wicket was perfect, keeping both
legs very straight.   The portrait in the picture of
the Sussex and Kent match best represents him at
the wicket: the one in the 'Cricket-Field' makes
him appear to stand too wide.   He played forward
a great deal, and his bat went down the wicket like
the pendulum of a clock.   He not only utilised his
forward play for defensive purposes, but scored from
it very frequently as well.   His best hit was one in
front of cover-point.   I do not think any one ever
excelled him in this stroke.   He was a powerful
driver when the ball came to him, but did not
leave his ground much.   He twice defeated Tom
Marsden for the Championship of England at single

E. G. WENMAN.

From the Collection of Mr A. J. Gaston, Brighton.

wicket, scoring 100 runs in one of his innings against the Sheffield crack. Pilch was a Norfolk man by birth, but receiving £100 a-year to live in Kent, he took up his abode there in 1835. He was a tall man, just over 6 feet, and was powerfully made. He was exceedingly good tempered, and very kind to all young players with whom he came in contact. He was a remarkably quiet man, with no conversation, and seemed never happier than when behind a churchwarden pipe, all by himself. Wenman was a tall man, about Pilch's height, but more bulky. After Pilch he was undoubtedly at one time the best batsman in the country; although not possessing Pilch's elegant style, still he was by no means a clumsy bat. He played back much more than most play-ers of his day. For hitting all round the wicket, I think he was even slightly superior to Pilch. He was also a first-rate wicket-keeper. He played for more than a quarter of a century for the famous Kent Eleven.

I played one more match with the All-England in 1850, and that was all. In the following year I played in every match. I think I took part in over forty matches this season, which was a very long one, our last match being played at Brighton on the 13th, 14th, and 16th (Sunday intervening) of October.

It took me a long time to get used to batting

against twenty-two in the field, and I soon found out that I must alter my play somewhat to score many runs. For a time I did not trouble to hit much, but went in more for placing balls for one or two, and always tried to keep the ball on the ground. I used to cut a great deal, as I always did in eleven-a-side matches, and scored a great many runs in this way, notwithstanding that the off-side was generally well packed with fielders for me. Playing so many matches and travelling so much was a great strain on one's constitution. We often had to travel all night and begin play at eleven o'clock on the morning we arrived at our place of destination, and I have often been so tired that I have almost fallen asleep while in the field. Clarke used to give us £4 a match at this time for the All-England matches. The All-England Eleven in 1851 was generally selected from the following players: W. Clarke, J. Guy, J. Cæsar, G. Parr, W. Caffyn, G. Anderson, J. Grundy, T. Box, J. Wisden, W. Hillyer, Mr Felix, Mr A. Mynn, W. Martingell, F. Pilch, and Daniel Day.

Bob Thoms, the now celebrated umpire, played with us a few times at the beginning of the season. He was not very successful with the bat, but was a very fine field. "Bob" was noted as a runner, and could give any of the eleven a start at 100 yards.

Daniel Day the Surrey player was a good "fast-medium" bowler, coming quick off the pitch with a slight break from leg.

Jemmy Dean of Sussex was about the finest long-stop in England in his day ("would seldom grant a bye," as the poem says of him), and was noted as a fast bowler at first and afterwards as a medium. He was a little man and very stout in his latter days. He had a queer shambling kind of walk, and indeed his appearance altogether was as unlike one's idea of a cricketer as could well be imagined. The picture of him in the All - England Eleven, as represented by Mr Felix, is a good likeness, but makes him appear absurdly small as compared with some of the other players. Jemmy did great things for Sussex, and was engaged, too, for many years at Lord's.

A splendid bowler was the famous Billy Hillyer of the Kent Eleven, being one of the very best of the early round-arm bowlers. He bowled medium pace, and had a big break from the leg. He obtained many wickets in the slips by bowling on, or just outside the off stumps, and making the ball "go away." I used to find him terribly difficult, as his ball went off the pitch so quickly, and one was very often too late for him when trying to cut near the wicket, as I generally used to do. His ball had a decided curl in the air. He could make the ball "get up," too, more than most bowlers of his time. His many feats with the ball are far too numerous to mention here. He had a remarkably easy delivery, as easy as that of Alfred Shaw of later times, and could bowl all day. A benefit match, England *v.* Eighteen Veterans, was played for him at the Oval in 1858 (a few years after his retirement), which brought him in nearly £400. This match had never been played before, and created a great amount of interest. England scored 196, G. Parr making 56 top score of the match, and the Veterans 82 and 164. Martingell made top score for the Veterans, 21, and Mr Mynn and Guy came next with 19 each. Mr Mynn hit a 5, a very fine drive, I recollect. Hillyer was a middle-sized, well-made man. He went by the nickname of "Topper." Towards the latter part of his time he was a martyr to rheumatics and gout in the feet, and sometimes could hardly bear any one to come near him for fear they should tread on his toes. Sam Parr, an elder brother of George, who played with us sometimes, and who was an inveterate practical joker, used to plague the life out of the old chap. Sometimes between the innings Sam would get hold of the ball, and coming near Hillyer, would, while engaging him in conversation, suddenly dash the ball on the ground within a few inches of his feet, causing poor "Billy" to jump nearly out of his skin. Another trick Sam was fond of playing off on him was to stick a lot of railway

W. CLARKE.

From the Collection of Mr A. J. Gaston, Brighton.

FULLER PILCH.

From the Collection of Mr A. J. Gaston, Brighton.

JAMES DEAN.

From the Collection of Mr A. J. Gaston, Brighton.

W. HILLYER.

From the Collection of Mr A. J. Gaston, Brighton.

labels all over his bat. On one occasion it is related that a scorer in one of the All - England matches spelt "Billy's" name with an *i* instead of a *y;* and the error appeared in the local paper after the first day's play. "Billy," on seeing this, went to the scorer as soon as he arrived on the ground and told him he had got his name spelt wrong in the book. "I don't think so," said the scorer. "I tell you, you have," "Billy" retorted, impatiently. "Well," exclaimed the scorer, "if a *haitch* and a *hi* and a *hel* and a *hel* and a *hi* and a *he* and a *har* doesn't spell 'Illyer, I don't know what will!"

William Martingell was an excellent "fast-medium" bowler, though he used, I thought, to allow rather too much for his leg-break, and was often a good deal punished by such players as George Parr in consequence. He was also a very decent bat against fast bowling, but was generally too eager to hit when playing against slow. He was by birth a Surrey man, but received a salary for residing in Kent, which was the great centre of cricket at that time. "Billy" was a fine judge of the game, and made an excellent coach. A story used to be told of how Martingell once managed to back a loser in a big race. He had an excellent tip about a horse a month or so before the race was to come off, and forthwith put some money on it. A week later he had another tip about another horse, and was also told that a third one would be very dangerous. So "Billy" had a little on each, and on yet *another* one which he rather fancied *himself.* As he journeyed about the country he heard other people's opinion as to what had a good chance of pulling the race off, and backed *their* fancy as well. By the time the race came off Billy found that out of the twenty-two runners he had backed twenty-one of them; so that his chagrin can well be imagined when the twenty-second horse — which he had allowed to "run loose" — won fairly easily! I can by no means vouch for the truth of the story, but I do know that it was always related when any one wanted to make old "Billy" angry.

Tom Box, the wicket-keeper for Sussex, and for a good many years for the England Eleven as well, was in his day probably the best that had yet appeared. Like most of the wicket-keepers of that time, he "set himself" to look after the off-balls, and allowed the leg ones, to a great extent, to look after themselves. Indeed, with the exception of Wenman, I don't think there was any wicket-keeper particularly noted for taking balls on the leg side before the advent of Tom Lockyer. Box, like all the old wicket-keepers, stood nearly upright, though close to the wicket. Besides being so fine a wicket-keeper, he was also a splendid bat, with a fine upright style, and many large scores are to be found attached to his name in the old matches.

Box began his career early and played for nearly thirty years. He was at one time proprietor of the famous Brunswick cricket-ground at Brighton, and also kept the Egremont Hotel in that town. He was a smart-looking man, below the middle size, with a florid complexion and light hair and whiskers. Poor "Tom" died with awful suddenness while working the telegraph in the Middlesex and Notts match at Prince's ground in 1876, the game being abandoned in consequence of this sad event, I believe.

Mr N. Felix (whose real name was Wanostrocht), like so many of the celebrated old-time cricketers, did not come into notice till comparatively late in life. Born in Surrey and residing in Kent, his name was familiar in both counties. It is as a member of the far-famed old Kent Eleven that he is best known. He was a beautiful bat (left hand), being especially noted for his brilliant cutting, more particularly in the direction of cover-point (with the right leg in his case advanced). Mr Felix was undoubtedly one of the very finest exponents of this stroke ever seen. I have seen no batsman from W. G. Grace downwards who could excel him in this particular. Being a left-handed bat, he had ample opportunities of indulging in this favourite hit of his, as most of the bowlers in those days did not change sides of the wicket when bowling to a left-handed man; and as they bowled round the wicket in most cases with a break from leg, a batsman like Felix had only to wait for a slightly over-tossed ball to punish it severely. He once told me that he learnt this stroke by suspending a ball from the ceiling with a piece of string and hitting it with a bat as it swung towards him (an old-fashioned method practised by many enthusiasts anxious to improve their batting in those days). The defensive play of Mr Felix was of the "forward" order. He made many large scores, and was of great assistance to the Gentlemen in their matches against the Players. He was also a good left under-hand bowler. He played Mr A. Mynn twice for the Championship of England at single wicket, but was defeated on each occasion. It is to this celebrated cricketer that we owe the invention of the modern batting-gloves. He is also said to have been the inventor of the catapulta. For many years he kept a school at Blackheath. He was an excellent artist. The picture of the old All-England Eleven (of about 1850) was done by him. He was a most agreeable man, and devoted a great deal of time to the study and improvement of cricket during the whole of his career. He was a little man, and rather stout.

Of his friend and fellow-player, the great Alfred Mynn, perhaps I can say no more than has been said already. Mr Mynn was without doubt the most popular cricketer of his day. When I played

THOMAS BOX

From the Collection of Mr A. J. Gaston, Brighton.

with him towards the end of his career he was
always the centre of attraction on every cricket-
field, and the spectators would crowd about him
when he walked round the ground like flies round
a honey-pot. His immense popularity threw even
the superior abilities of Pilch and Parr into the
shade. He was beloved by all sorts and conditions
of men, and he in return seemed to think kindly
of every one. He had an affectionate regard for
his old fellow-players who had fought shoulder to
shoulder with him through his brilliant career, and
there are many players who were just becoming
known to him in his latter days who could bear
witness to the kindness and encouragement he
showed to them. As a bowler he was very fast,
with a most stately delivery, bowling level with
his shoulder. As a batsman he was a fine powerful hitter. He played a driving game, setting
himself for this and not cutting much. Against
fast bowling he was magnificent, and against slow
of an inferior quality he was a great punisher.
Against the best slow bowling of the day he did
not show to so much advantage. He had not that
variety of play which enables a batsman to deal with
this sort of bowling to the best advantage. His
pluck and gameness were something wonderful, and
were shown in every department of the game. He
had an iron constitution which nothing seemed to
upset. He liked good living, and seemed especially

to enjoy his supper. I have often seen him eat a
hearty supper of cold pork and retire to bed almost
directly afterwards! A curious custom of his was
taking a tankard of light bitter beer to bed with
him to drink during the night. "My boy," he once
said to me when he saw me taking a cup of tea,
"beef and beer are the things to play cricket on!"
He was a fine single-wicket player, and was never
beaten. His batting and bowling were both emin-
ently adapted for success at single wicket, as he
got nearly all his runs in front of the wicket, and
his bowling was rather on the "short" side and
not easy to drive. His height was 6 feet 1 and his
weight 20 stone.

John Wisden, one of the best all-round cricketers
I ever saw, was in my young days one of the most
familiar figures on a first-class cricket-field. He
was for years one of the mainstays of Sussex, and
did an immense deal of bowling for the All-England
Eleven in its early days, and afterwards became
secretary to the United Eleven at its formation in
1852. Wisden was the best fast bowler I ever saw
for so small a man. His height was said to be
5 feet 4½ inches, but I should not think he stood
even as high as that. When I knew him he would
weigh perhaps a little under 10 stone. He was a
remarkably good-tempered little fellow, with a most
comical expression of face. He was a grand bowler,
with, I think, the easiest delivery I ever saw. In

"FELIX" (MR NICHOLAS WANOSTROCHT).

From the Collection of Mr A. J. Gaston, Brighton.

the days when the bowler was compelled to bowl level with the shoulder, Wisden was always spoken of as being remarkably "fair." Indeed I think he never gave the umpire any trouble as to the doubt-fulness of his delivery at any time. He had a great command of "pitch," was very straight, and likely to slick a batsman out even on a good wicket, how-ever well set, as his ball came in quick off the pitch, and he bowled many shooters. The most remarkable performance he ever did with the ball was the one already alluded to in the North and South match, where he clean bowled all 10 wickets of the South. As a batsman he was first-rate. He played with a beautifully straight bat, which he appeared to hold very lightly, but nevertheless he could hit hard and clean. In 1849 he scored exactly 100 in the Sussex and Kent match, and in 1855 his score of 148 for Sussex v. Yorkshire was much talked about. There is no doubt that if Wisden had had less bowling to do he would have been still more famous as a batsman. He was clever at making the old-fashioned "draw" between the right leg and the wicket. For so good a batsman he appears to have earned "spectacles" a great number of times. He played the famous Tom Sherman three times at single wicket, and defeated him on each occasion, and once when playing with three others at single wicket he bowled out his four opponents for no runs. He was once the victim of a bad piece of

c

luck when playing for England *v.* Sixteen of Oxford University. Wisden was caught off a no-ball on this occasion, and not having heard it "called" was on his way to the pavilion and had his wicket put down. Poor "Johnny" was terribly chaffed about this for a long time afterwards. In 1848 he and George Parr became joint proprietors of a ground at Leamington, which they had laid down, and on which many good matches were played. "George" always bought the horses which were required to do the rolling and mowing, and some curious specimens they were. Parr used to tell people that he always liked to give about "fifty" for one of these animals (meaning shillings!). Wisden was one of the first of the All-England players who quarrelled with Clarke, and when the United was formed he became its secretary. He fulfilled this office in a most efficient manner, being always a particularly keen man of business. He was a remarkably good pedestrian, and he and I have had many a long walk together in the winter season. He was also very fond of a day's shooting.

The name of James Grundy deserves to be bracketed with that of Wisden as an all-round man. For many years he did great execution both with bat and ball. He was one of the best-plucked men I ever saw on a cricket-field, and could generally rise to the occasion, either to keep runs down or to obtain them, when necessity re-

GENERAL PLAN OF FIELD FOR MR ALFRED MYNN'S FAST BOWLING.

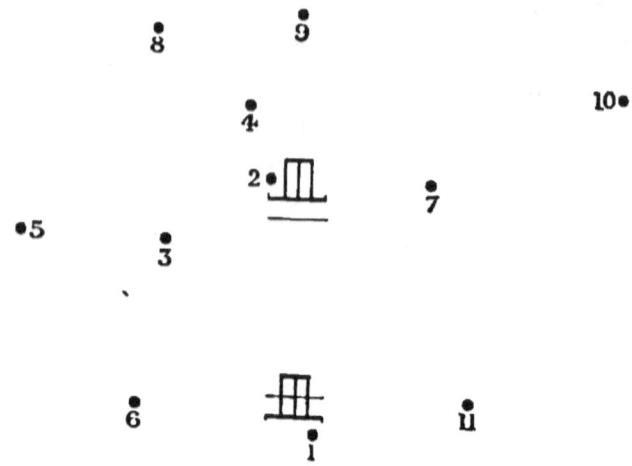

It will be noticed that point is placed much more forward, and cover-point more square, than is the case at the present day when a fast bowler is on.

1. Bowler.	5. Cover-point.	9. Long-stop.
2. Wicket-keeper.	6. Mid-off.	10. Long-leg.
3. Point.	7. Short-leg.	11. Mid-on.
4. Short-slip.	8. Long-slip.	

quired. His bowling may be described as fast medium, with just a *little* break-back. He bowled very straight, and could drop the ball on a cheese-plate all day if so minded. Indeed, this was the class of bowlers to which he belonged. He bowled "at the wicket," always endeavouring to beat the batsman *himself*, and not bowling for catches; so it may easily be imagined how successful he was when anything peculiar in the ground helped him. I sometimes used to think he did not "feed" the batsman enough, and would tell him to give him one to hit occasionally, to which Jemmy invariably replied, "Nay, I shan't! I shall gi'e him a *good* 'un: if he wants to hit me let him come and do it!" He possessed a nice easy delivery, and never tired. As a batsman he had excellent defence, and being always very cool and collected, could often keep his wicket up "till further orders," when required to do so. He rendered great service to his county (Notts) for many years, as indeed he did for all the elevens which he represented. Like Palmer the great Australian cricketer, Grundy was for some time much more successful as a bowler than as a bat; but after a time, like the celebrated Australian, he improved as a batsman almost beyond recognition. Grundy was engaged at Lord's in 1851, and remained there for very many seasons. He was about the middle height, and through his erect carriage looked taller than he really was. He was a strongly built man, had a fresh colour, and always looked "spick and span" when in the field. He was exceedingly good company, and always ready with a song when called upon.

The word "brilliant" may be used very appropriately when describing the batting of my fellow-countyman Julius Cæsar. He was one of those hard clean hitters whom it is so delightful to watch. Although only about 5 feet 7 inches, "Julie" was very powerfully made. He may be described as "a big man in little room." He had a wonderful knack of timing the ball, which had a great deal to do with his success as a batsman. He was not much of a cutter,—those who set themselves for a driving game seldom are,—still he had a good hard cut past cover-point, which he often made use of. The on-drive was his best hit, and he was also noted as a leg-hitter. He appeared at Lord's in 1850, and I believe was engaged by Clarke for the All-England Eleven about the end of the following year, with which he remained until Clarke's death, and continued to play under the captaincy of George Parr, when he succeeded to Clarke's office. "Julie" was a first-rate boxer, and exceedingly fond of the noble art. He was of a peculiarly nervous temperament, and, laughable as it may appear, was always afraid of sleeping in a room by himself at a strange hotel, for fear some one might have died in it at some time or other. When playing, I have frequently shared a double-bedded room with him, and when sound asleep have often been awoke by his calling out that he was sure the house was on fire! Poor "Julie" seemed to have a fixed idea that every hotel *must* be burnt down sooner or later, and always refused to be put higher than the first floor. I shall never forget once sharing the same room with him at Hereford. The streets were very quiet, it being almost morning. All at once I could hear a drunken man come staggering along, bawling something out by way of a song, as I thought. "Julie," however, who was half asleep, felt sure that some one was calling out "Fire!" He at once called out to me, but I pretended to be asleep. "Billy, the confounded place is on fire; can't you hear 'em calling out?" he shouted. I only replied by a feeble snore. "Julie" could stand it no longer, but jumped out of bed, rang the bell violently, rousing the whole house, calling me a fool all the time, and asking me if I wanted to be burnt to death! Another peculiar fancy of "Julie's" was, that whenever he happened to get a small score, he thought that he should at once be left out of the Surrey Eleven. He was very confident that this would happen just before he played his magnificent innings of 111 for Surrey v. Cambridgeshire in 1862. Of course nothing was further from the committee's thoughts than leaving him out; but, as I said before, "Julie" was of a very peculiar temperament, always

being very elated when successful and terribly de-
jected after getting a small score.   Both "Julie"
and George Parr used to make a point of taking a
certain amount of liquor before retiring to rest when
they were in the thick of the cricket season.   Once,
it is said, they each agreed to lessen the quantity by
half.   They were both unsuccessful with the bat on
the following day, but they nevertheless agreed to
give their new *régime* another trial on the following
night; but, alas! the result was the same as on
the previous day—viz., small scores in both cases.
"George," said "Julie" to the famous leg-hitter as
he came into the pavilion without having troubled
the scorer, "it is evident that we must take in our
'usual quantity' to-night."   "Right you are, my
lad!" promptly replied "George"; "and we'll make
up for what we went short of last night and night
before as well!"   "Julie" was a very good shot and
fond of the sport, but he had a sad experience on
one occasion.   When out shooting he happened to
accidentally let off his gun in getting over a stile or
through a hedge, and one of the keepers who was
with the party was shot dead.   Poor "Julie" was
in a terrible way, and I believe his mind never got
over the shock till the day of his death.   Cæsar was
a native of Godalming, where I believe his family
had long resided.   There is a match on record where
twelve Cæsars played another eleven at the time when
Julius was a young man.   It is many years now since

GEORGE ANDERSON.

From Photo by J. Yeoman, Bedale.

poor "Julie" passed away, but his name still lives in his native county and in many a little out-of-the-way corner in various parts of England which he visited with the All-England Eleven. He had a brother Fred, a very fair player, a great big strong fellow, who for some years officiated as turnkey in one of the London jails.

I now come to the two Georges—Anderson and Parr. The former has been truly described by Mr Daft as "one of the finest men Yorkshire ever produced." Anderson was in my earlier days one of the greatest batsmen who hailed from the "shire of broad acres." Anderson is best remembered as a great hitter; but he had an excellent defence as well, and when set it was indeed a treat to see him bat. He was one of the best men I ever saw at playing a hitting game on a sticky wicket. Often when others could do nothing on a pitch of this description, "George" would go in and make a good score. I once remember his knocking up 43 out of a total of 80 odd (10 of which were extras) when we played an All-England match against twenty-two at Manchester in 1854, the next highest score being 8 on the side of All-England. Box, by the way, was hurt in this match, and as H. H. Stephenson was required to bowl, the task of wicket-keeper devolved upon myself. I was very glad when the game was over, as we had nothing to give away. We won by 36 runs eventually. I managed to stump one and catch another, but was in mortal fear of "making a hash of it," especially when Old Clarke was bowling, in which case I should undoubtedly have had a good blowing up from him. George Anderson, too, once made 32 out of a total of 66 (9 of which were extras) for All-England v. Twenty-two of Reading, Willsher and H. H. Stephenson being next highest scorers with 5 each! On another occasion he scored 25 out of 46 at Lincoln, Daft being the next highest with 6! I could quote many more instances of how this great batsman has "come off" when others were unable to score, but the few I have mentioned will serve to show what an invaluable man he was on a side. What a fine strapping fellow "George" was, to be sure! Six feet high in his stockings. He had quite a military appearance when in ordinary dress. He nearly always wore a suit of "heather mixture." I saw a gentleman only the other day dressed in this kind of tweed, and the figure of George Anderson as he was forty years ago rose before my mind immediately. I look on his portrait as I write, and feel that it is impossible to think of him as an old man. "George" and myself are now the only survivors of Clarke's Famous Eleven. "George" was liked by everybody. I do not think he ever made an enemy in his life. I should very much like to see him once again, but as we live so far apart I fear my wish will not now be realised in this world.

CHAPTER IV.

THE LION OF THE NORTH.

I HAVE now come to one of the best-known names in the whole history of cricket. In 1845 a match was played at Lord's, "North *v.* M.C.C., with Pilch." In the ranks of the North there appeared a young player from Nottinghamshire, only just nineteen years of age, named George Parr. He was said to have been discovered at his native village of Radcliffe-on-Trent by William Clarke in the previous year. Clarke had given him a trial in a match got up by himself on the newly formed Trent Bridge ground, "Players of Notts *v.* Gentlemen of the County, with Mynn, Pilch, Box, Dean, and Hillyer." Young Parr had played with the Players and had made a creditable score of 20 against the bowling of Mynn and Hillyer, so on the strength of this performance, and on his reputation in village matches, he appeared at Lord's on the present occasion. The young player, who was to become a world's wonder in after-years, made one run only in his first match at

Lord's. There is, I am told, an implicit belief existing in his native village that George Parr scored heavily in this match, the story going that when he got to Lord's some of Clarke's London friends told him that he had brought the "wrong Parr" with him (they expecting to see Butler Parr, another noted Notts player, but not related to "George"), and that Clarke replied that they would soon see whether it was the *wrong* Parr or not after he had been in a bit, and that "George" fulfilled this prediction by making a big score. But, alas! for the truth of the story, the score-book declares that "George" had only one innings and was bowled by Hillyer for one run. Parr's only other feat worth recording in 1845 is his making 31 and 17—being not out in both innings —for his County *v.* Kent. In June of the following year he again appeared at Lord's in a match played in honour of Mr Felix. The match was Pilch's side *v.* Mr Felix's side. Parr played for the latter and scored 11 and 59, the second being the top score of the match. This, I have heard, was a very fine innings, obtained as it was against the bowling of Hillyer, Martingell, Sewell senior, and the veteran Lillywhite. "George" appeared three times more at Lord's in 1846—once for the North *v.* M.C.C., again for England *v.* Kent, and finally for the Players against the Gentlemen; but in none of these matches was he very successful. His first Gentlemen and Players match was a remarkable one. The

GEORGE PARR.

From the Collection of Mr A. J. Gaston, Brighton.

Gentlemen required 2 runs to win when Mr Walter Mynn came in last man, and the runs were obtained amidst the greatest excitement. The betting had been at the start 2 to 1 on the Players. Though Parr played in several other matches of importance this season, he did nothing wonderful except making 51 for a mixed team of Notts Gentlemen and Players (with Mr A. Mynn given) v. England at Southwell. A violent cold caught in this match prevented him from taking part in the first three All - England matches started by Clarke this year. These first three matches played by this afterwards famous organisation were at Sheffield (where they were defeated) and at Manchester and Leeds, where they won. The following year Clarke made a good number of these matches and Parr played in them, and his performances in these contests placed him in the front rank of English batsmen. In his first match with the All-England he scored 100 v. twenty-two of Leicester, and followed this up by making 78 not out at York v. eighteen, and 64 at Manchester, also against eighteen in the field,—being top scorer of the match each time. He scored consistently well in 1848; and I can well recollect that about this time he was talked of as the man who would succeed Pilch as the first batsman in England. Young men, as is generally the case in such instances, already began to declare that the Nottingham man was even now a finer bat than the great

Kent cricketer had ever been.   I distinctly remember
asking my uncle what his opinion was on the subject,
and he unhesitatingly gave the verdict in favour
of Pilch, and he was also of an opinion that Parr's
success would not last.   However, at the time I
joined the All-England Eleven in 1850 there is no
doubt that Parr was the most dangerous bat in
England.   He gave one the impression that he was
able to deal with all kinds of bowling on all kinds
of wickets.   When one has said that he played
thoroughly *sound* cricket, one has given a general
outline of the play of George Parr.   He certainly
played a different game to any one who had preceded him, using his feet and going out to drive
straight balls far more than any one else.   His
style of defence was "low down" both in playing
forward and back, and in this he presented a
strange contrast to Pilch.   When in attitude at
the wicket he bent his left knee and arched his
back a good deal; still he did not crouch down so
low as some other players we have seen.   He cut
hard and well in front of the wicket, with the right
foot advanced, but required a ball a good way from
the wicket to make an effective cut.   His late cut
was a hard chop striking the ground at the same
time as he struck the ball.   This stroke was the
best he had, barring of course his leg-hitting.   He
drove hard and well, and often left his ground to
do so.   As a leg-hitter he will always be best

known. The great secret of his success in this
respect was that he hit *more* balls to leg than any
one else. There is no doubt whatever that we have
seen as fine leg-hitters as Parr, but never one who
hit so many balls in that direction. His method
was to reach out with the left leg straight down
the wicket, bending the knee, and to sweep the
ball round in a sort of half-circle behind the wicket.
He would sometimes make a lofty square leg-hit;
but even this was done in a different manner to
the hits of Mr Mitchell, Oscroft, Carpenter, and
others. There seems to be an idea sprung up of
late years that Parr was in the habit of hitting
straight balls to leg, but this is a mistake. In
Parr's day it would have been considered decidedly
bad form to have even pulled a short ball round
in that direction, and to have attempted to make
a deliberate leg-hit from a ball on the wicket would
have been unpardonable. In none of the old books
which give a description of Parr's play can I find
any mention whatever of this now supposed habit
of his, and I must certainly say I never saw him
do it. For instance, John Lillywhite's Annual for
1866, in the hints on the game, advises young
gentlemen, in italics, not to *hit straight balls to leg*,
as "nothing can be worse cricket"; and shortly
afterwards goes on to say, "There is no doubt
that George Parr was the finest leg-hitter ever
known." It is true that he ran it very fine,

especially with a ball breaking in from leg, and when bowling against him I used always to remember this, knowing that if he hit round to leg and missed the ball I should most likely bowl him off his pads. I was attempting this when he hit me over the tavern at Lord's in the England and United match in 1860. This ball pitched outside his leg-stump and did not break in at all as I meant it to do, and it was promptly hit out of the ground. I bowled very well in that match and got "George's" wicket both times. George Parr never received any "coaching" at cricket. He had a *natural* gift for batting excelled by no one. He always played with a straight bat, and with a certain amount of wrist-work, but his body seemed so to smother his hands as it were (especially in his back-play) that this was not particularly noticeable.

"George's" was a well-known figure on the old cricket - fields, and easily spotted out amongst his fellow-players. He was rather over medium height, with round shoulders and powerful arms. He stooped slightly and limped somewhat in his walk, seeming to have a fagged and tired appearance. He had a florid complexion, large blue eyes, auburn hair, and thick chestnut-coloured moustache and whiskers. The portrait of him which appeared in 'Bailey's Magazine' many years ago is the exact image of him. He was a very queer - tempered man, but

THE OLD CRICKET-GROUND, RADCLIFFE-ON-TRENT.

(*Where Old Clarke "discovered" George Parr.*)

one of the easiest to get on with if one knew his peculiarities; but one had to make up one's mind never to take offence at his remarks. "If you'd bring what little brains you've got to the wicket with you, you might p'raps get a few runs!" he once remarked to one of his eleven who had got out with a wild stroke. The player to whom this remark was addressed merely replied, "I had 'em all there *yesterday*, 'George,' but what about *yours*?" At this "George" laughed heartily, for on the day before, the one without the brains had made a good many more runs than his captain. "George" used to bowl lobs very fairly. I once remember his getting a well-known batsman out with them, who feebly played one into point's hands. "That's d—d fine bowling to get anybody out with and no mistake!" the batsman remarked as he passed "George" on his way to the pavilion. "And d—d fine hitting too!" was "George's" prompt rejoinder.

Parr was an excellent captain—never a better I should say; he always played to win and would permit no "slackness" in the field. Rather curiously, he did not believe in having any batting practice on the day of a match. He has often told me he much preferred batting against a right-hand bowler than a left, which is not the case with most batsmen. Parr's long and brilliant career is known to most lovers of cricket, and to go through it here would only be to go over ground where others have been before.   He gave up first-class cricket before my return from Australia in 1871, and died in the village in which he was born, and where he learnt his cricket, in 1891.

CHAPTER V.

RETURNING to the year 1851, our first All-England
match was a curious one. We played at Lord's *v.*
fifteen of the M.C.C. and Metropolitan Clubs. The
fifteen only scored 95, but this was enough to beat us
by an innings and 18 runs. In our first innings we
made 30 and in the second 47, of which I scored
23 and Box 15. The first seven wickets of England
fell for 7 runs, and if an easy catch given by myself
had been taken we might not have reached double
figures. Wisden was run out, but allowed to continue his innings as his bat was knocked out of his
hand by one of the fielders, which caused him not
to be able to reach his ground. He was, however,
genuinely enough run out shortly afterwards. Jemmy
Dean obtained most of our wickets.

Our next match was at St Ives *v.* twenty-two, and
this again we lost. The twenty-two scored 55 and
75, and the All-England 36 and 64. No one reached

D

double figures in our first innings. The Twenty-two
had the assistance of the renowned Billy Buttress of
Cambridge, one of the cleverest bowlers and one of
the most eccentric characters that ever played cricket.
"Billy" was born at Cambridge in 1827, being one
year older than myself. He was a medium - paced
bowler with a tremendous break from leg. I never
saw a man in my life able to get more work on the
ball. There were some good batsmen who dreaded
to play against him. Woe betide the batsman who
got playing forward to one of "Billy's" that was not
right up to him ! Sometimes the batter would simply
play the air, and the ball went into the slips; but
what more often happened, he generally assisted it
there with the edge of his bat, where short-slip anxi-
ously awaited it. He once bowled me out round my
legs when hitting to leg at a ball; and I have seen
him get other wickets in this manner. "Billy"
played an immense lot of cricket with the twenty-
twos to which we were opposed. He was a most useful man for these matches too. It was bad enough
to have to play against him with only eleven in
the field; but one had to have all one's wits
about when he had the help of twenty-one fielders. "Billy" was a good ventriloquist, and could
imitate a cat to the life. He had a stuffed one
which he used to take about with him and secrete
under a railway-carriage seat sometimes. When the
compartment became full of passengers "Billy"

would commence "mewing" and cause no end of commotion, especially when the stuffed cat was discovered. "Billy" was a lamplighter by profession. He died at the early age of forty-one.

Our next match saw us again defeated by fourteen of Sheffield. The fourteen was a very strong one, including T. Hunt, G. Chatterton, H. Sampson, G. Anderson, Sam Baldwinson, &c. Hunt was a famous single-wicket player — said to have played more of these matches than any other man. He defeated G. Chatterton, Charley Brown, and Cris Tinley at single wicket, and challenged Wisden, but this match did not come off. If it had I should have been inclined to back the Sussex player. Hunt was a fine punishing bat and fast bowler. He was killed by a train near Rochdale while walking on the line. Chatterton was a big hitter and excellent wicket-keeper. At Stockton-on-Tees we won our first match, chiefly owing to the fine bowling of Clarke and Wisden.

We next played a drawn game against twenty-two of Newcastle. We scored over 300, the veteran Clarke knocking up a fine score of 72, another veteran of the team, Alfred Mynn, making 52. On the other side Harry Wright, a well-known Yorkshire player, scored a grand 65 run out. Our next match was at Thirsk, and a most exciting one it was, we winning eventually by 9 runs only. Wisden bowled grandly in this match, taking 14 wickets for 35 runs in the second innings. After playing several other matches, which are not worth recording here, Clarke took his eleven to Lord's to play fourteen of the M.C.C. This match excited a good deal of interest. The match was drawn—considerably in our favour it must be said. Tom Box and myself were in (with but 5 other wickets down), and we only wanted 1 run to win when time was called! There had been a good deal of betting going on amongst the spectators throughout the game, and there was a tremendous row at the finish. The fourteen of M.C.C. included some well-known men, such as Mr A. Haygarth, Mr C. Morse, Sir F. Bathurst, Mr W. Nicholson, H. Royston, old Tom Sewell, Jemmy Dean, and Jemmy Grundy.

Mr Haygarth was a player of the "stone-wall" type, and when once set was almost impossible to be got rid of. He had not much "hit," but possessed a wonderful defence. He assisted the Gentlemen on many occasions against the Players. He is well known as the compiler of 'Cricket Scores and Biographies,' a work which must have been an endless trouble and expense, and for which all old cricketers who have gone through it must feel truly grateful to the compiler. Mr Haygarth was rather tall and thin, and of a very dark complexion.

Mr Morse was a big tall man and a great hitter. He did not play much in first-class matches, but

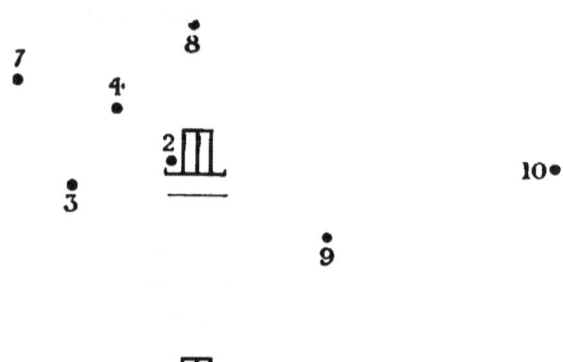

1. Bowler.	5. Cover-point.	9. Short-leg.
2. Wicket-keeper.	6. Mid-off.	10. Long-leg.
3. Point.	7. Long-slip.	11. Long-on.
4. Short-slip.	8. Long-stop.	

made many large scores for I Zingari, which had not been long formed before the time of which I write. This was a club composed entirely of amateurs who toured about playing other elevens. Mr Morse was best known as "Esrom" (Morse spelt backwards).

My next match was one I played *against* the All-England, being selected for fourteen of Surrey. This was unfinished. I represented the Players against the Gentlemen at Lord's, which match was easily won by the former. I scored 48, being second to Joe Guy, who compiled a beautiful innings of 65. Sixty-five was considered a large score at Lord's in those days. The wickets there were generally bad. They possessed only a very small roller, which we christened "the 2-ounce 'un." We had a very close match this year at Sleaford in Lincolnshire — the All-England *v.* twenty-two of that town. The wicket was a difficult one on this occasion, and the twenty-two had the assistance of Billy Buttress, who bowled extremely well. We ultimately lost the match by 10 runs. We had a dinner given to us at the hotel on one of the evenings we were there, to which a great number sat down at an immensely long table. After dinner churchwarden pipes were the order, and when all were lit up, on looking down the table we resembled a regiment with drawn swords. We had some excellent singing, I remember, after dinner.

This match at Sleaford became an annual thing, and we all looked forward to it with pleasure and left the place with regret.   I ought to mention that in this particular match there was not a double figure in our first innings, nor was there in the second venture of the twenty-two.   I played for South *v.* North twice this year, once at Lord's and once at the Oval; both matches were won by the North.

I took part in a memorable match this year at the Oval—Surrey *v.* Notts.   This was the first match ever played between these two famous counties, which were to become such keen rivals in after-years, and I am proud to think that I took part in this game.   Both these counties had a great history behind them, even as far back as 1851; and both had, as events turned out, a great history in the future.   We have records of cricket-matches played both in Surrey and Notts soon after the middle of the eighteenth century.   Neither county was nearly so strong in 1851 as they were a few years later.   Still on the present occasion they were two powerful elevens who met to do battle in this their first encounter.   Notts were without Cris Tinley, otherwise they had their full strength. The match created a great deal of interest, and was a very pleasant one both for players and spectators.   As will be seen by the score, Surrey were victorious by 75 runs.

SURREY.

FIRST INNINGS.	SCORE.	SECOND INNINGS.	SCORE.
J. Cæsar, b Nixon	0	st Brown, b Tinley	0
T. Sherman, run out	6	st Brown, b W. Clarke	0
G. Brockwell, b Grundy	14	b W. Clarke	2
W. Caffyn, c S. Parr, b W. Clarke	29	st Brown, b W. Clarke	14
W. Martingell, b Nixon	1	l b w, b Tinley	23
N. Felix, c Guy, b Nixon	4	b Grundy	10
J. Chester, b W. Clarke	42	c Brown, b Tinley	14
T. Lockyer, c G. Parr, b Grundy	14	run out	20
C. H. Hoare, b Grundy	5	b Grundy	15
J. Heath, not out	0	l b w, b Grundy	1
D. Day, b Grundy	1	not out	1
Extras	4	Extras	6
Total	120	Total	106

NOTTS.

FIRST INNINGS.	SCORE.	SECOND INNINGS.	SCORE.
F. Tinley, c Cæsar, b Day	5	c Felix, b Sherman	0
J. Guy, b Sherman	0	b Martingell	15
G. Parr, b Day	1	b Sherman	23
Butler Parr, b Sherman	4	c Hoare, b Sherman	16
J. Grundy, b Day	6	c and b Sherman	13
S. Parr, b Day	10	b Sherman	3
C. Brown, b Sherman	13	b Sherman	7
G. Butler, not out	3	run out	5
T. Nixon, c Felix, b Day	1	c and b Martingell	9
A. Clarke, b Day	0	not out	0
W. Clarke, b Day	0	c Lockyer, b Sherman	4
Extras	5	Extras	9
Total	48	Total	104

In this match the veteran William Clarke and his son Alfred are to be found playing together for Notts; and, strange to relate, when this same match took place on the same ground exactly forty years later, we again have an instance of a father and son

representing Nottinghamshire in the persons of
Richard Daft and H. B. Daft.

In the 1851 match two celebrated wicket-keepers
were seen, Tom Lockyer and Charley Brown.
Lockyer was undoubtedly the finest wicket-keeper
who had yet appeared, and in my opinion he has
never been excelled to the present time.   He was
the first to adopt the modern attitude for wicket-
keeping, and almost the first to take balls cleverly
on the leg-side.   Few wicket-keepers had hitherto
even attempted to trouble about these balls.   Lockyer was a big, strong, loosely made man, nearly 6
feet in height, and with tremendously long arms.
His reach was something wonderful.   The catches
I have seen him make on the leg-side have been
little short of miraculous.   He was also wonderfully
good at taking a ball and putting the wicket down
like a flash of lightning, even when it was badly
thrown in.   He was just as good against fast
bowling as against slow, which is more than can be
said of many celebrated wicket-keepers, some preferring one and some the other.   Lockyer was also
a fine bat, being a strong and powerful hitter, and
many large scores will be found attached to his
name, even against the best bowling of the day.
He was one of those plucky hard-working cricketers
who never know when their side is beaten; and
often, when his fellow-players were at their wits' end
to separate two batters, would pull off his pads and

gloves and go on to bowl himself, frequently with success. Indeed "Tom" was by no means a bad bowler (rather fast round) had he had more opportunity of developing it. He never knew what it was to give in. Hard knocks had no apparent effect on his nerves. I once remember his having a very bad split finger, and he had a large sort of tin thimble made, and into this he thrust two of his fingers together and kept wicket in this way for several matches, having, of course, the gloves altered on purpose to suit this contrivance. Tom was very queer-tempered at times, but it was soon over, when he became as cheery as possible again. For cricket in cold weather he had a sort of flannel jacket made, very short, almost like a waistcoat with sleeves in fact, which gave him a most peculiar appearance. This garment he had for a greater number of years than I can possibly remember. Julius Cæsar used to declare that it must have come out of the Ark! "Tom" had a glorious career, and no name stands higher in the list of great cricketers which his county produced.

Of the old wicket-keepers Charley Brown, if he had been of a less excitable and eccentric temperament, would in my opinion have ranked second to Lockyer. His natural quickness and his clever way of taking a ball which rose over the top of the wicket were astonishing. He was as quick as lightning and as clever as a monkey. When any one speaks of him, his knack of bowling behind his back is always mentioned, and this feat " Charley " could do to perfection. I have often, too, seen him knock out the flame of a candle from the other side of a room by throwing a bit of the stem of a tobacco-pipe from behind his back. As a bat " Charley " was a slashing hitter, and though by no means to be relied on, made runs at times. He was a good skittle-player, and, I have heard, a wonderfully fast skater. Like Lockyer, " Charley " was a big powerful man.

In the Surrey and Notts match before referred to, Tom Sherman bowled remarkably well. He was a very fast bowler, straight with a good length, and was of great assistance to Surrey for some years. After a time he lost some of his speed, however. "Tom," like nearly all fast bowlers of that time, did not attempt to get any break on the ball, but was content to keep pegging away at the stumps and keeping a good length, and as such bowlers received a good deal of assistance from the wickets in those days, it is not to be wondered at that they were so successful. " Tom " made runs at times, but was too fond of hitting to be a consistent scorer.

Owing to playing for my county against Yorkshire, I was unable to represent the Players against the Gentlemen at Lord's. The Surrey and Yorkshire match came off at the Hyde Park ground, Sheffield. The Bramall Lane ground was not made

until four years later. This was the first time
the two counties ever met. The result was almost
the same as the match we had lately played against
Notts, Surrey on this occasion being victorious by
72 runs. Surrey batted first and totalled 164, of
which I was responsible for 42, being the highest
score. Yorkshire responded with 95, of which Harry
Wright made 43 and George Anderson 28. In the
second innings of Surrey we were got rid of for 93,
and then put the Tykes out for 90. Yorkshire had
undoubtedly a good team now, and it is strange that
they did not at this time come more to the front in
the cricket world. They had good and experienced
bats in Tom Hunt, Harry Wright, Sam Baldwinson,
Harry Sampson, George Anderson, and others, and
good bowlers in Ellis and Armitage; still they played
very few matches at this period.

Clarke in the following week took his eleven to
Cranbrook to play against Kent, and I accompanied
him. This match was unfinished owing to rain.
Kent batted once and made 107, the only double
figures being made by the two veterans Pilch
and Wenman, who scored 37 and 30 respectively.
There was a crowd of people to witness this match,
many of them coming miles to see it. Here, I
recollect, there were a lot of farm-waggons placed
round the ground, in which people sat in chairs to
watch the cricket. It is a pity that this match was
left unfinished, as the result would in all probability

have been exciting. Kent had all their wickets in hand, and required exactly 100 to win.

A celebrated left-hand bowler's name appears on the side of the hop county—Edmund Hinkly. He was a fast bowler, delivering slightly below the shoulder. His ball swerved a good deal in the air, which caused it to be very puzzling at times; it also came quickly off the pitch and often got up high. It was noticed that he nearly always succeeded in getting George Parr's wicket when opposed to him. "George" at no time was fond of left-hand bowlers, as I remarked elsewhere, and he was particularly averse to Hinkly. Hinkly was born in Kent, but was twenty-nine years of age before he appeared at Lord's for his county against England. His *début* at headquarters was phenomenally successful. In the first innings he took 6 wickets and in the second 10. He very often played as a given man for the twenty-twos who opposed the All-England and United Elevens. It is a pity that he did not play more in first-class matches. He was one of those bowlers who require getting used to—that is to say, when one had played against him a few times and learnt his peculiarities he became less difficult. He was rather a short man, weighing about 10½ stones, and could bowl all day without much apparent effort.

Soon after this I took part in a match against Yorkshire as given man for Lancashire at Sheffield.

W. MARTINGELL.

*From the Collection of Mr A. J. Gaston,
Brighton.*

ALFRED MYNN, Esq.

*From the Collection of Mr A. J. Gaston,
Brighton.*

J. BICKLEY.

*From the Collection of Cobbet's Cricket
Bat Co., Ltd.*

EDGAR WILLSHER.

*From the Collection of Mr A. J. Gaston,
Brighton.*

Besides myself Lancashire had the help of Julius
Cæsar, Tom Adams, and Vincent Tinley (brother
of Cris). Yorkshire defeated this mixed eleven by
6 wickets.

Surrey met Yorkshire at the Oval this year, being
the return of the game played at Sheffield earlier in
the season. This match resulted in an easy win
for the home team by 10 wickets, Yorkshire scored
71 and 101, and we made 160 and 13 for no wickets.
The counties did not again meet on the cricket-field
until ten years had elapsed. Following this match
up, I journeyed to Newark-on-Trent with the All
England, where we had a close match, being defeated by 15 runs. The three brothers Tinley were
on the side of the twenty-two. The next three days
found me at Canterbury playing for England *v.* Kent.
England won this match by 4 wickets. Indeed Kent
at this time were no match for a picked eleven of
England. They had no new men worthy to wear
the armour of the old champions Mynn, Felix, Pilch,
and Wenman, all of whom had now seen their best
day. I made the winning hit of the match, being a
square-leg hit for 6.

We had a low-scoring match at Worcester—All
England *v.* twenty - two of Worcester with Jack
Bickley—a few weeks later. The ground here was
a very rough one, only a small square being laid, and
the remainder ridge and furrow. Our first 4 wickets
fell for 5 runs. A rather curious thing occurred

in this match. Pilch was caught and bowled by
Arnold, and the hit being a very hard one, hurt
his hand badly,—so much so that it caused him
to bowl 4 wides in one over and 3 in another,
after which he had to leave the field. We were
disposed of for 43, 10 of which were singles. We
then got rid of the twenty-two for 47, and in our
second innings we managed to make 89. Martingell
and Tom Box were responsible for 52 of these, and
there were 21 extras. There were six of our side
candidates for "specs." Wisden was the only one
who obtained them, however. I had luckily made
one run in the first innings, or should have kept
"Jack" company, as I failed to score in the second.
We got the twenty-two out for 47 in their second
attempt (which was just one more than was made
in their first), and won the match by 39 runs. The
wicket was of course a very queer one, and Bickley
bowled exceedingly well. I may take this opportunity of saying that this bowler was to my mind
one of the most difficult I ever played against, and
I think he certainly ought to have been selected to
take part in the great contests of the day oftener
than he was. Bickley was born in Nottinghamshire,
in the same village where in after - years William
Attewell first saw the light. He appeared at Lord's
for the first time in 1849, being then thirty years of
age. He was a middle-sized man, but tremendously
strongly built. He walked up to the crease and de-

livered the ball with an easy swinging action. The
ball came off the pitch with astonishing quickness,
something like those of George Freeman's of a later
period. He was just the kind of bowler to slick a
batsman out before he got set. He, like Frank
Tinley and others, often assisted the twenty-twos
against the England and United Elevens. He,
Buttress, and Hinkly formed a trio of great bowlers, who were much less known than they ought
to have been. In 1856 Bickley, when playing for
England against a combined team of Kent and
Sussex, actually took 8 wickets for 7 runs! He
was, I may add in conclusion, a noted sprint runner.

We played a delightfully enjoyable match at the
end of the August of 1851 in the Duke of Sutherland's
park at Trentham in Staffordshire. This was in every
sense of the term a holiday match for both players
and spectators. The gardens—perhaps the finest in
England—were thrown open, and a great treat it was
to have the privilege of inspecting them. We had a
good wicket for our match, and scored over 200 runs,
and rain alone prevented us from securing an easy
victory. We next took a trip to Yorkshire, staying
on the way to play a match at Ilkeston in Derbyshire.
We played four matches in Yorkshire—viz., at Sheffield, Huddersfield, Bradford, and Newbury Park—
the seat of Sir George Wombwell. This last match
we won by 11 runs, notwithstanding that we only
made 29 in our second innings (of which number I

made 18). Luckily we had a useful lead on the first innings. We then went on to Edinburgh and played twenty-two of Scotland. This match we won by 20 runs. We then proceeded to Glasgow; where we played an unfinished match. We went in to bat for our last innings requiring 65. Six of us fell for 31, so it is doubtful whether we should have obtained the desired number had the game been finished. After a day's interval we began a match at Birmingham against twenty-two, which was also left unfinished, as was also our next match v. twenty-two of Hereford at Hereford. We had a good deal of wet at this time, and as it was now quite the end of September stumps had to be drawn early. Our next match was at Teignbridge in Devonshire, where we were easily defeated. After playing at Southampton we proceeded to Brighton (it now being the middle of October), and played our last match of this memorable season of 1851 against sixteen of Sussex, the game being left drawn. This was the longest season I ever had, extending as it did for a period of twenty-two weeks, and having taken part in over forty matches. I had had a good season with the bat, but had not, comparatively speaking, much bowling to do this year.

It will be seen how successful Clarke had been with his travelling eleven in a short time. Two years before the idea of starting such an organisation had never entered his head, and now he found himself overwhelmed with letters requesting him to take his team to almost every corner of the United Kingdom. Some of the matches in 1851 had been made at short notice, and no doubt this accounted for the fact of the wickets in some places being in such a terrible state. In the following year we found an improvement in this respect. These All England matches did an immense amount of good in causing the spread of cricket, there is no doubt, but it must be confessed that they rather stopped the development of inter-county matches. Such matches, when played at that time, were often not representative, through their best players being engaged with the All England. I must acknowledge that I was heartily glad when the season of 1851 came to a close; indeed we all were, and looked forward with pleasure to a well-earned winter's rest.

CHAPTER VI

THE year 1852 was chiefly noticeable for the formation of the United Eleven. I played with the
England Eleven throughout this season, but we
did not have so many matches as in the previous
year, completing our programme nearly a month
sooner.

Our first match was at Edinburgh, and was rendered noticeable by the fact of George Parr scoring
54 out of a total of 89 (10 of which were extras).
.There was not another double figure scored on
our side. For this fine performance "George"
was presented with a beautiful silver cigar-
case. In a match against twenty-two of Preston
(with Buttress and two others given) we were disposed of for what I think was one of the smallest
scores we ever made—23. Buttress had the extraordinary analysis of 18 overs, 14 maidens, 5 runs,
and 7 wickets! We made 75 in our second innings,
and I had the unenviable distinction of making

spectacles, our captain, Clarke, bearing me company. The wicket was sticky, and Buttress was simply unplayable. We played a match at Lord's this year — I think it was at Whitsuntide — England v. Sussex and Surrey. This match had been played only once before, and that was sixty years previous. The match was chiefly remarkable for the fine bowling in the first innings of Bickley, who took 6 wickets for 15 runs, and for the equally fine bowling of Tom Sherman on the other side, as he captured 6 for 16—all bowled. England were defeated by 51 runs. Clarke arranged a match at the Oval after this, England v. Surrey (with Clarke, Parr, and Bickley given). Surrey won by 7 wickets. Mr Felix, the great Kent player, played on the Surrey side through his residing in the county. At Ipswich I made my as yet highest score for the All England — viz., 88 — against twenty - two of the district. I accomplished a rather remarkable feat at Lynn shortly afterwards, by scoring 28 not out, out of an innings of 41 (6 of which were extras). This was also against twenty - two. On the All England side there were no fewer than 8 duck-eggs in the innings of 41 alluded to. Old Clarke was so delighted with my performance that he presented me with a box of choice cigars. Our next match was a benefit at Broadwater, near Godalming, to Cæsar, Martingell, and myself, got up by the kindness of Mr Marshall, on whose ground it was played, and a few other gentlemen. The match was the All-England Eleven v. sixteen of Godalming and district. Cæsar, Martingell, and I playing for the sixteen. The famous old player William Beldham, of the Old Hambledon Club, came to see this match, having walked seven miles from his residence near Farnham. He was now between eighty and ninety years old. He, however, was in possession of all his faculties, and talked with us about the old cricket-matches in a most intelligent manner. He wore a tall hat, I can recollect, and a beautifully clean smock-frock. This was the only time I saw this celebrated veteran, but an old man who resides only a few doors from me at the present time knew him intimately. Beldham, I believe, was nearly a hundred years old when he died.

This season we of Surrey sustained a crushing defeat at the hands of Nottinghamshire at the Oval, the Midlanders thus turning the tables on us for our victory of last year. Notts scored 181, and Surrey 71 and 67. An old paper, speaking of this match, says, " Many of the patrons and players of Surrey are not a little chagrined at this defeat, while the lungs of the men of Trent 'crow like chanticleer.'" A rather curious match we played at Banbury — All England v. twenty-two (with Buttress). The twenty-two scored 52 and 42, and there was not a double figure made in either innings, 7 being the nearest approach to it. Buttress took

OLD PAVILION, TRENT BRIDGE GROUND, NOTTINGHAM.

Photo by Phillips & Co., Nottingham.

14 wickets against us in our two innings. I took part in the Kent and England match at Lord's, which the latter won by 7 wickets. This match is noted for two things—the fine batting of Mr W. Nicholson, who totalled 39 and 70 for England, and as being the first appearance of that prince of left-hand bowlers, Edgar Willsher, on this enclosure. Mr Nicholson's batting on the present occasion was a treat to see; indeed all his large innings were delightful to the spectators, as he was a very rapid scorer and a hard and clean hitter. He was, besides, a first-rate wicket-keeper, and filled this post for the Gentlemen on many occasions. He was also one of the most liberal supporters of the game that ever lived.

Of Edgar Willsher as a cricketer it is almost impossible to speak too highly. As an all-round man he may be classed with Wisden and Grundy, but as a bowler he occupies a higher place. From my own experience I should put him down as *the* most difficult of all bowlers I ever met. Though, as far as mere pace goes, he was not so fast as either Jackson or Tarrant, his ball was a more difficult one to play than those of either of those famous cricketers. Willsher had an extraordinary command over the ball. For accuracy of pitch he was almost the equal of Fred Morley,—so I have heard good judges say who have played against both. Willsher's ball came in a good bit from leg as a rule, and he seemed to have the knack

of being able to make a ball "get up" on almost
any wicket. We have all heard how his delivery
was objected to as being higher than the shoulder,
and that he was no-balled six times in succession
by John Lillywhite in the England v. Surrey match
of 1862 at the Oval for this offence; how the England team left the field in consequence, play ceasing
for that day, and continued on the following morning
with a fresh umpire. There is no doubt whatever
that Willsher was often in the habit of bowling
above the shoulder, but then so also were nine
out of every ten bowlers of that time. I myself
have often been no-balled for this, and have also
frequently committed the offence without paying
the penalty. The old law was an absurd one,
and one wonders that it should have remained in
force as long as it did. As a batsman Willsher
was a fine hitter, and had an excellent defence as
well. Indeed at one part of his career he might
have been classed amongst the "stone-wallers."
In a match, Kent and Surrey v. England, in 1855,
he batted for over three hours and a half for 20
runs. He joined the All England in the year I
left it, and was for years one of their bowlers on
whom a great deal of the work devolved. Willsher
was rather tall, and being very thin, looked taller
than he was. He was light in weight, and had a
very dark complexion. When in ordinary clothes
he had not at all the appearance of an athlete.

The Surrey and Kent match at the Oval in 1852 was a most exciting affair. We had 160 runs to make in our last innings, and obtained 154, thus losing the match by half-a-dozen runs. The excitement was intense towards the finish, our last wicket putting on 20 runs. Shortly afterwards Surrey met a picked team of England at Lord's, and defeated them by 2 wickets; but sustained a severe defeat at the hands of Sussex at the Oval the same week, chiefly due to the fine bowling of Wisden. In the first innings of Sussex G. Brown played a grand defensive innings of 86. He went in first, and was nearly carrying out his bat. We defeated the Gentlemen by 5 wickets this year at Lord's in the Gentlemen and Players match. The All England had an unenviable experience against twenty-two of Hungerford in Berkshire. This match was played in the park of Captain Willes, who had got a strong twenty-two together, and they succeeded in getting rid of us for the record score of 12 runs! Joe Guy being the highest individual scorer with 3. Mr G. Yonge, who was one of the best amateur bowlers of the day, took 5 of our wickets for 3 runs. Mr Yonge bowled very fast, and the wicket on the present occasion suited him to a nicety. He played against us in our next match v. twenty-two of the Landsdown Club at Bath, and here also he was very destructive. It is a pity that he did not follow his cricket up more than he did, or his name would have been better remembered than it is.

At Newark-on-Trent, on the three days following our match at Bath, we had opposed to us that terrible bowler John Jackson, rightly named the Demon indeed! Although only a youth at this time, he had all the making of a great bowler. Jackson was born at Bunay in Suffolk, but was brought up in the neighbourhood of Newark, in which district as a boy he was well known through running barefoot after the hounds in the hunting season, and for his mischievous propensities of throwing stones at all the milestones and guide-posts on the highroad. He went by the name of "Jim Crow" in those days. We little thought when we played this match at Newark that he was in after-years to make a name which should for years be a household word in cricket circles, and which is almost as well known to-day as when the owner of it was such a terror to his opponents. Poor old "Jack" has, I am told, fallen on evil days, and the hardest task I have had in the compiling of these pages is that to which I have now come. I cannot picture him as a lonely old man of sixty-six, but can only think of him as a great powerful figure, seeming to tower above every one else, full of life and animal spirits, and appearing to have strength enough to bowl both batsman and wicket down together! Jackson had one or two club en-

gagements in his native county before he appeared
in first-class cricket. He played his first match
at Lord's in 1856 for the North against the South.
"Jack" stood over 6 feet in height and weighed over
15 stones. He bowled level armed with a beautifully
easy delivery, and though of a terrific pace, always
gave one the idea that he was bowling well "within
himself." I have been often asked whether I considered he or Tarrant to have been the better bowler,
and can say without hesitation that Jackson was far
superior to the Cambridge man, fine bowler though
the latter unquestionably was. He was straighter
and could keep a better length than Tarrant, and
was equally as fast. His performances against some
of the twenty-twos he met are extraordinary; indeed many of these players were exceedingly glad
to get out and return to the pavilion without broken
bones. I myself have had many a nasty knock from
this great bowler, and I too have not been sorry at
times when my innings against him at Lord's has
come to an end. "Jack" was very fond of sending
one a full pitch when well set, and when this came in
the near vicinity of the head it was far from pleasant.
Jackson was also a fine punishing bat, and often
made large scores against first-class bowling. He
was quite a character, and always afforded a fund of
amusement to his fellow-cricketers. Daft has told
us of his peculiarity of blowing his nose when he
got a wicket, and how he was dubbed the "fog-

horn" in consequence. He never would take bank
notes in payment of his services, but always insisted
on·having gold. Once I can recollect he had a lot
of sovereigns in his trousers-pocket, which gave way
in the middle of an innings, and the coins went rolling all over the place. There was at once a rush
made to help "Jack" to collect them, but he waved
us all back in a most decided manner while he
did the picking up himself, calling out loudly in
his broad Nottinghamshire dialect, "Get out o' th'
road and let me pick it oop mysen!" Jackson
did not last so long as most cricketers, and there
is no doubt that his having to do so much bowling
against the twenty-twos for the All England had
much to do with this.

Tom Plumb, the famous wicket-keeper, played
against us for twenty-two of Northamptonshire in
1852. Some years afterwards he was celebrated as
a fine wicket-keeper and very fair bat.

Sussex and Surrey played a drawn game towards
the end of this year, but our All England engagements prevented both Cæsar and myself from taking
part in this match. The United Eleven played their
first match on August 26, 27, and 28, against twenty
Gentlemen of Hants, on a ground belonging to
Daniel Day at Portsmouth. There had long been
dissatisfaction among some of the Players against
Clarke. It was thought that Clarke was coining
money, and that they ought to be better paid. I

believe Wisden at the time put the matter straight to Clarke, who answered him somewhat roughly, and caused a breach between them. So the United Eleven was formed with Wisden and Dean as secretaries. Wisden was really the only regular All England man who took part in this first United match. They followed up their match at Portsmouth by one against twenty - two of Newmarket on the same days that the All England were engaged at Ilkeston in Derbyshire. The following week the United defeated fifteen of Sheffield on the same day that we of the All England were beaten by twenty - two of Bradford, which made Old Clarke feel very bitter against the renegades. It was after their victory at Sheffield that the United (who had now been joined by Grundy) drew up a document to the effect that none of their players would ever take part in another match of which Clarke had the management. The United played no more that year, but the All England played four more matches, finishing the season at Kelso in Scotland. This had been arranged as a three-days' fixture, but Clarke was persuaded to stay another day to finish it, and the result was that we won by 8 runs. This is the only four - days' match I ever took part in in the United Kingdom.

I cannot allow this chapter to end without giving some account of my first visit to Nottingham to take

part in the return Notts and Surrey contest at Trent
Bridge. A large and appreciative crowd gathered
together to witness this match, and the scene of
enthusiasm which ensued at the conclusion, when
the Notts men were victorious by 10 wickets, defies
description. Surrey batted first, and made 112.
Notts responded with 209, George Parr making 69,
and Charley Brown coming next with 36. In our
second innings we totalled 134, leaving Notts with
but 30 odd to win, which they obtained without
the loss of a wicket. The shouting and throwing
up of hats when the game was won was tremendous,
and for hours afterwards the quaint little old inn,
just outside the ground, was packed to overflowing
with the supporters of the home eleven. This old
Trent Bridge Inn stood partly in the borough
and partly in the county of Nottingham. Of the
four matches which had now taken place between
these world - famed counties, Surrey had won two
and Notts two. Nottingham people at the present
time complain of the slackness of their supporters,
but they had nothing to complain of in this respect
in the year of grace 1852.

NEW PAVILION, TRENT BRIDGE GROUND, NOTTINGHAM.

CHAPTER VII.

NOTWITHSTANDING the formation of a rival eleven
in the previous year, Clarke commenced his season
early in the following May with a powerful side, and
won his first match by 25 runs at St Helens. The
season at Lord's this year opened with a match
between Notts and England, which was won by
the Midlanders by 27 runs. Notts went in first
and scored 63; England then made 117. Notts
replied with 129, thus leaving England the apparently
easy task of obtaining 75 to win. Jack Bickley was,
however, so "on the spot" that he took 8 of our
wickets for 23 runs, the innings closing with a total
of 48. For this great bowling feat Bickley was
handsomely and deservedly rewarded. The betting
was 6 to 4 on England at the start and 2 to 1 on
them at the conclusion of Notts' first innings. There
were a lot of spectators from Nottingham on the
ground, many of whom won a hatful of money over
the result of the game. There is no disguising the

fact that Notts were a very powerful team at this
period, notwithstanding that several of their players
were veterans, such as Guy, Butler Parr, and Old
Clarke. Butler Parr, I may say in this place, had
now been playing for his county for nearly twenty
years. He was a fine manly cricketer, always obtaining his runs in a style well worth looking at. He
was a very hard cutter, and could drive beautifully
off his legs. His scores in local matches are said
to have been enormous, made as they were at a time
when even 40 runs or so was a large score. It is a
pity that this player did not devote more time to
the game. I have heard George Parr say that
against loose bowling he was, he considered, a more
effective bat than himself.

The renowned Cris Tinley made his bow at Lord's
in the Notts and England match. He was one of
the hardest-working cricketers I ever met. "Cris"
was a most useful bat, and although his style of
defence was somewhat marred by not playing with
a straight bat, still his hitting was almost unsur-
passed by any player of his time. He would jump
in and drive in a manner that was often startling
to a slow bowler who had followed his ball up. He
would often by his plucky hitting (nervousness was,
I believe, unknown to him) pull a match out of the
fire for his side when everything appeared to be
going against them. When I first knew Cris he
was a very fast round-arm bowler, and though good

at this, it is as a lob-bowler (which style he adopted in later years) that he is best known. As a bowler of this kind he must always rank amongst the very best. In my opinion he was second only to Clarke in this respect. He varied his length and his pace in a most puzzling manner, and a dodge he often adopted was to deliver a ball when standing a yard or so behind the crease. He was a magnificent point, being light and active as a kitten.

Samuel Parr, an elder brother of George, played first at Lord's in the same match as Cris Tinley. He was a less man than his more famous brother, with very sandy whiskers. He was a hard hitter both as to driving and leg-hitting, but was rather too fond of "having a pop at a bowler," as he called it, to be considered a reliable bat. Often, too, Sam would run himself or his partner out by attempting a short run, done to please the "gallery" when the game was becoming slow. He was notorious for playing practical jokes on his friends. These, how-ever entertaining they might be to the company generally, were often exceedingly annoying to the one whom Sam selected as the victim of his pranks.

When playing with the All England at Sleaford this year, George Parr, after making 64 runs, had his hat knocked off, and this falling on the wicket dislodged the bails. I shall never forget his look of disgust as he returned to the tent.

In the England and Kent match at Lord's this

year England were again victorious. This was
a bowler's match throughout. Clarke got up a
team from the North to play the South at the Oval
soon after this, and it is noticeable that no member
of the United took part in it. The South won by
70 runs. This again was a match where no large
score was made,—Hinkly, Hillyer, and Wisden on
one side, and Clarke, Frank Tinley, and Bickley on
the other, all bowling extremely well. We played
an interesting match at Lord's between the M.C.C.
and a picked team of England, the M.C.C. beating
us by 70 runs. This was the first time they had
ever won this match without assistance. Tom
Adams, the Kent man, made a square-leg hit off
Hillyer, which went through the door of the tavern
and down the cellar steps, and for this they ran
6. Adams was a fine free hitter, and made many
large scores for the famous old Kent Eleven. He
was a tall man, with an exceedingly good-tempered
countenance. He wore his hair rather long, with
a curl which he trained down each side of his
face. As a bowler he was useful, being one of
the few in those days who bowled over the wicket.
Before bowling he had a peculiar way of holding
the ball on a level with his eye, to take aim as it
were at the batsman. He was very fond of shooting,
and used to relate some wonderful stories of his
exploits in this line. He declared that he was so
well known in one district as a deadly shot, that

every hare or rabbit which he came across in the open never attempted to run away, knowing that it would be quite useless, but would sit quietly to be knocked over! "Tom" at one time owned a ground at Gravesend, where I believe he resided till his death, which took place only a few years ago, thus surviving all his old comrades of the old Kent Eleven.

The next match of importance in which I took part in 1853 was for the England Eleven *v.* twenty-two of the Zingari Club at the Oval. The Zingari, who were very strong, had the best of the match, which was unfinished owing to rain. This match was played for the benefit of Thomas Beagley, the famous old Hampshire player, a well-known bat and long-stop in the earlier part of the century. I have often seen the old man up at Lord's watching the cricket there. He it is, it will be remembered, whom Mr Pycroft mentions in the 'Cricket Field' as being pointed out to a young player as "Thomas Beagley"; and the young man inquiring, "Thomas *who?*" causes the author of the 'Cricket-Field' to exclaim, "One might as well expect to be asked 'Who is W. G. Grace?' or, 'Who is Daft?'"[1] This benefit match was so interfered with by the weather that it was played over again later in the season. I ought

---

[1] The names of Grace and Daft were in the later editions of the 'Cricket Field' substituted for those of Pilch and Parr of the earlier editions.—EDITOR.

F

to mention that that accomplished batsman Mr
C. G. Taylor played in both these matches for the
Zingari, and although he did not make many runs
on these two occasions, one could see that he still
possessed an elegance of style which perhaps in his
best day was only surpassed by Daft himself in the
whole history of cricket.   Mr Taylor was a middle-
sized man, slim, and of a very neat appearance.

The Gentlemen defeated the Players at Lord's
this year on a sticky wicket.   This was the last
match they won against the Players till 1865.

The next great match I took part in in 1853 was
for England v. Kent and Sussex at Tunbridge Wells,
and this fixture being arranged by William Clarke,
was marked by the absence of all United men on
either side.   This match was left drawn in favour
of England.   We next played a match at Lord's,
England v. Sussex, who had the assistance of George
Parr.   This match was played for the benefit of the
veteran William Lillywhite, who was now over sixty
years of age.   He was to have played himself—indeed he appeared in the field and commenced to
bowl, but was taken ill after the first over, and his
place was filled by mutual consent by Mr H. Hoare,
then the hon. treasurer of the Surrey Club.   England won the match by nearly 200 runs.

The All England again visited Hungerford Park
this year, where, it will be remembered, we were
got rid of for the small score of 12 in the previous

season. In the present match we very curiously made
the same score (54) in both our innings. Charlie
Arnold, a very fast bowler, played with us just now
in a few matches. He bowled a great pace, but was
not very straight. At Spalding we had the misfortune to be beaten by one run only. George Parr
had received a terrible blow in his first innings, and
had not intended going in to bat in the second, but
as the game became so close, was persuaded to do
so. He, however, did not have a chance of receiving
a ball, as the previous wicket had been obtained with
the last ball of the over, and Billy Hillyer, who was
"George's" partner, was got out with the next ball
that was sent down. During this match Mr Mynn
smashed down an old wooden four-post bedstead at
our hotel, in the middle of the night, alarming the
whole house. It is rather curious that we were only
2 runs behind the twenty-two in our *first* innings.

Our next match was at Arnold, near Nottingham.
This match I shall always remember. I stayed with
George Parr at his house at Radcliffe, where each
morning we had a little snipe-shooting down by the
Trent. "George," though unable to play in the match
at Arnold owing to the injury he had received at
Spalding, accompanied us there each day. We drove
over from Nottingham with a Mr Malpas, who kept
the "Flying Horse" Hotel near the market-place.
This gentleman was a great sportsman and very fond
of cricket. He always insisted on our cracking a few

bottles of champagne each morning before setting
out for Arnold, and took a case of the same with him
in the carriage.   George Parr, being "off duty" this
match, was in great form, and although his favourite
beverage used to be gin-and-water, he paid particular
attention to the champagne on the present occasion.
Every evening on our return to Radcliffe we spent
at the house of Mr Butler Parr, whose custom I
heard was to entertain "George's" cricketing friends
to supper whenever they stayed with him at Radcliffe, and jolly times we had on this and other
visits.   Mr Butler Parr was a brewer and maltster,
and resided in an old-fashioned house built all on
the ground-floor.   "George" told me that he had
often wished that his own house had been built on
the same principle, as he found stairs were uncommonly awkward things when returning home
after an evening out!   Mr Butler Parr was a non-
smoker, and when in company, in order not to
appear unsociable, generally pulled at an empty pipe.
He told me rather an interesting anecdote of Mr
Alfred Mynn.   The great Kentish cricketer always
visited him when playing at Nottingham; and his
arrival was the signal for a huge jug of strong ale
being produced.   Mr Mynn, it appears, never liked
to have a large glass when partaking of this old
English beverage, so Mr Parr used to always have
two glasses ready for him, and while his guest was
disposing of one he himself filled the other for him,

which performance was repeated until the jug was empty. Our match at Arnold we won by 4 runs only. I ought to mention that six players of the name of Oscroft played for Arnold, including, I believe, the father and several uncles of the afterwards famous William Oscroft.

Our next match at Leeds, against twenty-two of that town, we just contrived to win by *five* runs. In the second innings there were 5 run out and 5 l.b.w., Hillyer achieving the hat-trick with 3 leg befores. The famous George Atkinson was one of those run out. "George" was an excellent bowler, rather inclined to fast, and wonderfully straight, often delivering a great number of maiden overs in succession. He was for some years one of the best bowlers of the United Eleven. He also at times made some good scores with the bat. He was an excellent singer, and very good company at all times.

I took part in the England and Kent match at Canterbury, which resulted in an innings victory for England, notwithstanding the absence of George Parr. No Kent and England match was played again for nine years. Julius Cæsar played a magnificent innings of 101 for England, and I was next to him with 55. Most curiously, there were no fewer than five run out in the first innings of Kent, including Pilch, Mynn, Wenman, and Willsher. George Parr was able to appear *v*.

twenty-two of Bath, and although he went in rather late, managed to score 84 not out. Our next match at Torquay was the last All England match that that grand old batsman Mr Felix took part in, and it is to be regretted that a nought is found to his name in this his final match.

Surrey played a close match with Kent at the Oval this year, the home team winning by 12 runs amidst great excitement. Against their old rivals Notts they were not so fortunate. Both sides were strongly represented, but the bowling of the midland county was too good for us, and we were defeated by an innings. Hinkly, who was now residing in Surrey, played for us in this match.

A most curious thing happened when we were playing twenty-two of Ipswich. I was fielding behind Clarke, being placed for a sort of half-hit between mid-off and the long-field. I fielded a ball which had been hit rather sharply to me and threw it hard at the nearest wicket, which it hit and knocked off the bails, after doing which it rolled to the other end and knocked the other wicket down. The whole thing was done in much less time than it takes to relate, and there was an appeal made at both ends; but the umpires gave each batsman not out, considering each was in his crease.

We played a most enjoyable match towards the end of this season at Enville Hall, the seat of the

Earl of Stamford. Lord Stamford had for many
years at this period four or five first-class bowlers
engaged on his ground, and this year we had opposed to us Bickley, Cris Tinley, and others. We
won the match by 8 wickets, Clarke and myself
bowling with great success in the second innings
of the twenty-two. Bickley took all our wickets
in the first innings except that of Arnold, who
was run out. We were most hospitably entertained throughout the match by Lord Stamford,
who himself formed one of the twenty-two. This
was a most enjoyable finish to our season of
1853.

The United had not played so many matches as
ourselves, but had had on the whole a fairly successful season, being strengthened by the assistance
of Edgar Willsher during the latter part of the
season, though he subsequently joined the All
England. Amongst their other engagements the
United took a trip over to Ireland to play a
match at Dublin, in which they were defeated.

As far as myself went, I had had another good
season with the bat, and had done more bowling
than in 1852, having improved a good deal this
season in that department of the game. It was
about this time that I began to be known at the
Oval by the names of "The Surrey Pet" and
"Terrible Billy."

CHAPTER VIII.

THE SEASON OF 1854.

THE season of 1854 was my last as a member
of the All-England Eleven. The United got a
start of us this year, and played one or two
matches before we began our season towards the
end of May. I took part in the Notts *v.* England
match at Lord's, and helped to defeat the midland
shire by 59 runs. Mr W. Nicholson captained us
in this match. In our first innings Tom Lockyer
had to forfeit his innings. He was well in at
lunch-time, and adjourned to a tavern to partake
of refreshment, which was situated some distance
from the ground. Tom, it appears, thought the
interval would be an hour, as was the case generally in those days; but arrangements having been
made to only allow half that time, when Tom
was wanted to continue his innings he was no-
where to be found. He had not told a soul on
the ground where he had gone, so the game had
to be continued without him, and when he came

strolling leisurely on to the ground the innings had just come to a close. It was one of "Tom's" peculiarities to get away from every one at lunch-time and to enjoy a pipe afterwards all to himself, and when we played away from home he very often went and took lodgings somewhere all by himself.

Another remarkable incident occurred in this match. Cæsar, who was ill, was allowed a substitute (Billy Buttress) to run for him. "Julie" played a ball, and forgetting all about his substitute, ran a run himself, leaving Billy behind, whereupon Old Clarke with great presence of mind put down the wicket which "Julie" had reached and called out, "How's that?" Tom Sewell, who was umpire, replied, "Not out." But Clarke at once appealed to some of the committee of the M.C.C., who settled that "Julie" was run out. As a matter of fact it should have been "Julie's" partner (Wisden) who was out, as he and Billy Buttress, the substitute representing "Julie," were both at one end and had not crossed each other.

In this match Alfred Clarke, the son of the veteran, played first at Lord's. In one All England match this year he played *against* us, he representing twenty-two of St Helens and his father the Eleven.

In June of this year we played twenty-two of the West Gloucester Club at Bristol. Dr W. G. Grace mentions this match in his book, and tells us that

he himself was one of the spectators, being then
only six years old. Mr Alfred Mynn officiated as
one of the umpires in this match.

From Bristol we went to Salisbury, where we
were defeated by eighteen of Wiltshire by 3
runs. It is remarkable how many close finishes
we had about this time. In this match the
eighteen made 69 in each of their innings. Clarke
and Bickley bowled unchanged throughout this
match, and, most strange to relate, each bowled
the same number of balls; and in the second
innings bowled exactly the same number as in
the first. The eighteen had the assistance of
Hinkly, and also of one who was to become
shortly afterwards one of the best known players
in the world—H. H. Stephenson. Stephenson was
famous as a batsman, bowler, and wicket-keeper.
He was a tall man, and possessed a long reach
when batting, which he always made good use of.
He was a fine leg-hitter, generally hitting square,
and had also a splendid on-drive. His off-play
for so great a player was undoubtedly weak; nor
can I call to mind a batsman who scored so heavily
as he did, who was so little noted for his cutting.
His defence was very strong, and he always played
with a remarkably straight bat. He was an excellent man to send in when the bowling had been
"collared," rarely failing to make a good score on
such occasions. As a bowler he was a genius. He

bowled rather fast, with a tremendous break from the off. Indeed we may almost look upon Stephenson as the pioneer of *break-back* round-arm bowling. As a bowler he had his good days and bad. Sometimes he would bowl in a manner that was almost unplayable, while at another he would seem to lose his command over the pitch of the ball. For a few seasons he was, in my opinion, about the most difficult bowler in England. After a while he fell off in his bowling, which was chiefly owing to his having to do so much of it, and he in a manner lost the use of his fingers somewhat—so he often told me himself. As a wicket-keeper he was really first-class, and like his great fellow-county player, Lockyer, stood up to the wicket in the modern manner. Stephenson was a most popular man both as a cricketer and in social life. He it was, it will be remembered, who captained the first English team in Australia. From his often wearing a black frock-coat he acquired the nickname of "Spurgeon" from George Parr.

In the Surrey and Sussex match at Brighton this year no definite result was arrived at, the match being left in a very interesting state. Shortly afterwards we succeeded in defeating the great county of Nottingham at Trent Bridge by 97 runs. Lockyer, Stephenson, and myself were the chief scorers for our side, while George Parr and Charley Brown did best for Notts. Stephenson bowled very finely

throughout, taking in the first innings 4 wickets
for 4 runs.   This was a great and well-deserved
victory.   The Notts men were very disappointed,
as was only natural.   Our return match, played
this year at Broadwater towards the end of August,
was similar to the one at Nottingham, the victory
again remaining with Surrey, this time by 65 runs.
Four years elapsed before this match took place
again.

The All England were easily defeated by Lord
Stamford's twenty-two this year, his Lordship on
this occasion having a very powerful side, including
his four professionals, Charley Brown, Bickley,
Brampton, and Cris Tinley, also Mr John Walker,
Mr W. Nicholson, and other well-known amateurs.
H. H. Stephenson had now joined the All-England
Eleven, in whose ranks he remained for many years.
The Gentlemen and Players match was spoilt this
year, by reason of Clarke having had some difference
with the M.C.C.; and in consequence he not only
refused to take part in the match himself, but de-
clined to allow Cæsar, Parr, and myself to do so;
and when later in the season the M.C.C. played
v. England at Lord's, all Clarke's players were
conspicuous by their absence.

We played a match at a little town called Bingham
in Nottinghamshire against twenty-two of the district.
I happen to have the account of this match published
in the local paper of the time, which I think beats

anything I ever saw in cricket literature. Quite half of the article is taken up with an account of the town of Bingham from the days of the Romans. At last we come to the match, which is described in the most flowery language imaginable. George Parr going in to bat, is termed the "lion of the day; but that fickle jade Fortune deserted him" ("George" scored 3 only). The England Eleven is spoken of as one "whose name is Legion." However, the account of the match itself is soon over, and then comes a long description of the luncheons on the ground, with many compliments addressed to "the culinary talents" of the hostess of the "Chesterfield Arms" who did the catering, "which could not fail to please the most fastidious taste." The account concludes by stating that a brass band was in attendance each day, "whose rich music gave an additional charm to the gay and festive scene." I regret to say, that although I am quite ready to indorse all that is said about the luncheons, I am *not* prepared to agree with the gentleman who wrote the article in what he says about the brass band, which was about the worst I ever heard, and was heartily cursed by old Clarke from its advent to its departure.

We had a great match at my home at Reigate about this time — Reigate *v.* Godalming. H. H. Stephenson and I played for Reigate, while in the ranks of Godalming appeared Mr F. P. Miller, Mr A.

Marshall, Mr E. Napper, and Julius and Frederick
Cæsar. "Julie" was busy bowling in this match,
and was highly delighted at getting my wicket in
both innings. However, we managed to win the
match by nearly 100 runs. In the Kent and
England match at Canterbury this year the hop
county had the assistance of W. Clarke, Bickley,
G. Parr, and Wisden. England won by 7 wickets.
None of Clarke's All-England Eleven played for
England, hence the fact of Julius Cæsar and
myself being able to take part in the Reigate
and Godalming match, which was played on the
same days. We, however, played in the Sussex
v. England match at Brighton in the following
week. Sussex were assisted by G. Parr and old
Clarke, and defeated us by 68 runs, chiefly owing
to the fine bowling of Wisden. Mr F. P. Miller
of Surrey played for England on this occasion.
He was the same age as myself, but did not appear at Lord's till 1851. He was one of the most
brilliant batsmen of the great Surrey Eleven which
carried all before it in 1858. Though rather a short
man, he was strongly built and could hit very hard.
His best hit was perhaps the off-drive, but he was
essentially an all-round batsman, there being scarcely
any hit on the board which he was unable to make
successfully. His defence was excellent, and though
a quick run-getter he always played a correct game.
He was a fair bowler and a brilliant field. Some of

the catches I have seen him make have been little short of miraculous. He was a most enthusiastic cricketer, being as fond of the game, for itself alone, as I believe both Mr Mynn and Mr Felix had been. The great success of the Surrey Eleven was doubtless attributable to the interest taken in the players by this truly great cricketer. None of Clarke's Eleven were selected to play for England by the M.C.C. in the Notts *v.* England match at Trent Bridge in 1854, which resulted in an easy victory for England.

At the beginning of September we played a match at Hungerford Park (Major Willes's place in Berkshire)—the All England *v.* Major Willes's twenty-two. Here Mr W. Ridding made a record score of 68 against us, there never having been so many made before by a member of a "twenty-two" against the All-England Eleven. Mr Ridding was a fine bat of the "hitting" order, and an excellent wicket-keeper. He played cricket without a hat, and wore simply the *peak* of a cap over his eyes held on by an elastic band.

The United Eleven established a record this season by having to go in to get 279 runs to win against fifteen of Gravesend, and by obtaining them with 2 wickets to spare. This was said to have been the first time a side had been set to get so large a score and to have accomplished the feat. At Birmingham we had another of our All England close-

finished matches, defeating twenty-two there by 12
runs. The scoring was small throughout. Cris
Tinley in this match caught twelve men out at
point. This being a record, was much talked of
at the time. In a match towards the end of the
season we got out a twenty - two of Cheshire at
Macclesfield without a double figure being obtained
in either of their innings, notwithstanding that they
had the help of "Ducky" Diver. In our return
match Surrey v. Sussex we were victorious by 10
wickets. Tom Lockyer with 65 and myself with
41 were the chief scorers for Surrey, while Tiny
Wells played an excellent defensive innings of 43
for Sussex. Wells was nicknamed "Tiny" from
his being little more than five feet high. For his
size he was a remarkably hard hitter. His style
was very peculiar. He took his guard about the
distance of a couple of inches from the stumps;
after doing this he held his bat over his shoulder;
then when the bowler advanced to deliver the ball,
he too advanced as far as the popping crease. Tiny
was a fair medium-pace bowler, and could bowl lobs
too if required. He was a first-rate shot—one of
the best, in fact, I ever saw.

At the close of the season of 1854 a single-wicket
match was played at Chertsey between Tom Sherman
and Julius Cæsar and H. H. Stephenson and myself.
This match has, I see, been reported in the books as
being for £25 a-side; but as a matter of fact it was

WILLIAM CAFFYN.

From the Collection of Mr A. J. Gaston, Brighton.

just a match made overnight for no money whatever. Cæsar and Sherman defeated us by 12 runs.

The United Eleven had a successful season on the whole in 1854, taking a trip both to Dublin and to Edinburgh.

George Parr scored 933 runs this season for an average of 16, John Lillywhite just beating him with an average of 17, though he only scored 537 runs. I myself scored 875 runs for an average of 15. In eleven-a-side contests George Parr was top with 26; I ran him close with 25, being just 4 runs behind him in the total number we each obtained during the season. Julius Cæsar was next with 21, and John Lillywhite followed with an average of 20. Some one writing to one of the London papers on the subject of the averages for 1854, declares his belief that they are so large this year owing to the wickets receiving more attention than formerly; and also goes on to say that " if we now had a few bowlers like Redgate and old Lillywhite, batsmen would not score as heavily as they do." In the bowling the great veteran Clarke, who was now fifty-six years of age, obtained 476 wickets at a cost of a little more than 8 runs per wicket. Wisden took 210 wickets for an average of a little under 6, while Tom Sherman, with an average of 5 runs, took 180 wickets, being just behind Jemmy Grundy, who obtained 196 wickets at the cost of a trifle *under* 5 runs per wicket.

G

H. H. Stephenson had the same average, but took
16 wickets less than Grundy, while I myself had
110 wickets for an average of 4. I was particularly
anxious to beat George Parr in the batting averages
this season, and I can well remember at one time
I looked like doing so, but I was just beaten on
the post by that eminent cricketer.

There is a story told of one celebrated bowler who
was generally engaged by local twenty-twos to oppose
the All - England Eleven. The bowler, it appears,
owed a debt of £12 or so, for which he was greatly
pressed, and was at his wits' end to know how to pay
it. He, however, at last made an arrangement with
his creditor to have himself arrested on the ——
cricket-ground just prior to the commencement of
a match. This arrangement was carried out, the
bowler counterfeiting much surprise at the proceedings. The local cricketing authorities were in a
great way at the prospect of being deprived of the
services of their eminent bowler, and after a short
consultation sent the hat round and quickly collected
the required amount to set him at liberty—which
was exactly what the bowler had anticipated would
be done!

CHAPTER IX.

OWING to my being engaged at Eton College for
this season, I was unable to play so much cricket
as usual. I may add that during the seasons of
1853 and 1854 I had been engaged at Christchurch,
Oxford, for just the early part of the spring. Rare
times we had at the University in those days, and
no mistake! There were many other good men
engaged there besides myself, including the veteran Pilch, Jemmy Grundy, Willsher, Julius Cæsar,
Hinkly, and Billy Buttress. There was one gentleman at the 'Varsity in those days who used to
invite one or two of us to breakfast with him
before we started practice, and such breakfasts too!
I am afraid they sometimes interfered somewhat
with the practice afterwards. This same gentleman used also to have the great pugilist Aaron
Jones down to teach him to box. I remember
once when we were breakfasting with him that
his servant in opening a bottle of wine badly cut

his hand, which Aaron Jones very skilfully dressed
and bound up.   Our pay at Oxford was not very
large, but we made a good deal of money by the
gentlemen putting a shilling on the wicket for every
time we got them out.   The wicket had not merely
to be knocked down for us to obtain the coin, but
we used to set out an imaginary field, and whenever
the batsman gave a chance to the mythical fielders
he forfeited his shilling.   We have often made as
much as 18s. per hour at this game.   The wages
we received at Oxford used to be £1 a week, and
1s. 6d. per hour.   Well, as I said before, in 1855
I accepted an engagement at Eton, and not being
altogether satisfied with the way poor Old Clarke
had treated me, I severed my connection with the
All-England Eleven.

The North and South at Lord's was the first
great match of the season of 1855.   This was a
most interesting contest, the North winning by 18
runs.   Jemmy Dean declared that the over in which
he got rid of George Parr here was the best he
ever bowled.   The first three balls completely beat
"George," and the fourth clean bowled him.   John
Lillywhite played a good innings for the South in
this match.   "John" was a son of the famous old
Sussex bowler, and although inferior to his father
in the bowling line, was an infinitely better bat.
He was a little, square, strongly built man, and a
very powerful hitter.   His style, though by no

THOMAS BEAGLEY.

From the Collection of Cobbet's Cricket Bat Co., Ltd.

C. G. TAYLOR, Esq.

From the Collection of Mr A. J. Gaston, Brighton.

F. P. MILLER, Esq.

From the Collection of Mr A. J. Gaston, Brighton.

V. E. WALKER, Esq.

From the Collection of Mr A. J. Gaston, Brighton.

means elegant, was sound and correct.	For a few seasons he was one of the very best bats in England, but did not maintain his form for so long as many other cricketers of note.	This was in a great measure owing to his eyesight becoming slightly defective.	He was one of the leading players of the United after he left the All England in 1852.

We had a fine match, Surrey *v.* England, at the Oval this year.	Clarke got up the England side, which was scarcely a representative one in consequence, as none of the United Eleven were asked to play.	We set England 87 to get to win in their last innings, which they did not look like obtaining at one part of the game.	However, they got the required number while old Clarke, the last wicket, was in.	James Southerton played in this match, but was not put on to bowl.	Before going in to bat in my second innings, Mr Miller promised me a handsome present if I got 50.	I made 52, and received my promised reward from that gentleman.

In our match Surrey *v.* Sussex at Brighton we were defeated by 2 runs only.	We wanted about 25 to win when our last wicket was in.	Tom Sherman obtained 20 of these, and then in attempting a short run was run out.	Jim Chester and I made a good stand in the early part of our last innings, and at one time we looked like getting the runs off, but after our separation there was a complete collapse. Chester was a fine free hitter, being a strong powerful man. Although his career was not a long one, he played many extremely useful innings for his county. In our return with Sussex we were defeated by 5 wickets. Surrey, I should observe, were handicapped by the absence of Julius Cæsar and H. H. Stephenson, who had had a dispute with the executive about this time. The names of Messrs Edwin and William Napper are still to be found in the Sussex ranks this year. Both were left-handed batsmen, Mr Edwin, the elder brother, being the better of the two. He was a fine hitter in his day, and made many large scores.

In place of the usual Kent and England match at Lord's this year, a match was arranged "England v. a combined team of Kent and Surrey." This match had taken place only once before, and that was as far back as 1796. In spite of the combined team being very strong we were easily defeated. Owing to Cæsar and Stephenson not taking part in this match, Pilch and Wenman both refused (it was said at the time) to play with the combined counties. Mr (afterwards the Rev.) E. T. Drake took several wickets with his lobs in our second innings. He was at one time one of the best lob-bowlers in England, and although not quite so tricky with them as Tinley or Mr V. E. Walker, still he bowled with an excellent length and with a lot of twist. He was also a great hitter: being a tall thin man, loosely made, he was evidently designed by nature as such. He was likewise a magnificent field.

We once more defeated the Gentlemen in the Gentlemen and Players match this season, disposing of them for 43 in their second innings. George Parr played a grand innings of 77 for us—said to have been the best he ever played in these encounters.

My first match with the United Eleven was at Enville Hall against Lord Stamford's twenty-two. I scored 10 and 2 in this match, and obtained a few wickets. Fred Bell of Cambridge now played regularly with the United. Although not a great cricketer, he was useful as a bat and bowler, and was a wonderfully fine field, being an uncommonly fast runner. I have seen him come off an easy winner in many an impromptu foot-race. He formed one of the famous Cambridge Eleven in after-years, when Hayward, Carpenter, and Tarrant were all in their prime. My second experience with the United was a defeat at Langton Wold in York-shire, where we met a strong twenty-two. Mr F. P. Miller, who was elected president of the United about this time, played for us in this match.

Wisden and Dean next arranged a North and South match at Tunbridge Wells; but there was by no means a representative team from the North on this occasion, as none of the All England would take part in the match, and the South obtained an easy victory in consequence. We reversed the tables on England in the England *v.* Kent and Surrey match at Canterbury by defeating them by 9 runs. England had 147 to get in their last innings, but only obtained 138. I caught and bowled 4 in this match, and was the highest scorer with 60. This match was played in the Canterbury week. A military band was on the ground, and all festivities, almost as at the present day, were in vogue. We all visited Fuller Pilch on this occasion, who had lately become proprietor of the "Saracen's Head," and had practically retired from active cricket, although for this match he had had the superintendence of the preparation of the wicket.

In a match this year against twenty-two of Chichester the United captured the last 8 wickets of the twenty-two for no runs at all, Wisden and Jemmy Dean being the bowlers.

Against twenty-two of Bedfordshire at Luton this year the United made the large score of 334. Wisden, who was in great batting form just now, scored 80, myself 57, and Mr F. Burbidge, the famous Surrey player, 54. Mr Burbidge was one of the leading members of the Surrey Eleven, who a few years later than the time I am now writing of were almost invincible. He was a splendid batsman, combining brilliant hitting powers with a most ex-

cellent defence. Like Mr Miller, he could hit well
all round the wicket, and could often make runs
when others were unable to do so. He was a
splendid field, especially at point. His pluck was
something extraordinary. I once remember his
getting a tremendous smack on the forehead while
standing point (I think it was in a Surrey and Notts
match at the Oval), and although the blow almost
knocked him senseless he refused to leave his post,
where he made several magnificent catches in the
same innings. He did a great deal to help cricket
in Surrey, and was very popular with his fellow-
players.

The United played two curious matches in the
same week towards the close of the season of 1855.
The first was at Rotherham, where we required 27
to win when our last man (Fred Bell) went in to
Chatterton, who had then only scored 2. Bell kept
his end up while his partner hit away and knocked
off the runs, leaving us victorious by 1 wicket. In
our next match at Bradford we also came off the
victors by 1 wicket; this time having 5 runs to get
when our last man went in. We played our last
match at Edinburgh, where we were defeated.

George Parr headed the averages in both eleven-a-
side contests and for the whole season in 1855, his
average being 32 and 22 respectively. He and Mr
Burbidge were the only two who scored over 1000
runs. My own average was 22 and 16, the former

being for eleven-a-side matches and the latter for all. In the bowling Jack Wisden took 223 wickets in all matches at a cost of 5 runs per wicket, and as he had an average of 23 with the bat, his season may be looked upon as a remarkable one.   In the wicket-keeping Lockyer caught out 40 and stumped 21. Box (who had kept in one more innings than Tom) caught out 29 and stumped 29.   Lockyer was now in great form at the wicket, being scarcely ever known to miss anything at this part of his career.

CHAPTER X.

THE SEASON OF 1856.

OWING to a spell of ill-health I did not commence playing this season till rather late, my first match being for Surrey *v.* Sussex at Brighton towards the end of June. Here on a wet wicket we defeated the home side by 9 wickets. A great name figures in the Surrey Eleven who played in this match—that of Mr C. G. Lane, one of the great trio of gentlemen players who helped to place Surrey in the proud position which she occupied a few years later. To say that he was the finest bat I ever saw against fast bowling would be perhaps saying too much, but I certainly never saw a finer. He was a splendidly built man of 6 feet, and carried no unnecessary weight. His style of batting was very correct, always playing with a perfectly straight bat. For brilliancy and precision of playing fast bowling he never had a superior. He had an uncommonly hard stroke, something between a push and a drive past the mid-wickets, quite peculiar to himself. Jackson

when at his best used to say he would sooner bowl
at any one in England than Mr Lane.   He was a
grand field out in the country or at cover-point, and
always threw himself heart and soul into every game
he played.

The North and South match at Lord's was won
by the latter by 6 wickets this year.   Wisden and
Willsher bowled finely in this match, which is
noticeable as being the first match at Lord's in
which the " Demon " Jackson took part.   Mr R.
Hankey made the top score of the match—38.   This
batsman was one of the finest that England ever
produced.   Like Mr Lane, he was about 6 feet high,
but weighed nearly 14 stone.   His batting was a
treat to behold.   His leg-hitting and driving were
something to wonder at, and he possessed a fine bold
style of defence.   His innings of 70 made for the
Gentlemen against the Players in 1857 has become
historical, and it is strange to relate that he said to
us on arriving at the wicket, " I am far from well
to-day, I shan't trouble you long ! "   He commenced
his innings by hitting Willsher for two 4's, and
continued to force the game until he was at length
caught out by Willsher from a fine drive off H. H.
Stephenson.   He hit one 6 and several 5's, only
making very few singles.   It was a fine performance
when one considers the amount of bowling we
possessed.   Willsher, Stephenson, Wisden, and myself all had a turn at him, as had also George Parr

REGINALD HANKEY, Esq.

From the Collection of Cobbet's Cricket Bat Co., Ltd.

with lobs. "Well," sighed Jack Wisden when he was at length disposed of, "if that's his form when he's ill, I'll be hanged if I ever want to play against him when he's well!" It is a fact, nevertheless, that Mr Hankey's innings would have been larger if he had been in better condition for running. Mr Hankey was a good field and a fair change bowler, but had not a very good length. He was born in Middlesex, but played afterwards a little for Surrey. His career was a short one, which is to be regretted by all admirers of cricket.

Harking back to the season of 1856, Surrey easily beat Oxfordshire in their return match at the Oval by 6 wickets. A most memorable match I took part in this year at Lord's—England *v.* Kent and Sussex. In their last innings the combined counties had only 44 to get to win, but owing to the extraordinary bowling of Bickley they only made 39, Bickley actually taking 8 wickets for 7 runs! 7 of which were clean bowled. It is also a remarkable fact that 6 of these 7 runs were made from *the first over*. After the match Bickley received a new ball from the M.C.C. and several sums of money from different members. In the account of this match the players are described as "receiving almost as many blows as they obtained runs." On the middle day of the match there was no play on account of rain. So a meeting was called in the pavilion to consider the subject of the "Cricketers Fund Friendly Society."

On the third day we arranged to begin play at ten
o'clock, but it was somewhat later than that before
we got a start. A curious incident occurred when
Mr Nicholson was batting in the second innings of
England. Box stumped him, and John Lillywhite
gave him "not out," meaning, as he at once afterwards declared, to have said "out"!

Surrey inflicted a severe defeat on Sussex at the
Oval shortly after this match, being victorious by
240 runs. I made 88, the largest score of the
match. Mr Alfred Mynn officiated as umpire on
this occasion.

The Players once more defeated the Gentlemen
at Lord's, this time by 2 wickets. We had to
take the last innings to get only 70 runs to win;
but had it not been for the stand of George Parr,
who made 27, we should in all probability have
been defeated. In the account of the match it is
described as being "the most exciting game played
between the Gentlemen and Players for years, and
'hedging' was consequently the order of the day
after dinner." The betting had been 2 to 1 on us
at the start, I may mention. This was the first time
Julius Cæsar had taken part in this match, of which
he was top scorer with a fine 51 made in the first
innings. Messrs C. D. Marsham and A. Payne
bowled well for the Gentlemen on this occasion.
Mr Marsham was a fine medium-pace bowler. He
had a very pretty delivery, and on a wet wicket

wanted a lot of watching. He was of great assistance to the Gentlemen for years, being a hard-hitting
and effective bat, as well as being in the front rank
of bowlers. He was also an excellent field. He was
a fine man, standing well over 6 feet in height. Mr
Payne was a very fast left-hand bowler, rather erratic:
sometimes sending you a couple of balls almost out of
reach, and the next, a regular trimmer, right on the
middle stump, and often making it fly out of the
ground, too, in a most alarming manner. As a bat
he was also left-handed and was a most terrific hitter.

The United Eleven had a most enjoyable match
at Lord Stamford's seat at Enville this year, where
we were, however, easily defeated. Indeed no eleven
could well contend against twenty-two such players
as Lord Stamford used to get together. An excellent band from London played on the ground each
day, and every one who took part in the match
was treated in the most sumptuous fashion. On
the middle day there were said to be over 10,000
people to witness the cricket, and at the conclusion
of the match nearly 80,000 people were assembled
in the grounds to behold a grand exhibition of
fireworks. When the magnificent gardens were
all illuminated the sight was one which could
never be forgotten. We were, I may mention,
again opposed to Mr Payne's bowling in this
match. He was, I believe, private secretary to
the Earl of Stamford at this time.

Tom Lockyer and I assisted the M.C.C. against
England at Lord's this season, where we were
defeated by 200 runs.   The chief feature of the
match was the splendid hitting of Cris Tinley,
who knocked up 50 in just over the hour in the
second innings of England.   Shortly after this I
made my first century for the United—viz., 104—
v. twenty-two of Luton.   Our total, 358, being at
that time the highest ever made against twenty-
two, caused a great stir in the cricket world.   I
took part in a North and South match at Manchester this year, which was unfinished owing to
rain, and chiefly noted for the grand innings of
102 made by the Yorkshireman, Tom Hunt.   In
the return match England v. Kent and Sussex the
tables were turned on England, the counties defeating us by 6 wickets.   Willsher and Wisden
bowled magnificently throughout.   The wicket at
Canterbury was prepared by the veteran Pilch
about this time, and was undoubtedly the best in
England.

We had an interesting match at my native place,
Reigate, this year—sixteen of Reigate v. the United
Eleven.   I assisted the sixteen, who also borrowed
the services of Mr Alfred Mynn and other gentlemen.   The sixteen won by 43 runs.   We had
several pleasant United Eleven matches towards
the close of the season of 1856 in Wales and
Ireland, playing a very close game against eighteen

of Dublin in the Phœnix Park, who defeated us by 6 runs only. That capital player Mr (now Canon) M'Cormick played for the eighteen, and had the unenviable distinction of making "spectacles." He was a fine, powerfully built man of more than 6 feet, and would, I should say, weigh over 14 stones. He was a most brilliant hitter, and had an excellent defence as well. Unfortunately he was unable to devote much time to cricket, otherwise his name would have been better remembered than it is. Mr M'Cormick was also a very useful bowler, slow round-arm, and very tricky.

When playing for the United at Hereford this year, Julius Cæsar, Bell, and myself had an unpleasant experience. We stayed at Derby overnight, and being terribly tired, overslept ourselves and missed our train in the morning. Consequently we were unable to reach Hereford till late in the afternoon, and missed our innings accordingly.

The All England had a successful season, on the whole, in 1856, George Parr succeeding Clarke in the management of that body at the close of the season. "George" had not played so much as usual this year, owing to having hurt his finger badly. In the season's bowling averages it is shown that in 1856 the slow bowlers had not been so effective as the fast, Wisden and Willsher being at the top of the list. An old newspaper which I have before me declares that if a few more Wisdens and Willshers do not turn up "it will be found prudent to adopt some alteration in the size of the stumps, or some other plan to favour the bowler." This sounds rather strange to us now, when the same paper informs us that "John Lillywhite carries off the palm of victory" (in the batting averages) "with an average of 24."

CHAPTER XI.

THE SEASON OF 1857.

THE season of 1857 found me once more engaged
at Oxford for a short time. After making my score
of 104 at Luton the previous year, I had accepted
an engagement with a gentleman near Hitchin;
but, owing to his going abroad in 1857, it fell
through. Charley Brown, Tom Lockyer, Julius
Cæsar, Hinkly, and others, were all engaged at
Oxford in 1857. I scored 87 in a match between
eleven players engaged at the University and eleven
undergraduates early in the season. My first big
match was for Surrey *v.* Cambridgeshire at Cambridge. This was the first time the two counties
had met, and we had the satisfaction of beating
them by 56 runs. Cambridgeshire were not very
strong, however. Mr Henry Perkins (afterwards
the well-known secretary of the M.C.C.) played for
them, as also did Ducky Diver, who was for years
one of their best players. He was a remarkably
pretty bat, a good change bowler, and fine field,
especially at long-stop; and as a coach, was one of

the very best that ever lived. He was a little man,
but well put together. He was an excellent judge of
the game, and capable of captaining any eleven in
any match, however important. I have often heard
George Parr declare that he was always glad to take
his cue from Diver as to when he changed the
bowling. "Not very straight!" the little long-stop
would whisper to "George" as he changed for the
over; "take him off."

At the commencement of June 1857 was played
the first of the matches between the England and
United Elevens at Lord's. This first match was
organised for the benefit of the Cricketers Fund.
There had been attempts made during Clarke's
lifetime to arrange this match, but the veteran
never would consent to it so long as he had the
management of the All England. A crowd of 10,000
people witnessed the first day's play, being then the
largest "gate" which had ever assembled at Lord's.
The match did not begin till noon, but as early as
half-past nine the spectators had begun to arrive.
The United scored 143 and 140; All England 206
and 78 for 4, being thus victorious by 6 wickets. I
received a terrible smack in the ribs from Jackson in
my second innings, which made me feel very queer.
Over £150 were cleared for the fund, after deducting
all expenses. Mr Dark, the owner of the ground,
entertained both teams to roast - beef and plum-
pudding each day at lunch.

Surrey defeated Oxfordshire this year by exactly the same number of runs with which we had beaten Cambridgeshire—viz., 56; and we followed up this by a victory over Kent by 7 wickets, and managed to again beat Cambridgeshire at the Oval by 36 runs in the return. The famous Tom Hayward assisted his county in this match, but made few runs in either innings. Volumes almost have been written about this player, and little can be said of him which has not been said already. He was a beautiful player to watch, and was a remarkably effective bat, as well as possessing a graceful style. He had a decided flourish in his style of defence, which might have been considered bad form in a less skilful batsman, but the flourish in Tom's case was natural, and was never the cause of his getting out. He was one of the very best "on-side" players I ever saw, his finest stroke perhaps being made between short-leg and mid-on. He also drove freely, but somewhat loftily. His wrist play was perfect. He was remarkable for the way he could put down a rising ball, and was also very safe at stopping a shooter. He was seen to great advantage on a fast wicket. His style of defence may be considered as forward and "half-forward." This latter stroke he used more frequently than any player I ever saw, and used it to a ball which most batsman would play back to. Though in my opinion he was not as reliable a bat as Carpenter, he was of course a more

attractive one to look at. For a first-class bat, he
was, I think, the worst judge of a run I ever saw,
and should say he was responsible for more "runs
out" to his side than almost any other player. As
a bowler he was also very good, being medium pace,
with a break back, He was also an excellent field
at cover - point. He was a thin man of medium
height, had a very dark complexion, and rather a
"sour" expression of face. Soon after he appeared
in first - class cricket he joined the All - England
Eleven, and made many large scores for them for
years.

Surrey, continuing their victorious career, next
defeated Sussex at Brighton by 9 wickets; and
followed this up by a victory over the North of
England at the Oval by 6 wickets. In our second
innings, when we wanted 2 runs to win, Jackson
got out Stephenson, Mr Miller, and Griffith in one
over. I scored 60 in our first innings, for which
the old newspaper says that I "received some
'California' from the Surrey Club." Victories
over Sussex, Oxfordshire, and the North of England once more were obtained by our county, who
were only once defeated this season—viz., against
Manchester assisted by Wisden and John Lillywhite; and here we were only defeated by 3 runs.
There is no doubt that we were at this time by a
long way the strongest county in England. The
Gentleman and Players match was a very close one,

the latter winning by 13 runs. This was the match
when Mr Hankey made his famous 70 before alluded to. Towards the finish we looked like being
defeated, as in the second innings of the Gentlemen
Mr Drake was hitting our bowling all over the place.
He hit a 6, two 5's, and three 4's, and just before he
got out the Gentlemen only required 16 to win with
2 wickets to go down. I luckily managed to snap
Mr Drake at short-slip off Willsher at this state of
the game, and we contrived to run the last man
out (Mr Walter Fellows), and thus won amidst the
greatest excitement. The betting had been at one
time 6 to 4 on the Gentlemen.

There were three North and South matches
in 1857,—one at Lord's, which was won by the
South by 14 runs; another at Tunbridge Wells,
which was won by the North; and the third
match, played at Nottingham, which was left unfinished. In the match at Lord's I scored 90, but
gave three easy chances. I well remember this
match. I think I never saw Jackson bowl so
fast as on this occasion. The wicket was fiery,
and was, I recollect, pitched much nearer the
pavilion than usual. It is wonderful how one
remembers these details when one has made a
large score in a match. If I had got out for a
duck, perhaps I should have even forgotten to
mention the match at all!

We played two interesting matches this year,

Surrey and Sussex combined *v.* England.   The first
was at the Oval and the return at Brighton.   The
counties were successful in both contests.   There
was some good batting shown on both sides in
the match at the Oval, — George Parr, Jackson,
Lillywhite, and Tom Lockyer all receiving a handsome donation, which, as was then the custom,
was presented publicly in front of the pavilion
amidst the cheers of the spectators.   I was also
liberally rewarded for my bowling in the second
innings, when I took 9 wickets for 29 runs.   Teddy
Stephenson of Yorkshire played a very useful innings of 42 in this match.   The papers were rather
down on him for not hitting more, but predicted
that he would make a good bat if he learnt to
lay on the wood.   Teddy could, however, hit as
hard as any one when in the humour to do so,
but he had a most stubborn defence as well.   Like
his great Surrey namesake—to whom, by the way,
he was not related — he was a bat, bowler, and
wicket - keeper, being much distinguished in the
last capacity.   He bowled fast round - arm, and
had his services not been so much in requisition behind the sticks, he would have made a very good
bowler indeed.   Teddy was a Yorkshireman, and
quite a character.   He was always saying something to put a roomful into a roar of laughter.
He was a strongly made man of medium height.

We had a second match between the England

and United Elevens at Lord's in 1857, this one being for the benefit of Jemmy Dean. Many thousands of people were again present, and "Jemmy" cleared a handsome sum of money. George Anderson was ill and unable to play for the All England, who wanted to play E. Stephenson in his place; but this was objected to on the ground that he could not then be considered an All-England man. Eventually Tom Adams was played by mutual consent, he having been a member of the *old* All-England Eleven. The matter took a lot of arranging, and at one time there looked like being unpleasantness. The All England won the match easily, chiefly owing to the fine bowling of Willsher in the second innings.

There were fewer matches than usual played against twenty-twos this year, owing to the inter-eleven, North and South matches, &c. No one scored 1000 runs in the season, although John Lillywhite and I each scored over 900 and George Parr more than 800. I may mention that I played with the M.C.C. on one or two occasions in 1857, but was never permanently engaged by them. It was, I believe, this year that Mr William Burrup succeeded to the hon. secretaryship of Surrey, vacated by his brother Mr John Burrup.

CHAPTER XII.

THE SEASON OF 1858.

THIS season I was engaged at Winchester College, where I remained for four seasons in all. I enjoyed my engagements there very much. I was kindly treated by every one, and found the coaching of the boys very interesting. My first important match in 1858 was for the United v. Eighteen of Christ-church, Oxford, when I totalled 77. In the "Two Elevens" match at Lord's this year the United had the satisfaction of coming off victorious by 4 wickets. This again was played for the benefit of the Cricketers Fund. Another large concourse of spectators assembled, and great improvements had been made for their accommodation, amongst others being the erection of a huge marquee for luncheons. I was in good bowling form in this match, securing 7 wickets for 39 in the first innings and 5 for 64 in the second. The match is remarkable for the first appearance at Lord's of Bob Carpenter. Never perhaps did a colt do so well at Lord's in his first venture, when the importance of the match and the quality of the bowling is taken into consideration. Carpenter played a faultless and plucky innings of 45, most of which he obtained from the bowling of Jackson. I have called Carpenter a colt; but he could hardly be so termed, being at the time twenty-seven years of age. Carpenter has been popularly described as "the champion back-player of the century," and he may be considered as being justly entitled to the appellation. Never was there a batsman who played so *much* back as Carpenter. Even when he played forward he generally got back in order to do so, pushing his bat down the wicket at the last moment. But it must be remembered that Carpenter went out and drove many balls which another batsman would have played forward to. Like Tiny Wells, he was one of the few batsmen who appear to greater advantage against slow bowling than against fast. Being a strong man, and very quick on his legs, he was able to get down the wicket and hit with tremendous force, generally contriving to drive the ball on the ground or at about the height of a man's head. He was also a magnificent square-leg hitter, though he was often caught out by making this hit. He was of medium height and strongly built, being much stouter in his cricketing time than he is at present. He was first-rate at point, and made many fine catches there. Sometimes when playing against twenty-twos he would purposely miss a ball in order to let the batsman attempt a run, and leave it to Tom Hayward at cover, who was in at the trick, to run out the victim. He bowled lobs occasionally with success. Carpenter played with the United for many years, but assisted the All England a good deal during the latter part of his career. The last time I saw him was a few years ago, when I accidentally met him in London.

Another famous name appears in the ranks of the United in the match when Carpenter made his *début*—viz., that of Tom Hearne, who played excellently for 54 not out in the second innings. Like Carpenter, Tom began his public career rather late in life, being nearly thirty years old before he appeared at Lord's. As a bat he was a fine hitter, but did not possess at all an elegant style. He was a quick run-getter, being a splendid driver. He was also very clever at making the old "draw" between his legs and the wicket. As a bowler Tom was of medium pace of the Jemmy Dean type, and was on certain wickets very effective. He was a tall man, but carried no superfluous flesh.

Surrey again defeated the combined counties of Sussex and Kent at Brighton after we had been headed over 100 on the first innings. I made 81 in the second innings. In the return at the Oval the weather prevented a definite result from being arrived at. I scored 59 in this match, being bowled by a full pitch from Stubberfield, which I was trying to hit round to leg. In justice to myself I must say that the light was very bad at the time. Stubberfield, who was a Sussex man, was a fair bowler, rather fast, but was not much of a bat. He was a great tall fellow of more than 6 feet. He possessed the longest feet I ever saw on either a cricketer or any one else. He used to say jokingly himself, that in order to keep them clear of the wicket he should have to stand at short-leg when batting! ·

The famous slow bowler James Southerton was now assisting Sussex, which was the county of his birth. He was one of the very best slow round-arm bowlers of his day, getting a good deal of work on the ball. He not only played for Sussex, but became qualified for Hampshire, and finally for Surrey, through his living at Mitcham. When getting on in life, for a cricketer, he was for years of the greatest assistance to Surrey, at a time when they were rather short of bowling. He had a nice easy delivery, and never seemed to tire. By the time I returned from Australia in 1871 he had altered his action a good deal, having then a much higher delivery than in earlier years. Southerton was a little man, who was much liked by all who came in contact with him.

I may here say that Surrey were in great form

this season, not losing a single match, and it was to commemorate this fact that the white marble tablet, so well known by frequenters of the Oval, recording the doings of the team, was presented by Mr A. Marshall of Godalming.

This year we defeated Kent and Sussex combined, Cambridgeshire, Notts, England, and . the North. Our closest match, strange to say, was against the weakest side, Cambridgeshire, who were without several of their best men. Our match with Notts was rather a curious one. George Parr was ill and could not play, and Bickley and Cris Tinley were engaged at Lord Stamford's and unable to come; so almost at the last moment it was arranged that Diver should play as a given man for the midland shire, and he proved very useful to them, making 28 and 46. The two counties had not met since 1854; indeed Notts had played no county since then, owing to the All England matches, no doubt. The success of Surrey in the present encounter produced the following letter in one of the leading newspapers, which perhaps was the cause of Notts rousing themselves to arrange . to meet Surrey the following season :—

MR EDITOR,—I am sorry to find the patrons of cricket in Notts so devoid of patriotism as to allow Surrey to gain all the laurels in the cricketing world without another trial. As a demonstration of the love of cricket in the county, the great quantity of clubs that exist in the towns and

villages need only be referred to, and I should be inclined to think, if an influential person were to interest
himself in the matter, a sufficient amount of money might
be collected to pay the expenses of a match between
Surrey and Notts. The only drawback is the unwilling-
ness of Lord Stamford to let his three bowlers play; but
surely if a deputation were to wait upon that nobleman
he would be liberal enough to grant the services of Bickley,
Brampton, and Tinley. I suppose the ill feeling existing
between Lord Stamford and the Surrey Committee is the
reason of his objection. If this is the case, would it not
be a worthy retaliation to give Nottingham a chance of
plucking the laurels from the Surrey Club? On the other
hand, supposing he will *not* let them play, could not an
eleven be selected from the following names that would
not disgrace Nottingham?—viz., C. Brown, A. Clarke,
R. Daft, Esq., T. Davis, R. B. Earle, Esq., R. Gibson,
J. Grundy, A. Hoyles, Esq., J. Jackson, A. W. M'Dougal,
Esq., G. Parr, H. Parr, J. Watson, Esq., F. Tinley, H.
Chatterton, and Gregory. Hoping yet to see the an-
nouncement of a match between the two counties, I am,
yours, &c.,   JUVENIS.

"Juvenis" saw his wish realised the following
season, when Notts came up to the Oval and easily
beat us. In the 1858 match Henry Parr, a brother
of "George," came to represent his county, this .
being his first visit to London. I shall never forget
riding on a 'bus with him. He seemed to have a
fixed idea that we were going to run into every
vehicle we passed, and when we had safely passed
one he would call out, "That wasn't two inches

off!" or, "By Jingo, that *was* a shave!" When
he first saw the Thames, too, he remarked that
"The Trent was a deal wider here than it was at
Nottingham"! "Oh, what a big Trent!" he kept
exclaiming.

The Surrey and Notts match of 1858 is celebrated
as being the first time the famous Richard Daft
played for his county. A great name, indeed, this
in the annals of cricket! It has become the custom,
when comparing the merits of one batsman with
another, to bar the name of W. G. Grace. So
also when the subject of gracefulness of style of
different batsmen is brought up, the name of
Richard Daft should in like manner be set aside.
The Rev. R. S. Holmes and Prince Ranjitsinhji
speak in no spirit of exaggeration when the former
declares him to have been "the most finished batsman that ever handled willow," and the latter, "the
most graceful and stylish batsman that ever adorned
the cricket-field." What was the cause of Daft
being entitled to have this said of him? Was it
his wrist-play? Partly, for beautiful wrist-play
he undoubtedly possessed, but then so in as great
a degree perhaps did William Barnes. No, it was
not only his style of batting that was elegant, but
he was graceful in every movement he made and
every attitude he assumed. He had a perfectly pro-
portioned figure, somewhat above medium height,
but owing to his erect carriage looked taller than

he was. His attitude at the wicket was an exact counterpart of that of Pilch. Like Tom Hayward and myself, Daft held the bat very lightly as regards his left hand, putting great pressure on the handle with the forefinger of his right. His style of play was without the slightest suspicion of flourish. The easy way he would play back at a good length ball on the off-stump was worth going miles to see. Willsher once said to me, "When Richard plays that ball I always feel as if he said, 'If that's all you can do, Ned, you'd better put somebody else on at once!'" He had also a very clever way of putting down a bumping ball in the slips, often scoring 4 by doing so. He was very quick on his feet, and, like Carpenter, would frequently go out of his ground and drive a bowler hard along the ground. Then there was the stroke under his leg, which no man ever played so hard or so successfully. Daft was the only man I ever saw who deliberately turned the course of the ball when making this stroke: practically it was a leg-hit made under the leg as it were, and not by any means like a "glance." In his style of defence Mr Murdoch reminds me more of Daft than any one, except that Daft played "higher" than the great Australian batsman. Like Shrewsbury, Daft could play with success on all kinds of wickets. His large scores will be found to have been made on bumpy, slow, and sticky wickets as well as on

I

easy pitches.   Daft was more modern in his style
of play than most of his contemporaries, and this
is borne out by the fact of the enormous scores
he made in local cricket after his retirement —
scores often made against a first-class bowler too.
He was a very fair lob-bowler and a magnificent
field, especially out in the country.

Notwithstanding the absence of George Parr, the
Players defeated the Gentlemen by 3 wickets at the
Oval, in 1858.   Daft played for the Gentlemen in
this match, he and Mr V. E. Walker making a
long stand in the second innings, for which they
each received a prize bat.   Kent with the help of
Jackson, Parr, and myself played England at Lord's.
It was a small-scoring match.   Mr C. D. Marsham
and H. H. Stephenson bowled unchanged in both
innings for England, and Jackson and myself did
the same for the county.   In the Gentlemen and
Players match at Lord's I regret to have to relate
that I did not score in either innings.   The Players
were this time victorious by nearly 300 runs.

The great match between Surrey and England at
the Oval immediately followed this.   George Parr
and Wisden got up the England team, which was
particularly strong.   I had the satisfaction of making
102 in this match, which, by the way, Surrey won in
one innings.   I received the usual talent-money,
and £13 was collected for me besides.   All the
other Surrey players had a sovereign each given

to them, and Messrs Lane, Miller, and Burbidge each a prize bat. The "prize bats" of those days were only for ornament as a rule, being made usually of some fancy wood and highly polished. After the match a dinner was given to the professionals of England by the Surrey Club in the pavilion. A great number were present. On this occasion we of the Surrey team presented Mr Burrup, the hon. secretary, who had done so much towards bringing our county to its present high position, with a meerschaum pipe mounted in gold. H. H. Stephenson made the presentation.

The All England and United match was this year played for the benefit of George Parr at Lord's. There was a great crowd each day (the match was over in two days), although the weather was not very good. An easy victory for the All England by an innings and nearly 100 runs was the result. Jackson's bowling was almost unplayable in this match, although for Lord's the wicket was not such a bad one. The Surrey *v.* North of England match was won by the county after having to follow our innings. An interesting match was played at the Oval this year for the benefit of Billy Hillyer—England *v.* Eighteen Veterans. I alluded to this match, it will be remembered, when speaking of Hillyer. Mynn, Wenman, and Guy figured for the old ones, whom we beat by 9 wickets.

A match, Married *v.* Single, was the last match

of note played in London in 1858.   This took place
at the Oval, and was a most exciting affair.   The
Single (of which I was then one) went in first and
scored 188.   The Married replied with 221, to
which Bob Carpenter contributed a splendid 84.
The Single were disposed of for 124 in their
second venture, and the Married had to go in
to get 92 to win; but owing to Wisden and H.
H. Stephenson being so "on the spot," we got
rid of them for 75, and thus won the match by
16 runs.   I never saw a bit of better bowling in
my life than that of Wisden and Stephenson,
neither of whom sent down a single loose ball.

George Parr had an average of 18 with 935 runs
for the whole season, while I myself scored 809 runs
for an average of 17.   I was also well up in the
bowling.   I think this was the year—I am not quite
sure, but think it was in 1858—that I was backed
by Mr Charles Chadband of Epsom to shoot Mr
Wood of that town in a pigeon-shooting match,
for £25 a-side.   I was a very good shot at that
time and won the match alluded to, which took
place at the Rosemary Branch ground at Peckham
Rye, of which Mr Fred Chadband, my backer's
brother, was the proprietor.   Mr Alfred Mynn and
Mr John Walker were present to see the match.
It snowed very hard, I remember, on the day it
came off.   Wood was about the best shot in Surrey,
so beating him was very satisfactory to myself.   I

RICHARD DAFT.

used to be very fond of pigeon - shooting in my young days. Sometimes we would get up a sweepstakes for a fat pig or something of that kind. I have won several of these at different times. Julius Cæsar was one of the best shots I knew. I could hold my own with him at the traps, but he could beat me at ordinary shooting in the open. I remember once losing a shooting match against Tiny Wells for a case of wine. On this occasion we shot sparrows under flower-pots. From a boy I had been exceedingly fond of all kinds of shooting. Mr Paley, a gentleman of Reigate and a keen cricketer, used to give me leave to shoot blackbirds in his fields, and, I am sorry to say, I by no means restricted myself to blackbirds at such times!

CHAPTER XIII.

THE SEASON OF 1859.

EARLY in 1859 I made the largest score I ever made
in my career. This was 157 for Surrey *v.* sixteen
Undergraduates of Cambridge on Fenner's ground.
Tom Hayward had, about a fortnight before, scored
220 when assisting the gentlemen of Cambridgeshire
against *eleven* undergraduates of the 'Varsity. When
I made my 157 " Tom " was one of the umpires, and
at different parts of my innings he kept saying that he
was sure I was going to beat that record score of his.
Perhaps if I had been playing against eleven I should
have done so. The England and United match this
year was a bowler's match, the ground being very
dead. Wisden captained the United, and having
won the toss decided to go in, although the majority
of us thought it would have been better to have put
in our opponents. However, the result was a win
for the United by 38 runs. This was the fifth time
the two elevens had met, England having now won
three matches and the United two. The North and

South match at Lord's was easily won by the latter
by 10 wickets. Mr Haygarth was the top scorer of
either side with 45, which he took over three hours
and a half to make.

A Gentlemen and Players match was again played
at the Oval in 1859, and resulted in an innings victory
for the Players. George Parr played a fine innings
of 73. Mr V. E. Walker took 6 of our wickets with
his lobs. He was, without doubt, one of the finest
lob-bowlers ever seen, and for fielding to his own
bowling I never saw his equal. As a bat he was, in
my humble opinion, the best of all the Walkers.
He was an exceedingly fine hitter, with a splendid
defence. Although his younger brother, the late
Mr "I. D.," may have been a more effective bat,
still he certainly was not so attractive to look at
as Mr V. E. In the Surrey v. England match of
1859 he performed the extraordinary and unparal-
leled feat of scoring 100 runs and taking in one
innings the whole of his opponents' wickets. Clarke,
Cris. Tinley, and Mr Walker form the finest trio of
lob-bowlers I ever saw. Mr Walker was a splendid
field, and could not be placed in a wrong position.
He was altogether one of the best all-round cricketers
who ever donned flannels.

The second England and United match of 1859
was again won by the latter, thus making each to
have won three matches of the six played. Carpenter and Tom Hearne, going in first for the United,

knocked up 149 runs before they were separated. Carpenter eventually made 97, and batted for four hours and a half. I played for England shortly afterwards against sixteen Undergraduates of Oxford at Lord's. Jemmy Grundy played an excellent innings of 103, taking six and a half hours to make them.

One of the great events of the season of 1859 was the match between Surrey and Notts at the Oval. Only one match between these counties took place this year, and it resulted in a win for the midland county by 8 wickets. George Parr obtained in this match the highest score he ever made—viz., 130. He received a nasty knock on the finger when he had made about 60, and, unless my memory misleads me, he also ricked his side at one period of his innings and had Daft to run for him. His innings was played without a chance, and £20 was collected for him on the ground. The Notts innings closed at 7.15 on the first day for 329. The betting at the start had been 6 to 4 on Surrey, but on Friday morning, before commencing our first innings, it was 5 to 1 against us. We scored 213 (of which I made 76), and following on made 172, thus leaving Notts 50 odd to get, which they obtained for the loss of 2 wickets. The Surrey Club paid all the expenses of the Notts players on this occasion, amounting to about £120 I believe. I must take this opportunity of saying that the Surrey Club were very liberal in rewarding their players at this period. In the match I have spoken of I received £2 for my 76, as also did Tom Lockyer for getting 61 in the second innings, and several of the Notts players also were awarded talent-money.

The Players this year again obtained an easy victory over the Gentlemen at Lord's. George Parr was unable to play owing to the injured finger he had received at the Oval. It began to be suggested about this time that the Gentlemen should be allowed a few extra players, and one eminent authority wrote to one of the newspapers proposing that the Gentlemen should play with wickets of less width. Neither suggestion was, however, adopted. The England and Surrey match (which may be called Mr V. E. Walker's match, owing to his unique performance already alluded to) resulted in disaster for the county, we being defeated by nearly 400 runs. In our match against the North of England we were more fortunate, as we won by 2 wickets. George Parr was unable to bat in the second innings, having been taken ill overnight, or the result might have been different. The game became most exciting at the finish, as Jackson was bowling in fine form, and when Tom Lockyer made the winning hit the strain was intense. Tom played a grand innings of 51 not out, and was handsomely rewarded for his services. We had a delightful match shortly afterwards, the United Eleven against Mr John Walker's

Sixteen, played on Mr Walker's ground at Southgate. Six out of the seven Walkers played against
us, the absentee being Mr "I. D." I was top scorer
with 124 for the United, and Mr V. E. Walker with
88 for the sixteen. This was not the first time I had
played at Southgate. It was always a most pleasant
place to play at. The ground was an excellent one,
and several thousands of spectators would often be
there to witness a good match.

Surrey defeated a combined eleven of Kent and
Sussex at the Oval. The match is remarkable for
the fact of Surrey putting on 128 runs out of a
total of 234 for the last wicket, Mudie making 79
and young Tom Sewell 39. Mudie was a useful
bat, though never quite first-class, and was also a
good lob - bowler. He was a tall man and very
thin, and was nicknamed in consequence "The
Surrey Shadow." George Griffith was now playing regularly in the Surrey Eleven, and was for
years one of its most distinguished players. As
an all-round man he had few equals in the kingdom. As a batsman he was one of the hardest
hitters that ever lived, and his opponents were
always delighted to see the back of him. "Ben,"
as he was always called, was just the man to go
in and pull a match out of the fire. He was, I
should say, the best left - hand batsman that had
been out up to his own time, with the exception of
Mr Felix, who of course was a batter of another

type. "Ben" bowled as well as batted left-hand, being fast round with a nice amount of break. On certain wickets his bowling was about as nasty as anything which can be imagined. He was also a fine field anywhere, and could throw a great distance. Towards the latter part of his time he bowled under-hand lobs very well indeed. At the time Mr Jackson of Fairfield was ready to back Hayward and Carpenter to play any two in England at single wicket. I was anxious to make a match for Ben Griffith and myself to take on the two Cambridge cracks. I remember once meeting Carpenter at a hotel in London and suggesting this to him, and £25 to back Ben and myself was quickly collected in the room; but for some reason or other the match never came off. With all due respect to the two Cambridgeshire stars, I may perhaps be pardoned for saying, that had we played them I think we ought to have beaten them, as there would practically have been only Hayward to have bowled against us, whereas both "Ben" and myself were bowlers. Fast bowling is of course an important factor in single wicket; and then there would have been "Ben's" great hitting powers to be dealt with. I have always regretted that for the sake of sport this match never came off. Griffith was only of medium height, but was tremendously strongly built. He stooped a little, and having a short neck, his head appeared to be partially buried between his immense shoulders. His career was somewhat cut short by his severely straining himself while catching a ball.

The match Surrey won by 34 runs against the North at Broughton, Manchester, towards the end of August in 1859 was rendered rather unpleasant by the following incident. On the first day Surrey were batting (having gone in first), and Teddy Stephenson, who was keeping wicket for the North, had his finger badly hurt early in the game. The injured finger was so painful that one of the other players (Cris Tinley, I believe) took the gloves, and Stephenson went into the field. Surrey were got out just before time on the first day, and the North began batting the next morning. After they had lost 6 wickets or so, Mr Miller, our captain, was asked if a substitute could be allowed to bat in place of Stephenson. This he refused to permit, and after a rather heated discussion, Stephenson came in to bat amidst the cheers of the crowd, intending to play with one hand, but before a ball could be bowled to him George Parr came out of the pavilion and peremptorily ordered him to come back. Stephenson did so, and the North thus played a man short in both innings, which perhaps was the cause of their losing the game.

And now a great event occurred, as a team of English cricketers paid their first visit to America.

Carpenter. Caffyn. Lockyer. Wisden. Stephenson. G. Parr. Grundy. Cæsar. Hayward. Jackson.
Diver. John Lillywhite.

FIRST AMERICAN TEAM.

Photographed on board ship at Liverpool, Sept. 7, 1859.

CHAPTER XIV.

THE FIRST ENGLISH TEAM IN AMERICA.

On the 7th of September 1859 the first team of English cricketers set sail to America from Liverpool in the Nova Scotia. We all arrived at Liverpool overnight and put up at the George Hotel, while we were photographed on a vessel in the docks before proceeding on board the Nova Scotia. The English twelve were a very powerful lot, consisting of H. H. Stephenson, Julius Cæsar, Tom Lockyer, and myself from Surrey; George Parr, Grundy, and Jackson from Notts; Hayward, Carpenter, and Diver (Cambridge); and Wisden and John Lillywhite from Sussex. Fred Lillywhite too accompanied us as reporter, and took his printing-press and scoring-tent along with him. There was not a single member of the team who could not bowl, two lob-bowlers being found in Parr and Carpenter. Our team rather curiously was composed of six All England and six United Players. We were just over a fortnight making the voyage, and experienced some rather rough weather. Some of us were very bad sailors, the worst being John Lillywhite, H. H. Stephenson, and old Jackson. There were also one or two of the others who were not much better. Parr, Wisden, Hayward, and Carpenter were just the same as if they had been on land, especially Wisden, who seemed thoroughly to enjoy the voyage at first. George Parr was all right except when it got a bit rough, whereupon he always became extremely nervous for fear we should "go down"; and at once tried to give himself a little Dutch courage by imbibing a copious supply of gin-and-water, which always seemed to me to have the opposite effect to what "George" desired, and made him more nervous than ever. After some days we most of us found our "sea-legs," and passed the time by day in playing "shuffle-board," there being generally a bottle or two of champagne depending on the result of each game. In the evenings we often had a little harmony. Our Captain (Mr Borland was his name) was, I recollect, particularly delighted with Bob Carpenter's song, "The sweet little cherub that sits up aloft," and at his request "Bob" rendered this very effectively at all our concerts. Diver and Jemmy Grundy too were much called upon as vocalists. Towards the end of our voyage we passed some enormous icebergs, which were very beautiful. They however at once drove old "George" to gin-and-water for fear we might encounter some of them

in the dark. Indeed, what with rough weather, icebergs, and a good thick fog which came on at one
time, poor "George" had by no means a pleasant
time of it. We landed at Quebec on the 22nd of
September, and proceeded to Montreal by special
train, where we were to play our first match. We
put up at the St Lawrence Hotel (an immense
building it was), where we were most kindly
treated. While we were there, nearly 300 people
used to sit down at the *table d'hôte*. The proprietors of this hotel had, we found out, sub-
scribed liberally towards the expenses of our tour.

Our first match was delayed for a day owing to
rain. There was great excitement on the day of the
match, and several thousands of spectators were assembled long before the time for commencing play.
There were a lot of people from the States as well as
the natives. We were to encounter twenty-two of
Lower Canada, and as we lost the toss we had to
take the field. I had the honour of bowling the first
ball, Jackson taking the other end. My first ball
was hit for 4, but with the next I got a wicket.
When the sixth wicket fell for only 12 runs there
were loud cries round the ground of "Bravo, England!" The innings terminated for 85, George Parr
obtaining the latter wickets with his lobs. We had
not much time to bat that day, as stumps had to
be drawn early. Grundy and Diver opened the batting, and "Jemmy" was got out very quickly. Tom

Hayward was next in, and he and Diver played out time. The day being Saturday, we of course had to wait till Monday before the game was resumed. A splendid banquet was given to us at the hotel on the Saturday night. On Monday morning there was more excitement, the spectators crowding round us in great numbers while we were practising before the match. The English eleven totalled 117 in the first innings, George Parr being top scorer with 24; Tom Lockyer next with 19 not out; I was next with 18, and Hayward just after me with one less. The only "duck" was made by Julius Cæsar. We got out the twenty - two for 63 in their second attempt, which left us about 30 to win. A good deal of betting was made that these would be knocked off by our two first batsmen—Lockyer and Hayward; but they were both disposed of, and it remained for Diver and myself to make the necessary runs. Bob Carpenter had not taken part in this our first match, but had officiated as umpire. As the game was over early on the Tuesday, another match had been arranged to commence as soon as the first was concluded. The six All England men were put on one side and the six United on the other; five gentlemen of Lower Canada assisting each to make up eleven a-side. The United batted first and scored 188. There was great excitement to see Carpenter bat, as he had not yet done so, and the spectators were delighted to see him knock up 32.

All England were got out for 90, and having to follow on, were got rid of for 44, thus losing the match (which we stayed an extra day to finish) by an innings and 54 runs.

On the following morning we left Montreal very early to proceed to New York. After a long and tedious journey and a lot of changing we arrived at Albany. I recollect that Fred Lillywhite's printing-tent was a great nuisance to us on the journey. It was a most complicated arrangement, and took a lot of carting about, and he was always complaining that the railway porters did not stow it away properly, until at last George Parr lost all patience and in pretty plain language consigned both Fred and his tent to an unmentionable region. It was night when we reached Albany, where a steamer awaited us, and everything being got on board, including the tent which had so annoyed poor George, we, after partaking of a meal, all turned in to bed. We arrived at New York on the Sunday morning, and put up at the Astor House Hotel. There was great excitement evinced on our arrival, about 2000 persons visiting the cricket-ground on the Sunday afternoon ! The ground was that of the St George's Club, and here on the Monday morning was a great crowd of nearly 10,000 people. We were absolutely mobbed when we arrived on the field, so eager were they all to get a look at us. Many of them had arrived at our hotel before we left, and followed us as we drove

K

to the ground, cheering us like mad.   A band was on the ground, and everything was as lively as possible.   We won the toss and put our opponents (twenty-two of the States) in to bat.   John Lilly- white acted as our umpire.   The bowling was in- trusted to George Parr and Jackson.   The twenty- two did not appear to at all understand the break on " George's " lobs, and as there was a stiff wind blow- ing they attributed the break to that.   They were all disposed of for the small score of 38.   Hayward and Carpenter opened the innings of the Englishmen to the strain of " Rule Britannia," and the two quickly knocked off the runs.   John Lillywhite had occasion to " no-ball " one of the two American bowlers who opened the attack, in his first over, and for doing this the unfortunate bowler was taken off by the American captain when the over was completed, although only 1 run had been scored off him !   Our innings closed for 156, Hayward being the largest scorer with 33 and his fellow-townsman next with 26.   George Parr only made 7, but contrived to make one of his grand leg-hits, which went right over the heads of the spectators.   The twenty-two only made 54 in the second innings.   I captured 16 of their wickets at a cost of only 24 runs.

The next day we played a match on the same ground—T. Lockyer's side v. Stephenson's side.   Wis- den, Grundy, Parr, Lockyer, Cæsar, and myself with five Americans made up one eleven; while the rest of our team and five more composed the other side. Lockyer's side were victorious by 74 runs. George Parr, in the second innings, was batting grandly when he received a tremendous blow from Jackson on the elbow. He, however, continued his innings, but after a while his elbow swelled to an enormous size. I dressed it for him, and continued to do so for many days; but he was unable to again take part in a match, which was a great source of disappointment to every one. We had a dinner given to us at our hotel in New York, and very enjoyable it was, there being some excellent music and singing; and being a pretty good judge of this sort of thing myself, it was very delightful to me. Poor George, in spite of his injury, was present, and had to make a speech, a task he did not at all like, for he was but a poor orator. One gentleman at this dinner read out a verse of poetry, describing our play, which he had composed during the match,—

> "In fielding nimble and in bowling strong,
> In batting skilful,—all their innings long,
> Well formed to catch, to run, to strike the ball,
> The many points in cricket—good in all."

On the Saturday night we left New York for Philadelphia, arriving there about eleven o'clock. An immense crowd awaited us at the station. A grand supper also awaited us at our hotel, to which many of the Philadelphian gentlemen sat down, and it was very late before we adjourned to bed.

We passed a quiet day on Sunday, and were all ready for cricket once more on Monday morning. A lot of rain had fallen in the night, and it was afternoon before a start could be made. Even then play would have been out of the question had we been in England. The match was against twenty-two of Philadelphia, nine of whom were got out on the first day for 40 runs. On the next day we had no cricket, owing to an election taking place. On Wednesday, however, we had a full day. An immense number of people were on the ground, about a thousand ladies, whose brilliant costumes lit up the whole scene, occupying one stand. Here, as at New York, a band was in attendance. We defeated the twenty-two by 7 wickets. This was the match in which Carpenter was caught off the famous wide ball! Bob, however, continued his innings. A North and South match was got up at the conclusion of the game, which was unfinished. The match against the twenty-two had been played for the benefit of the English Players. The Yankees were, many of them, much surprised to find that our captain was not a much older man; in fact, I believe some of them expected to find George an octogenarian. "Old Parr," however, was the name by which they always continued to call him all the time we were in the States.

On the Saturday afternoon we proceeded to Buffalo, on our way to Hamilton, where we were engaged to play our next match *v.* twenty-two of Upper Canada. The journey to Buffalo was a very tedious one, and we went a great length of time before we were able to get anything to eat. We arrived at Buffalo on Sunday morning, from whence we had arranged to go on to Niagara; but when we arrived at Buffalo we found the train for the Falls had already started, so we were obliged to take a conveyance, and we were nearly five hours doing a distance of twenty-two miles or so. It was evening before we reached our destination and took up our abode at the International Hotel on the American side. Arriving so late prevented us from seeing so much of the world - renowned Falls as we could have wished. We were up very early, however, on the Monday morning, as we had to leave at about nine o'clock, and saw all we could of them, but unfortunately we had not time to go on to the Canadian side. On our arrival at Hamilton—"the ambitious city," as it was called—we were met by so dense a crowd of people that we had great difficulty in getting out of the station. Fred Lillywhite's printing-tent had been lost on the journey, and consequently there were "no cards" on the first day at Hamilton. The weather was terribly cold, it now being the 17th of October. The twenty-two batted first and scored 66. Lockyer's wicket-keeping elicited a great amount of applause in this match, and Tom went through a lot of "by-play" to still more astonish the spectators. Every time he took the ball he would return it like a flash of lightning to the bowler, and each time he did so there was a round of applause from the spectators. The English team scored 79, and the twenty-two made 53 in the second innings, leaving us with about 40 to win, which we obtained without the loss of a wicket.

We left Hamilton that night and travelled to Rochester. It had been intended that our match at Hamilton should be the last of the tour; but while we were at New York the match was arranged, to be played against twenty-two of Canada and the States combined. It was morning before we arrived at Rochester, and the cold was now intense. We got the twenty-two out for 39 on the first day. On the second there was no play owing to a fall of snow, so we had a turn at base-ball. The Yankees paid me the compliment of saying that I was the best player amongst the Englishmen at this game. Sunday intervening, we all took the opportunity of going to Niagara Falls—a long journey—and we were thus able to view them from the Canadian side. The visit well repaid the trouble of getting there, the sight of the Falls being most impressive, in fact never to be forgotten. Returning to Rochester, we resumed our match on the Monday and scored 171 runs. When we took the field for the last time most of us had overcoats and gloves on! George Parr had tried a turn at umpiring, but he was not long in finding a substitute, and adjourned to the pavilion to hot gin-and-water.

We left Rochester that evening, and very early in the morning found ourselves at a place called Rome. There were no beds vacant at the hotel there, so we had to get a few hours' rest as best we could in the smoke-room. We next took train to Cape St Vincent, from whence we proceeded in a river-boat up a narrow canal to Kingston. On our arrival there we found the railway station was several miles away, and that we should never get there in time, with our great quantity of baggage, to catch the train to Montreal. One or two gentlemen, however, drove over to the railway in a trap and induced the authorities to delay the starting of the train for an hour. This saved us waiting at Kingston till the following day, but as it was, we reached Montreal that night. Having spent a day there, where we went to a steeplechase meeting, we proceeded to Quebec, whence we were to return to England in the North Briton. About two hundred miles up the river we passed the Nova Scotia, which had brought us out. The captain of the North Briton ordered a large board to be brought on deck, and chalked on it in large characters, "Won all our matches." This was no sooner seen by those on board the Nova Scotia than they began to cheer lustily, waving their hats and clapping their hands like anything. After a

few days' fairly smooth sailing a fearful gale sprang
up. Oh, dear me! all we had gone through on the
outward journey we had to go through again, only
this was much worse. Jemmy Grundy declared we
should never see land again; poor George Parr was
nearly out of his mind; old Jackson dropped on
his knees; and indeed our situation was rather a
critical one. Our jib-boom was broken, and one
poor old sailor had both his legs broken while he
and some of the crew were endeavouring to set
matters right. A subscription was got up for the
injured man; and we also arranged a concert in
the saloon a few days later for his benefit, at which
Carpenter, Grundy, John Lillywhite, Diver, and myself assisted. The poor fellow, I regret to say, died
of the injuries he had received a few days afterwards. We were all pleased to see Liverpool once
more, where Jemmy Grundy was detained for some
time at the custom-house for having a box or two
of cigars amongst his luggage. We had had, on
the whole, a most eventful trip, and had experienced
the greatest kindness from every one both in Canada
and in the States.

A few weeks later a banquet was given to the
Southern cricketers who had formed part of the
English team, at Godalming. There were over
100 persons present, including Mr John Walker,
Mr W. Burrup, Mr Edwin Napper, and others.
Mr Henry Marshall occupied the chair and Mr

Alexander Marshall the vice - chair. It was a
splendid affair, and greatly appreciated by those
in whose honour it had been arranged. I may
say that we cleared about £90 each over the
Canadian-American tour.

I was at the top of the Surrey averages this
year with 26, and scored just over 1000 runs in
all matches of the season, with an average of 23.

CHAPTER XV.

THE SEASON OF 1860.

I WAS engaged again at Winchester College this year, and while there had rather a novel experience at single wicket, being matched by Mr Burt, a hotel proprietor, to play an eleven of the town, including the Mayor. I was to have the assistance of two fields. The affair caused a good deal of excitement in Winchester before the match came off. It took us two days to finish it. I went in first and scored 20. This, with the help of 14 wides and 1 no-ball, brought my total up to 35. I remember the gentleman who fielded point (and who stood very close in) chaffed me a good deal at the beginning of my innings about the folly of my attempting to play eleven of them, whereupon, being rather nettled at this, I offered to lay 10 to 1 on myself, and at the same time strongly advised him to stand farther away or I might injure him! I got my opponents out for 4 runs only (one of them being absent). I only made 1 in my second innings. On the next day, when my opponents had to go in to bat once more, there were *two* absentees. I once more succeeded in getting them out for 4, and thus was victorious by 28 runs. The officers at the barracks had arranged a cricket match, but scratched it in order to come and see this match of mine. These kind of contests are often made light of, but are not so easily won as some people imagine. Let it be remembered that there are ten men all in front of the batter, in addition to the bowler, and that all runs are obliged to be made in front of the wicket, and that the batsman is not allowed to leave his ground to hit. I received, I believe, £10 for winning this match. There are several other cases on record of one playing eleven. Old Clarke, I think, once did so; also that famous fast Nottingham bowler Sam Redgate, whom I only once saw at Derby. I give the score of the match at Winchester in full :—

FIRST INNINGS.	SCORE.	SECOND INNINGS.	SCORE.
W. Caffyn, b W. Collins	20	c Sharpe, b W. Collins	1
wides 14, no-balls 1	15	wides, &c.	0
Total	35	Total	1

ELEVEN OF WINCHESTER.

S. Sherry, b Caffyn	1	b Caffyn	2
J. Nash, b Caffyn	0	absent	0
E. Powell, c and b Caffyn	0	c Chamberlayne, b Caffyn	0
T. Forder, b Caffyn	0	b Caffyn	1
J. Tubb, b Caffyn	0	b Caffyn	1
T. Birt, c and b Caffyn	2	b Caffyn	0
— Sharpe, b Caffyn	0	b Caffyn	0
W. Collins, b Caffyn	0	b Caffyn	0
J. Blake, b Caffyn	0	b Caffyn	0
W. Judd, c Simpson, b Caffyn	1	c Chamberlayne, b Caffyn	0
T. Collins, absent	0	absent	0
wides, &c.	0	wides, &c.	0
Total	4	Total	4

Amongst others whom I had the honour of coaching at Winchester College was Mr Herbert Stewart, who afterwards entered the army, eventually becoming General Stewart, and who, it will well be remembered, lost his life for his country in the Soudan.

The summer of 1860 was one of the most wet and miserable cricket seasons I ever remember. We never seemed to get anything but soft wickets that year. We had a great match at Reigate in May, the United paying us a visit to play sixteen of us, with Jackson given. Owing to rain the match was drawn. The annual "Two Elevens" match at Lord's was won by the All England by 21 runs. The wicket was a very sticky one. This was the match where George Parr hit me over the tavern. I, however, got him caught at long-leg afterwards, but not before he had scored 55.

Two fine bowlers, one on either side, first played on the famous St John's Wood enclosure in this match—George Tarrant for the All England and William Slinn for the United. Tarrant was one of the fastest bowlers that ever lived. He was right hand, and delivered level with his shoulder, taking a long run before doing so. He would be just about the same pace as Jackson, I should say, though he was not able to make the ball get up so much. Tarrant had a great way of getting a batsman out by the ball cannoning off his legs into the wicket. He did this oftener perhaps than any bowler of his time. Tarrant always bowled at the stumps, and never relied much on his field to get his wickets. He was also a very good bat, and at times made large scores, as he hit wonderfully well. Besides this, he was a first-rate field. He was rather a short man and very lightly built. He was of a most excitable temper, and his nickname of "Tear 'em" I used to think suited him to perfection.

In 1861 Hayward and Carpenter were backed by Mr Jackson, the owner of the famous race-horse Blair Athol, to play the three "Toms" of Stockton —Tom Robinson, Tom Darnton, and Tom Hornby —at single wicket for £200. The Cambridge pair were victorious. Later on the two, with Tarrant added, were matched to play the three Stockton players, with Halton and George Atkinson added. The stakes were doubled and the match played at Sheffield, and once more the Cambridge men were the conquerors. The celebrated trio were, however, defeated by Richard Daft, John Jackson, and Alfred Clarke at Nottingham twelve months later.

William Slinn, the Yorkshireman, was a beautiful fast bowler, with a perfect delivery and an excellent length. He was a tall man, and seemed to give the ball an elevation in the air after it left his hand. He was also able to make a good-length ball get up high from the pitch in a way which was very awkward for the batsman. Slinn, like the famous

J. C. Shaw, was a bowler only. With the bat he was completely helpless, and in the field he was very indifferent.

My county drew with Sussex at the Oval in 1860, but beat them in the return, Mr Miller and young Tom Sewell knocking up over 150 before the first wicket fell. In this match I got Tiny Wells out in a most remarkable way. In playing a ball from me a piece of his bat was chipped off, which flew into the wicket and knocked off a bail. It has appeared in print that the broken piece went over "Tiny's" shoulder, but this was not the case.

Our two great matches this season were against Notts. At the Oval we had a most exciting game. The wicket was a dead one and in favour of the bowlers. The game fluctuated a great deal from time to time. In our last innings we had to go in to get about 120 runs, and 50 of these were obtained when the first wicket fell, and 2 to 1 was betted on us. After lunch, however, Jackson got to work, and an hour later the betting was 6 to 4 on Notts, who eventually beat us by the small majority of 15 runs. Jackson took nine wickets in our second innings for 20 odd runs. I took 12 wickets in the match. On the second day we played as late as half-past seven. There was a dispute about one of our players being bowled, I remember, it being thought that Charley Brown the wicket-keeper had touched the wicket with his foot and dislodged the bail. The umpires (Tom Barker and old Tom Sewell) being in doubt, of course ought to have given the batsman the benefit of it, instead of which they appealed to Charley Brown himself as to whether his foot had touched the wicket. "Charley" promptly replied that his foot had never been near the stumps, and on hearing this the umpires decided that our man was out.

In the return match at Nottingham we were victorious, although we only won by 30 runs after being over 80 behind on the first innings. George Parr, having strained his side, decided not to play at the last moment, and so the betting was even at the start, but had been 6 to 4 against us when it was thought that "George" would take part in the match. Surrey batted first, but only succeeded in making 109, Cris Tinley with his lobs obtaining most of our wickets. Notts then scored 196, so it will be seen the outlook for Surrey was not very rosy. In our second innings, however, we collared the bowling at one period, and ran up a total of 247. Of these I made 91. This, I believe, was the best innings I ever played, and I feel proud to hear that it is still remembered by old cricket enthusiasts at Nottingham. Notts had about 160 to win when they commenced the second innings, but only managed to get 130. I was in good form with the ball fortunately, and took 6 of their wickets

for 30 odd runs.   There was some talk, I remember,
about the two counties playing off the "conqueror"
match on neutral ground; but nothing came of it.
What enthusiasm there was at Nottingham in those
days, to be sure!   A huge crowd collected each day
on the Trent Bridge.   Their cheering and clapping
of hands for every bit of good play I can hear now!
There was no hotel one could go into in the evening
but cricket, cricket, cricket greeted us at every turn.
The whole town seemed to have gone mad on the
game.   I remember, when we were on our way to
the Trent Bridge one morning, seeing Bendigo the
ex-champion prize-fighter fishing from one of the
recesses of the old bridge which used to span the
Trent.   Some one suggested throwing a stone at
his float, which was done; but when Bendy got
up in a towering rage and looked like making for
us we sheered off in double-quick time.   I saw a
good deal of Bendigo at Nottingham, where he
was looked on as a mighty hero.   He used to
show us how he stopped a blow of Deaf Burke's
—which was aimed at his ear—by jerking up his
shoulder, which trick Bendigo could do in a most
amazingly clever manner.

There were two novel matches played in 1860.
One was the eleven which had been to America the
previous year against another picked eleven of England.   This was called the "Champion match," and
was played at Manchester.   The Anglo-Americans

were defeated by 3 wickets.   The ground was dead, and the slows of Cris Tinley were very effective. Mr W. P. Lockhart kept wicket against us, and stumped 4 or 5 off Tinley in the match.   He was presented with a silver cigar-case by the Manchester Club for his fine wicket-keeping.   As soon as this match was concluded a violent thunderstorm came on, and had this occurred five minutes earlier the game must have been drawn, for the ground soon became a sheet of water.

Another match of interest was one played at Lord's, — the first eleven of England against the next fourteen.   I believe it was Lord Charles Russell who originated this match.   The fourteen beat us by 8 wickets.   There was much grumbling at the time, I recollect, about the selection of the two teams, many being of opinion that several of the fourteen ought to have been chosen in the eleven and *vice versâ.*

The return between the "two Elevens" at the Oval was drawn greatly in favour of All England.   It was, I believe, the first time this, the eighth match between the rival elevens, had been drawn.   One evening during the match we were all entertained at dinner by the Surrey Club.   The match was played for the benefit of Billy Martingell, and was wonderfully well patronised.   Surrey played two matches with the North of England.   We were well beaten in the one at the Oval.   Tom Lockyer

L

fielded in this match, because we required his
bowling, and H. H. Stephenson kept wicket. The
return at Manchester was unfinished. In this
match that fine bat Mr Joseph Makinson played
against us. He was a most attractive batsman to
see, obtaining his runs quickly, and able to hit
brilliantly all round the wicket; and though rather
a short man, was a very powerful driver, not being
afraid to come out of his ground. He was also a
fair bowler, and as good a field as could be seen. It
is a pity that he was not able to take part in the
national game more than he did. In the match at
the Oval, Surrey *v.* England, the weather prevented
us from bringing it to a conclusion, otherwise I
think we should have gained the victory.

The two Gentlemen and Players matches were
again easily won by the Players by 8 wickets at the
Oval, and by an innings and 180 runs at Lord's.
The two matches are chiefly noticeable for the
innings of 119 made by Bob Carpenter at the Oval,
and that of Tom Hayward for 132 at Lord's. Both
were wonderfully fine performances. Carpenter
made some tremendous hits, creating a record by
sending one ball clean out of the Oval. Hayward's
innings was a fine display of free hitting and
scientific defence, and was, I believe, the largest
score ever made in a Gentlemen and Players match.
He was about five hours at the wickets. There is
no denying that the bowling of the Gentlemen was

weak at this period, and it was much easier to obtain runs against them than it was to do so when one was opposed to professional bowling.

The All England and United had, as had become usual now, most of their work to do towards the close of the season, there being more good eleven-a-side matches than formerly. For this the public had to thank the hon. secretary of the Surrey Club, Mr W. Burrup, to a great extent, who always contrived to provide an attractive programme at the Oval. The wickets there, too, were greatly in advance of most other grounds. While playing for the United at Bradford early in September 1860 I fell down while making a run and displaced a bone in my knee. I continued my innings in great pain, and this accident placed me on the shelf for the rest of the season. My knee never got thoroughly sound again, and I wear a bandage round it to this day.

Tom Hayward made over 1000 runs this season for an average of 17. George Anderson was at the top of the list with an average of 20, having totalled 800 runs. Cris Tinley took over 300 wickets this season, which being so wet was of course greatly in favour of slow bowling.

CHAPTER XVI.

THE SEASON OF 1861.

THE season of 1861 was a run-getting one. Great things were done with the bat, Hayward, Carpenter, and Daft being very much to the fore. Surrey succeeded in vanquishing her formidable adversary Nottinghamshire twice, and highly delighted we were at doing so. The rival counties had now played ten matches, of which Surrey had won six, although our victory of 1858 can scarcely be counted, as several of the best Notts men were away and they played Diver as a given man. Surrey and Cambridgeshire met this year at Cambridge. This was a great run-getting match, we totalling 252 and Cambridgeshire 325. Two centuries were made, I scoring 103 and Tom Hayward just beating my score by 9 runs. The Prince of Wales, who was at Cambridge at the time, was present at this match on one of the days. This match was left unfinished. In the return we were defeated by 2 wickets. In this match no fewer than three centuries were made—

R. CARPENTER,   A. DIVER.   T. HAYWARD.

Cæsar 111 for Surrey, Hayward 108 and Carpenter exactly 100 for Cambridge. Three centuries had not been scored in one match since 1817. Kent twice defeated us this year. In the match at the Oval we were much handicapped by losing the services of Julius Cæsar, who was taken suddenly ill, causing us only to play ten men. The Players scored heavily in their two matches against the Gentlemen, Carpenter knocking up 106 in the Lord's match. The Hon. C. G. Lyttelton[1] played against us in both these matches. He was one of the finest bats I ever saw. He greatly resembled his younger brother, the Hon. Alfred, in style. He was a grand hitter, especially in front of the wicket, and was exceedingly quick on his feet, being a bad subject for a slow bowler to tackle. He could hit in front of cover - point like a flash of lightning. Richard Daft, in a letter I once saw, said, "All the Lytteltons possessed an electric quickness in their forward off-hitting *which I never saw equalled in any other batsman.*" The term "electric quickness" aptly described the off-hitting of the Hon. C. G. The ball seemed to arrive at the boundary almost before he had ceased making the stroke. He was also a good lob - bowler and an excellent wicket-keeper.

I played a long innings of 98 at the Oval for my county against the North this year. Tom Lockyer

[1] Now Viscount Cobham.—EDITOR.

made 69, and was in with me for a long time. I
had made 97 not out on the Friday night and felt
pretty sure of running into three figures, but was
got out next morning after adding but one run.
Daft, Hayward, and Carpenter each made 60 odd
for the North, but we had the satisfaction of leaving
off the winners. Our return "North" match ended
in a very even draw. Ted Pooley played for us in
this match. He was afterwards one of the best
wicket-keepers ever known, and a fine vigorous bat
too. If he had had less wicket-keeping to do he
would, in my opinion, have been more to the front
as a batsman. He had a lively style of play which
somewhat reminded one of Julius Cæsar.

We had the honour of defeating England at the
Oval this year. My knee gave way again in this
match; Tom Sewell put his thumb out; Mr Burbidge had his finger knocked up; and Mudie was
badly hurt by Jackson. We were indeed "in the
wars," although the wicket was a good one. The
top scorer of the match was Mr E. Dowson, who
played a magnificent innings of 80 in our first
innings. Mr Dowson had not a particularly taking
style, as his attitude was somewhat crouching. He
was, however, a most useful and reliable bat, with
a considerable variety of strokes.

The first match played between the England and
United Elevens at Lord's in 1861 was the most
exciting I ever remember. Up to their meeting

on the present occasion the All England had won
four times and the United three, the other game
having been drawn. A large number of people were
present on the opening day. Our opponents batted
first, and I had the satisfaction of getting two wickets
when 5 runs had been scored, Carpenter catching
both batsmen (Daft and Diver) at point. The
innings closed for the small score of 74. Billy
Buttress (who was secured to play for us at the last
moment in place of George Wootton of Notts) and
myself bowled unchanged. Notwithstanding our
good fortune in getting rid of our opponents for so
small a score, we were only able to make 61, seven
of us falling victims to the "Demon" Jackson.
"Jack" was making the ball jump about in the most
alarming fashion, I remember. He gave Jemmy
Grundy one on the arm which completely de-
moralised him, causing him to stamp and swear like
a lunatic. And I may here remark that "Jemmy"
had a great dislike to being hit, and used to rather
funk bowlers like Jackson and Wilsher accordingly.
The All England scored 152 in their second innings,
Daft being top scorer with a well-obtained 48. A
curious thing happened while he and Anderson
were in. Daft played a ball from me and ran;
Anderson was about to do so when he stumbled
against me and fell down just as Daft crossed him,
and he was thus run out. With 166 to win the
United commenced their second innings. When

play closed for the day we had made 118 for 7 wickets. Wisden was out next morning without the score being improved. Tom Sewell came in next, and he and Tom Hearne brought the score up to within 5 of a tie when the former was caught. Six to win when Billy Buttress came in last man! What excitement there was! old Jack Wisden had been doing nothing but walk round the ground. Jemmy Grundy, on the other hand, sat like a statue, afraid to move. For the last hour George Parr had been taking off his hat and rubbing his head, as he stood at short-slip, on an average of about twenty times a minute. This was always a habit of his when excited. We all congratulated ourselves, when Buttress came in, that he had not to receive the ball, Tom Sewell his partner being the striker. "Tom" hit the first ball he received after his partner arrived, called "Billy" to run, who was unable to get home and was run out. Thus ended this most memorable match in a victory for the All England by only 5 runs.

Twice more did the rival elevens meet this year: once at the Oval, where we won; and again at Manchester, where the match was drawn, somewhat in favour of All England. The United were on paper slightly inferior to their great rivals at this time; Jackson, Willsher, and Tarrant being quite unequalled by any other three fast bowlers in the country. Carpenter was a "host" in himself, and his advent in the United ranks was a great boon to us. Billy Mortlock, too, was now coming to the fore. He first came out as a long-stop, and was, I think, the very best man I ever saw in that position. He was for a few years a very fine bat indeed. He was of medium height and of a powerful build. He was of great assistance to Surrey, and to the United Eleven also for some years. He also formed one of the first Anglo-Australian team. Young Tom Sewell, too, was another noted Surrey and United player. He was always called "Young Tom" to distinguish him from his father, the old All-England man. Young Tom was a fine fast bowler, and an exceedingly useful bat, being a clean and hard hitter. He was in great form both with bat and ball in the season of which I am now writing. "Tom" was Surrey born, hailing from Mitcham, but played for Kent a few times through his residing there with his father, who removed from Surrey to Sevenoaks to keep an inn there. Young "Tom" was of very short stature, but was strongly and compactly put together. His father was for many years after his retirement from cricket engaged as umpire at the Oval. He had been noted as an underhand bowler in his day, and could also bat well at times, but was considered to lack patience and caution. Though not a big man he was considerably taller than his son.

The batting averages of 1861 were larger than they had ever been before, Hayward, Daft, and Carpenter all making over 1300 runs for averages of more than 20. George Griffith was the only other player who reached four figures, but several others—myself included—almost succeeded in doing so. I headed the bowling averages for Surrey this year, taking 47 wickets at the cost of 2·5 runs per wicket.

CHAPTER XVII.

VISIT OF THE FIRST ENGLISH TEAM TO AUSTRALIA.

THE idea of importing a team of English cricketers
to the Antipodes, to play a series of matches there,
originated with Messrs Spiers & Pond, the famous
refreshment contractors. This firm sent over an
agent—Mr Mallam—with instructions to procure
the best English eleven he could obtain. On
arriving in England, he, to the best of my belief,
went first to Mr Burrup, the Surrey hon. secretary,
for advice. When we were playing a North and
South match at Birmingham we were given a
dinner one evening by Captain Marshall[1] (who
formed one of the Southern Eleven) at the Hen
and Chickens Hotel at which Mr Mallam was
present, and it was on this occasion that he
unfolded his views to the two elevens present.
They were to the effect that we were each to
receive £150 for the trip and to have all our
first-class travelling expenses paid. George Parr

---

[1] Now General Sir Frederick Marshall.—EDITOR.

and the Northern players did not seem to relish the scheme at all, thinking that the sum of money offered was quite inadequate; and as it would have been impossible for anything like a representative team to have been formed without including some of the great players of the North, the affair was considered to be as good as "off." After seeing Mr Burrup again, however, Mr Mallam succeeded in inducing H. H. Stephenson, Mortlock, Griffith, Tom Sewell, Charles Lawrence, and myself (all of course of the Surrey Eleven) to make the proposed trip. To this nucleus of a tolerably strong side Mr Mallam succeeded in adding W. Mudie of Surrey, Tom Hearne of Middlesex, "Tiny" Wells of Sussex, Roger Iddison and E. Stephenson of Yorkshire, and George Bennett of Kent. The team was a good one, but was not of course anything like representative. There was a talk of Richard Daft joining us at one time, and I know that Mr Mallam brought all his persuasive powers to work to induce the great Notts batsman to accompany us, but without success. "Tiny" Wells, who took his wife with him, sailed before the rest of the team.

Before proceeding to Liverpool we were given a banquet at the London Bridge Hotel, when success to the English cricketers was enthusiastically drunk. There was, I remember, a celebrated comic singer present, although his name has escaped my memory,

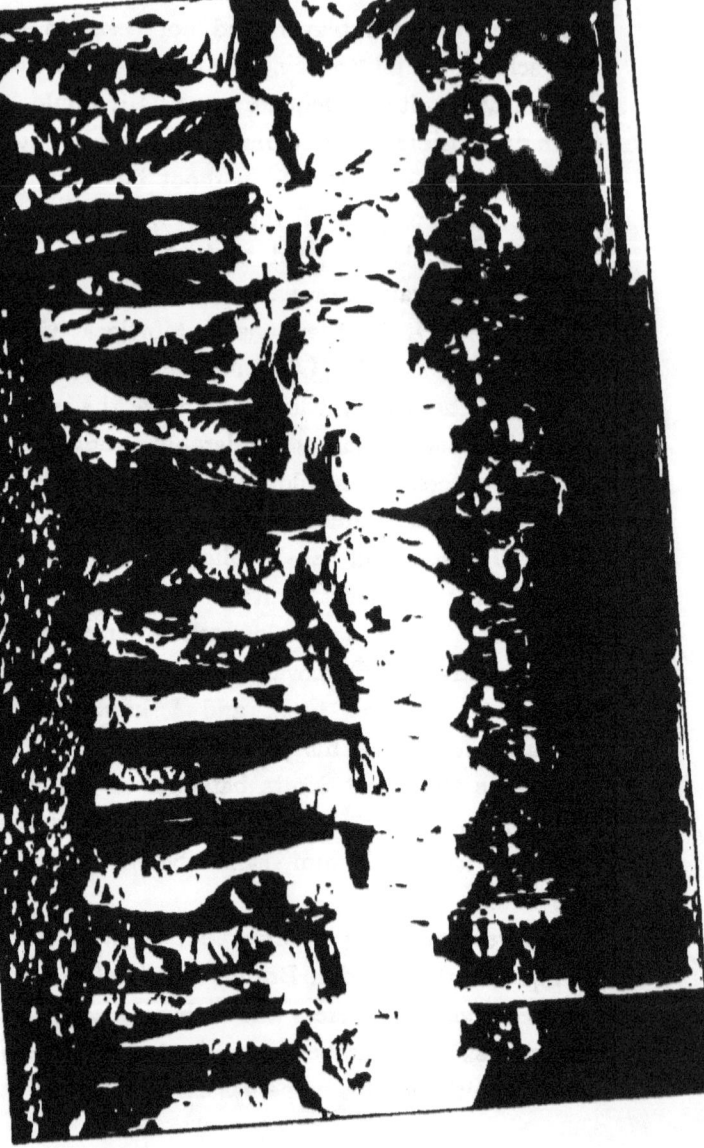

Morlock. Mudie. Bennett. Lawrence. H. H. Stephenson. Cafyn. Griffith. Hearne. Iddison. Sewell. E. Stephenson.

Mr W. B. Mallam.

FIRST ENGLAND ELEVEN IN AUSTRALIA.

Taken just previous to their departure for Australia, October 1861.

who rendered in fine style a song specially composed for the occasion, the chorus of which I have never forgotten :—

> " Success to the Eleven of England !
> The toast is three times and one more.
> May they all meet success o'er the briny,
> And safely return to our shore ! "

The night before we left London we all spent at the Anglesea Hotel in the Haymarket, and were photographed in the stable-yard the next morning. I have a copy of this photograph at the present time. Mr Burrup and Mr F. P. Miller accompanied us to Liverpool, and saw us safely on board the Great Britain. The team sang " The Anchor's weighed," and I gave them " Cheer, Boys, Cheer," on the cornet as the vessel moved off.

This passage was a very different thing from what our crossing the Atlantic had been two years before. It was like taking a sail down the Thames in comparison. The only unpleasant part of the voyage was the trouble caused by the mosquitoes. These tiresome insects seem to have singled me out as their special prey, and tormented the life out of me. I was quite ill for a time and had to consult the doctor. I used to get a large piece of muslin and wrap round my head before going to bed, and also put a pair of stockings on my arms. I shall never forget the laugh that was raised when my fellow-cricketers first saw me in this disguise.

There were several of the passengers who were sorely puzzled to know who and what we were, and when they were informed that we were English cricketers they did not appear to be much wiser than before. There was one lady who was going out to Australia to be married, and who knew Reigate very well, and happening to hear that I came from there, used often to chat to me about the old place. We used to practise cricket on deck a good deal to while away the time, which hung somewhat heavily on our hands.

There were great demonstrations on our arriving at Melbourne, flags being hoisted on most of the ships in the harbour, and a crowd of over 10,000 people gathered to welcome us as we came ashore. Previous to our leaving the Great Britain Messrs Spiers and Pond came aboard and presented us with an address of welcome. As soon as we got on *terra firma* we were driven off in a coach-and-four to the café of Messrs Spiers & Pond in Burke Street, a great crowd of people following us. We were photographed on the coach before alighting. We all wore white pot-hats with a blue ribbon. The following day we were driven seven miles into the bush to practise on a piece of ground which had been previously selected by Spiers & Pond. The locality had been kept a secret, as had it been known we should have been followed by a mob of people. There were many inquiries as to what was our destination when we drove off, but there were few who found it out. A few days later we had some practice at St Kilda, a suburb of Melbourne, and a lot of people came there to see us. Some of the Melbourne Club practised with us. When the people had seen old Ben Griffith make a few of his long-distance hits they forthwith named him "the Lion Hitter." We also had some nice practice at Richmond.

I think I have described at different times all the players who composed our team except Iddison, Charlie Lawrence, and Bennett. Iddison was a fine bat, with good defence combined with hard hitting. He was also a good bowler, round-arm, and could send up "slows" for a change if required. He was a strong, stout, red-faced, healthy-looking man— a true type of the old-fashioned Yorkshireman. Lawrence was a Middlesex man by birth, but through residing at Mitcham became qualified for Surrey, for whom he played a few times. Then he went to live at Edinburgh for some years, and afterwards crossed over to Dublin, where he became secretary to the United All-Ireland Eleven. He was a fast bowler and a good bat, though not a powerful hitter. He was, besides, an excellent judge of the game—one of the best, in fact, I ever knew. He was a light man of medium height. George Bennett was a slow bowler, somewhat of the Southerton stamp, giving the ball a lot of flight in the air. He was the bowler whom Griffith hit the four 6's from in one over at Hastings in 1864. "Farmer" Bennett, as he was always called, was an extremely useful bat, and made many large scores.

Our first match in Australia commenced on New Year's Day 1862, we having eighteen of Melbourne for our opponents. There was a great stir in the city at an early hour of the morning. People flocked in from the surrounding country in all directions, in coaches, waggons, cars, and conveyances of every description. The trains, too, were filled to overflowing. More than 15,000 people were on the ground when the English Eleven arrived. We lost the toss, and H. H. Stephenson, who had been appointed our captain, led us into the field. We had all been supplied with very light white hats of the helmet shape. Each of us had a coloured sash and a ribbon round his hat—one man's colour being blue, another green, another crimson, and so on. These colours were printed against each of our names on the score-card, so that any one provided with one of these could at once identify every member of our team. My own colour was dark blue. The National Anthem was played as we entered the field, amidst the silence of the vast concourse of spectators. When the band stopped playing a tremendous burst of cheering rent the air. The weather was so hot as

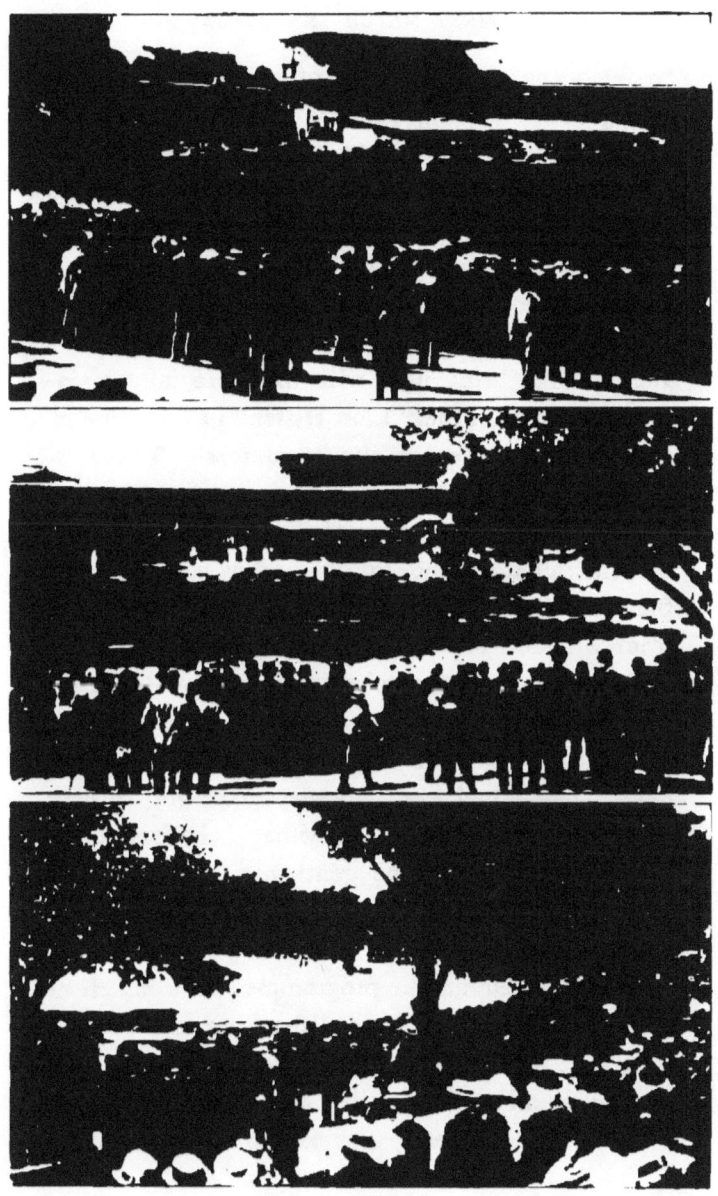

MELBOURNE CRICKET-GROUND (1898).

From the Collection of Mr A. J. Gaston, Brighton.

to fetch the skin off some of our faces. I commenced the bowling, but was obliged to come off
after a short time owing to my arm being so painful from mosquito-bites, which had again troubled
me while at Melbourne. The eighteen scored 118.
The eleven, on their taking the willow, knocked up
the large score of 305, to which I had the satisfaction of contributing 79 — the highest score —
Ben Griffith being next with 61. He fully main-
tained his title of the " Lion Hitter " in this innings,
and greatly impressed the spectators. The Australians only scored 91 in their second innings,
thus leaving us the victors of the first match played
on Australian ground by an innings and 96 runs.
Sam Cosstick, a fast right-hand bowler, who hailed
from Croydon in Surrey, played against us in this
and our subsequent matches in Melbourne. " Tiny "
Wells was the one to stand down in this match,
and acted as umpire. This first match lasted four
days. There had been a sweepstakes got up over
the match, the first prize being, I believe, quite
£100. I remember the gentleman who drew me
gave me a £10 note for making the highest score
and thus winning him the first prize.

The next item on our programme was a match at
Beechworth, in the Ovens district, against twenty-
two. To get to Beechworth we had to make a
journey of about 200 miles by coach. This conveyance was drawn by five horses—three in front

M

and a pair behind them. A very shaky and fatiguing journey this was, and glad indeed were we all when it was over. Here, at Beechworth, we obtained an easy victory, scoring 264 and disposing of our opponents for 20 in the first innings (in which there were a dozen noughts) and 53 in the second. Griffith was our highest scorer with 46. After the match "Ben" took on eleven at single wicket, and actually succeeded in getting them out without their scoring a single run! "Ben" himself scored 6 and won the match. He used afterwards to tell me that I was not in it now as a single-wicket player, and that he had put my Winchester performance completely in the shade!

A week later found us once more at Melbourne, again contending against twenty-two. This match proved to be a very different affair from the first one. We were got out for 101, "Tiny" Wells making the highest score (32), Mr "Extras" coming next with 20. The twenty-two made 153 and 144. This match ended in a draw. There was again a very large attendance, and much enthusiasm was displayed. We next defeated twenty-two at Geelong by 9 wickets. Sewell was in great bowling form, taking no fewer than 15 wickets in the second innings of the twenty-two.

Our next match was at Sydney, where we

SYDNEY CRICKET-GROUND (1898).

From the Collection of Mr A. J. Gaston, Brighton.

went by sea. As when we had landed at Melbourne, there was a great demonstration in our honour. More than 15,000 people were awaiting us on the quay, who cheered us loudly when we landed. We were at once entertained at a public breakfast, and at a dinner at the Victorian Club in the evening. There was an enormous and fashionable crowd each day on the Sydney ground when the match against twenty-two of New South Wales was played. The Governor Sir John and Lady Young and suite honoured us with their presence each day. The English Eleven batted first and scored 175, Mortlock playing a grand innings of 76, for which he afterwards received £20, which had been collected on the ground. The twenty-two scored 127, and succeeded in getting us out the second time for the small score of 66. The twenty-two had now 115 to win, but we succeeded in getting them out for 65, thus winning by 48 runs, the game having lasted four days. After the match a grand banquet was given to us in the Exchange, at which Sir John Young and other noblemen and gentlemen were present.

Our next move was to Bathurst. Here, too, we met with a very warm welcome. When we had reached within about four miles of Bathurst in our coach drawn by six splendid greys, we were met by a large cavalcade, which with a band of music had sallied forth to welcome us. When we arrived at

the town itself we were most enthusiastically received. The match, again *versus* twenty-two, was
drawn owing to the weather. Towards the close
of the second day a violent storm came on, flooding
the ground and destroying several of the refresh-
ment-booths. The next day the weather was still
unfavourable and the match was abandoned. We
scored 211, the extras being higher than the runs
made by any one of us—viz., 45. The twenty-two
scored 49 and 25 for 6 wickets.

We now returned to Sydney, to contend against
a twenty-two selected from New South Wales and
Victoria combined. Here we met with defeat, the
twenty-two beating us by 12 wickets. The Eleven
only scored 60 and 75, of which latter Griffith and
Mortlock were responsible for 58. The twenty-two
made 101 and 35 for 8 wickets. We once more had
high jinks at Sydney during our second stay there.
Scarcely a day passed without our being entertained
to champagne breakfasts, luncheons, and dinners.
A performance at the Victorian Theatre was given
for our benefit, the house being simply packed.
Between the pieces H. H. Stephenson read out
a farewell address. After various speeches had
been made we adjourned to Tattersall's, where
parting bumpers were drained. A large body of
people then escorted us to the Circular Quay to
see us start on our voyage to Tasmania. Rockets
and blue-lights were fired as we set out to sea.

At Hobart Town we had another hearty reception, being met by a deputation of gentlemen greatly interested in cricket, who, together with a band of the rifle corps, escorted us to our hotel. We had to face twenty-two of Tasmania in our match here, whom we beat by 4 wickets. After the game was concluded we played a match, E. Stephenson's side against one chosen by his namesake H. H.

We had to return to Melbourne, where a match styled " Surrey *v.* The World" had been arranged. The six Surrey players had the assistance of five more who hailed from that county, the remaining six of our team being of course helped by five colonists. "The World" batted first and made 211, Bennett playing grandly for 72. "Surrey" were only able to reply with 115, and having to follow scored 179, of which I made 75 not out. This left "The World" 80 odd to win, but they lost 5 wickets in making the required number. Bennett and myself were presented with £10 each by the Melbourne Club for being the highest scorers. Every kindness was shown us both by the Melbourne Club and the people generally, and we left the city with regret.

Our next match was at Ballarat, which was drawn. Here again we were opposed by twenty-two players, who scored 122 and 107. England scored 155 in the first innings, the match ending in a draw. At Ballarat we had, as at Sydney, a benefit given to us

at the theatre, where Tom Hearne was presented
with a prize bat for obtaining the highest score (37
not out) of the match. H. H. Stephenson here
made a neat little speech thanking the inhabitants
of Ballarat for giving us such a hearty welcome.

From Ballarat we proceeded to Sandhurst to meet
twenty-two of Bendigo. This match we won in an
innings. The twenty-two made 81 and 103 and the
eleven 257. I was top scorer with 57, and Bennett just behind me with 56. At the conclusion
of the game Lawrence played one of the Bendigo
players at single wicket, Lawrence allowing his
opponent the privilege of eleven fielders. They
had two innings each, and scored no runs at all.
Luckily for Lawrence, his opponent bowled a wide,
which caused him to win. In our next encounter
we were just beaten by 3 wickets at Castlemaine
by the twenty-two there. We made small scores
—89 and 68 in both our innings. Afterwards
Griffith, Lawrence, and Iddison defeated an eleven
chosen from the twenty-two at single wicket. At
Castlemaine we, in company with the opposing
twenty-two, appeared on the stage of the theatre.
Here we were presented with an address, H. H.
Stephenson once more replied in a nice little
speech, and we finished by giving three cheers
for the twenty-two.

We now paid our final visit to Melbourne, where
we once again had a hearty welcome. Here we

had to play our farewell match against twenty-two of Victoria. This was drawn, the English Eleven requiring 12 runs to win and having 3 wickets in hand. After the match twelve elm-trees were planted on the outskirts of the ground by our team. Messrs Spiers & Pond divided half the receipts of this, our last match, amongst the English players. We were offered £1200 to stay another .month in Australia, but were compelled to decline owing to our engagements in England. Griffith headed the batting averages and scored the greatest number of runs—viz., 372, average just over 21. Mortlock came next with an average of 21. I was the only other batsman to make an average of 20 with 331 runs.

We returned home by P. & O., and had a very pleasant voyage. Charley Lawrence we left behind, he having accepted a permanent engagement with the Albert Club at Sydney. We used to play cricket on deck sometimes — rather, I am afraid, to the annoyance of the lady passengers, but some of the gentlemen often joined us. We played with soft balls manufactured by the sailors, and for a bat had a large iron sort of "pin" used for some purpose or other on the vessel. Once George Bennett while batting let this slip from his hand and struck a gentleman over the eye. When we came to the Red Sea old Teddy Stephenson, after contemplating the water for some time with a very grave countenance, observed that he could not see that the water was any redder here than in any other sea! During the voyage some one got up a show of parrots, toads, and other curiosities which the different passengers were taking home. Of course a little music was necessary to make the thing pass off nicely, so I had to oblige with the cornet, while our cook sported the trombone and some one else the cymbals. The trombone made such a horrible row that Ted Stephenson stuffed a towel into it while the cook had retired for refreshment. We were all very glad to get on *terra firma* once more, and all landed fit and well in Old England, having spent a most enjoyable time.

CHAPTER XVIII.

THE SEASON OF 1862.

IN my first match with the United at Southsea *v.* twenty-two of East Hants I was run out for small scores both innings. Bob Carpenter made 122 in this match, thus beating R. Daft's record made at Walsall against twenty-two the previous year by 8 runs. The All England defeated the United at Lord's by 4 wickets, but the match was not such a runaway affair as at first appears. The All England had only 50 odd to get in their second innings, and we had six of their best bats out for under 20. Alfred Clarke and George Anderson then made a stand and wiped off the deficit. The fielding of both sides in this match I never saw surpassed.

There was a lot of run-getting in the Gentlemen and Players match at the Oval this year, over 200 being scored in all four innings. The Gentlemen scored 276 first innings, the Players running up 244. The Gentlemen made 211 in their second venture, and the match was drawn by the Players scoring

211 for 8 wickets. We had 80 runs to get and 3
wickets to fall at one time, but still managed to
make a draw of it. Mr John Walker in his first
innings played a brilliant innings of 98. Mr John
Walker, as most lovers of cricket are aware, was
the eldest of the seven brothers of the famous Southgate family. He was a tall, powerful man, standing
6 feet high and weighing heavy in proportion. He
was an exceptionally fine hitter, especially on the
off-side. Against fast bowling he was particularly
brilliant. He was also a very good lob-bowler, an
excellent wicket-keeper, and could field well anywhere. He was one of the most liberal supporters
of the game I ever knew. He had a splendid ground
at Southgate, and got up a great number of good
matches to be played there. There was no Gentlemen and Players match at Lord's this year, but the
Gentlemen under thirty years of age played the
Players under thirty instead. The match was easily
won by the latter.

The North and South match of 1862, played at
Lord's for the benefit of Jemmy Grundy, is best
remembered from the fact of Richard Daft's magnificent innings of 118. This innings was the talk of
the season. One of the London papers declared
that the Notts batsman had now "immortalised
himself." It certainly was a fine performance, as
the wicket was a very bumpy one, even for Lord's.
Daft batted for over four hours and never gave the

ghost of a chance, and was at length got out through an accident, Willsher hitting him on the hand and the ball dropping on to the wicket. The North won the match by an innings. Tarrant took 9 of our wickets in the first innings, and George Wootton of Notts bowled remarkably well in the second. Wootton was a fine, rather fast, left-hand bowler, who for years rendered great services to his county at the time they were exceptionally strong. He was not much of a bat, but made runs occasionally.

We drew with our old rivals Notts at the Oval this year, only getting one innings each owing to the weather. We were 60 odd behind on the one innings played, but we had somewhat the worst of the wicket. In the return match at Trent Bridge we sustained a defeat by 5 wickets. An immense amount of interest was felt in regard to this contest all over the country. It was hot weather at the time, and we had an excellent wicket to play on. Surrey batted first and made 133. Notts headed us by 91, totalling 224, a Mr Bateman, who seldom represented his county, being top scorer with 63. We made 187 in our second innings, leaving our opponents just under 100 to win, which they obtained for the loss of half their wickets. Prize bats were presented to the highest scorer on both sides. This was the last time, as it happened, that I was to play against the famous county of Nottingham-

shire, as they did not meet Surrey in the following
year, which was my last season in England before
my seven years' sojourn in Australia. Tom Humphrey, the afterwards world-famed "partner" of
Jupp, played in the above match. "Tom" was a
grand little batter, with an exceptional excellence in
cutting. He not only never let off an off-ball, but
could score 4 at times from one on the off-stump by
cutting it. His wrist-play was perfection. He gave
one the impression that he was "on wires." He
was also a beautiful field. Tom was an old-
fashioned-looking chap, of very short stature. He
was an excellent man to send in first, as he was
always a good beginner, which can by no means be
said about all good batsmen.

In the North v. Surrey match at the Oval, where
we were defeated by 10 wickets, the name of Harry
Jupp appears. Although a fine bat and afterwards
a heavy scorer, he had, unlike his "comrade-in-
arms," Tom Humphrey, not an attractive style of
play. Jupp was a little man, and played very low
down, generally adopting back-play in his defence.
He was not a brilliant cutter, and sometimes, owing
to excessive caution, would allow off-balls to pass
untouched even on good wickets when there was
no need to do so. He was a fine driver, however,
and when he set himself to play a hitting game
could make runs very rapidly. Mr W. Burrup
used to speak of Jupp and Humphrey as "his boys."

I believe this gentleman was the first to discover the merits of both players.

In our return Surrey and North match at Manchester we were beaten by one wicket after a most exciting contest. The great match Surrey *v.* England was played this year at the Oval, when the notorious "no-ball" incident of Willsher's career occurred. This was a remarkable match altogether. The England side was a very strong one indeed. They won the toss, and on an excellent wicket compiled the enormous score of 503. Tom Hayward scored 117, Jemmy Grundy 95, Bob Carpenter 94, and Willsher 54. Daft, who came in first wicket down, I was lucky enough to get out, caught at the wicket from a very bad ball, for a "duck." When Surrey took the bat Willsher was promptly no-balled by John Lillywhite half-a-dozen times. I have alluded to this unpleasant incident before, and have stated how the England side left the field (with the exception of the Hon. C. G. Lyttelton and Mr V. E. Walker). There was no more play that day, and the next morning the England team refused to go into the field unless another umpire was provided. So at this pass Street was substituted for Lillywhite. We were easily defeated in this match, as we only made about 250 in our two innings. The "no-balling" caused a lot of unpleasantness for a long time afterwards, some of the Northern players becoming bitterly prejudiced against Surrey and the Oval. It was very freely rumoured in the north of England that Lillywhite had been specially engaged to no-ball Willsher in the match in question.

I went with the United down to Cornwall this year, and also to the Isle of Wight.

CHAPTER XIX.

THE SEASON OF 1863.

I SHOULD have expressed great surprise if at the
beginning of the season of 1863 any one had told
me that this would practically be my last season
of first-class cricket in England. Yet such was to
be the case, as it so happened.

There were many large scores made this year,
the wickets on most of the principal grounds now
being much more carefully prepared than formerly.
The followers of Surrey cricket presented their
energetic honorary secretary, Mr William Burrup,
with a handsome silver cup and a purse of £300 at
the beginning of the season. Surrey had, as usual,
an attractive programme, and a successful season.
We beat Sussex at the Oval and drew with them
at Brighton, where the wicket was too good to allow
of the game being finished in three days. There
was heavy scoring on both sides in these matches.
At the Oval Mortlock made 106 and Mr Dowson
87, while at Brighton Mr Burbidge scored 101 and

George Griffith 89 and 142.   Griffith's hitting was
terrific, he obtaining his 89 in little more than an
hour.   For Sussex John Lillywhite played a grand
innings of 101 and Ellis scored 83.   We defeated
Kent twice : by an innings at Tunbridge Wells—
where I was top scorer with 70—and by 9 wickets
at the Oval.   We had 190 odd to get in our second
innings in this match, and we obtained them with
the loss of but one wicket.   The only county who
lowered our colours was Yorkshire, who managed
to defeat us by 3 wickets at Sheffield.   We defeated
the North at the Oval by 3 wickets.   George Atkinson met with a curious accident in this match.
When bowling he rushed to field a ball rather
wide of him, and falling down ricked his kneecap
and had to be carried off the ground.   In the return
Surrey and North match at Manchester we were
defeated by 20 runs.

The Surrey and England match produced some
rather remarkable cricket in 1863.   Surrey went
in first, and had scored nearly 150 for one wicket
at lunch-time.   After the interval, however, George
Bennett disposed of four of us in four balls.   Two
famous cricketers played for England in this match
—viz., Messrs R. A. H. Mitchell and E. M. Grace.
Mr Mitchell was one of the very finest batsmen
who ever existed, being not only one of the hardest
hitters we have had, but his defence was equal to his

punishing powers. His style of batting, too, was manly and commanding. As a leg-hitter he should be spoken of with George Parr, for in my opinion he was the next finest exponent of this hit after the Notts batsman. Mr Mitchell stood considerably over 6 feet, and was a Hercules in build. Mr E. M. Grace's play is difficult to describe. Quickness of eye and hand were the secret of his success as a batsman. He could detect the length of a ball to a nicety, and was able to make up his mind what to do with it in less time than most players. He was a tiresome bat to bowl against, for one never knew what he would do with the best ball one could send up to him. A really good-length ball on the middle stump he would despatch to the on boundary without the slightest regard to the feelings of the poor bowler. He was one of the few bats I have seen who could hit with as great a certainty when he first went in as when he had got well set. When occasion required, however, he could defend his wicket as well as any one. Had Mr Grace never got 10 runs in an innings, he would have been worth playing in any team for his unique fielding at point. Such a point had never been seen before, and perhaps never will be again.

The United had the satisfaction of defeating the All England at Lord's this year. The match was played at the beginning of the season, and great

interest was evinced on account of its being Willsher's first appearance since the "no-ball" episode
of the previous year.   The United batted after
the All England, and Willsher commenced the
bowling.   Nothing happened, however, in the opinion of the umpire to justify his no-balling the great
Kent bowler, and it soon became evident to the
spectators that there would be no "sensation," and
I believe many of them were disappointed accordingly.   The wicket in this match was one of the
worst I ever played on, and it required more than
ordinary courage for a batsman to stand up to two
such bowlers as Jackson and Willsher.   One ball
of Jackson's, I remember, struck the wicket-keeper
(H. Stephenson) with great force on the head,
nearly knocking him senseless, and causing him
to give up the stumping for the rest of the day.
While batting I myself received a terrible blow
on the elbow, which took all the play out of me.
Jemmy Grundy during the short time he was in
frequently drew his body away from the wicket,
and held the bat with one hand in front of the
stumps to take its chance.

I only took part in one of the Gentlemen and
Players matches in 1863, that at the Oval, which
we won by 7 wickets.   Mortlock, Willsher, and
Tom Lockyer all made over 70.   I once more
scored nearly 900 runs this season, while Hayward,

Carpenter, and E. M. Grace each reached over four figures. Lovers of cricket had been full of excitement during the past summer on account of the second trip to Australia coming off, the particulars of which I will endeavour to give in my next chapter.

CHAPTER XX.

VISIT OF THE SECOND TEAM TO AUSTRALIA.

IT was owing to the Melbourne Club that the visit of the second team to Australia was brought about. George Parr was entrusted to get up the team, and amongst others was told to try and get Dr E. M. Grace, H. H. Stephenson, Mortlock, Griffith, and myself. I distinctly remember getting "George's" letter requesting me to make one of the team while my father and I were at breakfast one morning in our house at Reigate. I asked my father what he thought about it, and he replied, "Oh, go by all means." So I wrote to "George" to say that I would make one of the twelve. "George" went to work with a will, and succeeded in getting a fine team together—far stronger, in fact, than the one which had gone to the Antipodes two years before. Mortlock at first agreed to go, but altered his mind later. His place was filled by Alfred Clarke of Nottingham, a son of the great All-England veteran. Alfred was an exceedingly useful cricketer, being

Carpenter. J. Cæsar. R. C. Tilney. A. Clarke. Tarrant. Dr E. Grace. Parr. Lockyer. Jackson. Hayward. Anderson. Caffyn.

THE AUSTRALIAN TWELVE.

TAKEN AT LORD'S CRICKET-GROUND, OCT. 1, 1863.

From the Collection of Mr A. J. Gaston, Brighton.

an excellent bat and fine field. Indeed he was scarcely to be excelled as an out-fielder, his only fault being that he was apt to get ".bustled" when he had a chance of running a man out. This sometimes caused him to lose his head and throw the ball in rather badly. Like his father, he was a very intelligent man, and made a most agreeable travelling companion. Julius Cæsar, Lockyer, and myself were the Surrey players who went with Parr's team. Parr himself, Jackson, Tinley, and Alfred Clarke represented Nottinghamshire; Cambridgeshire sent the famous trio, Hayward, Carpenter, and Tarrant. George Anderson was the only man from Yorkshire, and Dr Grace was sole representative of the then unknown county (from a cricket point of view) of Gloucester. It was doubtless a very strong combination, though not, in my opinion, such a powerful one as the Anglo-American team of 1859. It will be noticed that I was the only player who had made the first voyage to Australia two years previous.

Cæsar, Lockyer, and myself arrived late at Liverpool the night before we were to sail, all the rest of the team having preceded us by some hours. Having experienced a good deal of inconvenience on the last occasion of my going to Australia, in the way of leave-taking, I profited by experience on the present occasion by slipping off very quietly after bidding farewell to my own family. When we arrived at our hotel we found all the team had retired to rest except our captain, George Parr. "George" had evidently dined well, and had thoroughly enjoyed himself after dinner. One or two old friends were sitting up with him and making a night of it. "George" told me I was to share a double-bedded room with George Anderson. On repairing to this apartment, I found the great Yorkshire player wide awake, and the first words he said to me were, "Oh, I *have* had a job to get away from my relations! They all think I shall never come back alive!"

We set sail the next day. Richard Daft, Butler Parr, and a few other friends made the journey from Nottingham to Liverpool to see us off. We were entertained to a farewell luncheon at the Adelphi Hotel by Mr Whitaker, a great supporter of cricket, before we proceeded on board the Great Britain in the afternoon. George Parr was rather nervous just before we weighed anchor, and kept looking at the weather in a very anxious manner, although I assured him that the voyage would be quite a treat as compared with a trip across the Atlantic. Poor George Anderson, who was a wretched sailor, did not at all appear to relish the idea of the long voyage. When he wished Daft good-bye, I remember him saying, "If *you* had been coming, Richard, I shouldn't have minded so much, for then I should have been sure of some one to keep me company in my sea-sickness!" We

had not been many hours in the open sea before the
vessel began to roll a bit, causing several of our
team to retire to bed. Poor George Anderson's prediction was fulfilled, and he became wretchedly ill.
I never saw any one suffer so much from sea-sickness. He was unable to leave his berth for several
days, and even when he had "found his sea-legs"
the malady always returned to him whenever the
ocean became at all rough. Poor "George" was
reduced to quite a skeleton. I used to valet him
when he was getting over an attack—cut his hair,
shampoo him, and so on. There were about ninety
saloon passengers on board our vessel besides ourselves.

We had a very pleasant voyage altogether, and
used to beguile the time by day with a little cricket
practice, "bull-board," &c. We had some great
fun when we started "cock-fighting." This game
was played between two opponents, who had a stick
passed at the back of their knee-joints, and held it
there with their arms. While in this position each
had to try to knock the other over. In the evenings
we sometimes had a concert in the saloon, at which
several of our men assisted. At one of these a
gentleman sang a song specially composed in honour of our cricketers. On one occasion we had a
great "judge and jury trial," one gentleman bringing a charge of "attempted poisoning" against one
of his fellow-passengers. The case was, however,

decided against him, and he was fined a bottle of champagne! On another occasion we had a most enjoyable magic-lantern entertainment. Then there was often dancing on deck on fine evenings. At one part of our voyage we encountered large flocks of "Mother Carey's chickens." I recollect seeing a hawk capture one of these, which he came and devoured on one of the masts of our ship. When we were off the coast of Madeira we saw shoals of flying-fish, which had a most curious appearance in the sunlight. When we sighted the Canaries there was great excitement, caused by the appearance of a large whale. Later on we viewed an albatross, and this set Tom Lockyer on to fish for one with a piece of meat for a bait. He never succeeded in catching it, however. When we crossed the line a lighted tar-barrel was thrown overboard. This we could see after we had left it miles behind, and it produced a grand effect in the darkness of the night. The captain of the Great Britain (Mr Gray) was a remarkably nice man, and endeared himself to all of us by his many little acts of kindness. His birthday was celebrated by us during the voyage. We had a champagne dinner in the saloon; the captain's health was drunk with three times three, and many speeches were made. Towards the end of our voyage he entertained the saloon passengers at supper, on which occasion an address was presented to him. On Sundays when it was fine we always had divine service on deck, and when the weather was unfavourable it was held in the saloon. To see the sailors attending these services, all attired in beautiful clean white jackets and trousers, was very pleasing. We had rather rough weather towards the end of our voyage, which terminated on the 16th of December, having lasted sixty-one days. We arrived " off Melbourne " early in the afternoon; but it was arranged that we should stay on board till the following morning, and then make a public entry into the city. Lots of people, however, came on board to see us, including several whom I had met on my former visit to Melbourne.

We entered Melbourne about noon on the following day and had a tremendous reception. We put up at a hotel kept by Mr G. Marshall (who was one of the best bats in Australia) in Swanson Street. We were most enthusiastically cheered by the great crowd of people on our way from the station. We had a fortnight to prepare for our first match, which was to take place on New Year's Day. Shortly before our arrival there had been a vast flood in Melbourne, which had caused a great destruction of property, and even loss of life. We had some practice most days between our landing and the first match. On Christmas Day we were invited to Sandridge to visit the ships Dover Castle and Agincourt. A few days later we had a picnic at Sunbury, which was very enjoyable. Towards the

end of December there was a match played between
Melbourne and Sydney, which we went to see. The
Mayor of Melbourne gave a large dinner after the
match to the two Australian Elevens, and most of
our players were present as well. Between the time
of our landing and New Year's Day we had some
excellent quail-shooting. We killed over forty brace
one day, I recollect.

There was an immense crowd to witness our first
match, which was against twenty-two of Victoria.
I believe there were about 15,000 people present,
including a great number of ladies. It was a very
fine day, this 1st of January 1864, and was not
uncomfortably hot. The twenty-two won the toss
and we had to take the field. We all wore white
"helmets," but had not each a distinguishing colour
as on the visit of the first team two years previous;
and we all had white flannel shirts with a red spot.
The match lasted four days—a Sunday intervening.
The twenty-two scored 146, the English Eleven
beating this total by 30 on the first innings.
Hayward and Carpenter made a long stand, the
former scoring 61 and his fellow - townsman 59.
The Australians put on 143 in their second innings, leaving us 114 to win. We were within 9
runs of winning, having 6 wickets in hand, when
time was called, the match being thus—for us—
provokingly drawn.

Our next match was at Bendigo against twenty-

two of the district. Here the wicket was a very
rough one. We disposed of the twenty - two for
74 and 46, Tinley and Jackson doing the bowling.
We eventually won the game by 140 odd runs.
Rain came on heavily towards the finish, and we
all got wet through. George Parr, our captain,
did not play in this match, being laid up with a
bad attack of erysipelas.

Ballarat was the next place where we were booked
to play, and here we easily defeated a twenty-two by
an innings and a few runs to spare. Parr was too
ill to play, and had remained behind at Melbourne.
E. M. Grace and Tom Hayward ran a race of 100
yards here, in which Tom was just defeated. Julius
Cæsar and I were the highest scorers at Ballarat
with 40 and 39. Tinley was once more very successful with his lobs. When the game was over
Dr Grace and Tarrant played eight of Ballarat at
single wicket. One innings each only was played,
the two Englishmen scoring 20 and their opponents 11.

After this match we journeyed by coach to Ararat,
where we were to meet another twenty - two the
following day. We started on this journey at mid-
night, and reached our destination about nine the
next morning. The road was a rough one, and we
all felt thoroughly done up by the jolting. The
twenty-two here were a very poor lot, Tinley and
Jackson getting them out as fast as they came in.

They scored 35 in their first innings and just one less in the second, Lockyer stumping seven of them in this innings. Our side made 137, and thus won easily by an innings and 68 runs. The match being over early on the third day, Tarrant agreed to play eleven out of the twenty-two at single wicket. This match ended in a tie. Only one innings was played, and each side scored 4 runs. While we were here we all went to the Diggings except Carpenter, who remained behind playing cribbage with a gentleman. When we returned we told Bob we had "found gold." He promptly replied that he thought *he* had found more than we had, and at once produced a handful which he had won at cards during our absence! George Anderson had a great fright while at Ararat. We were shown a large snake here which had been lately killed. The next night "George" was out for a little 'possum-shooting, and trod on something about 3 feet long, which reared up and struck him over the leg. George at once cried out that he was bitten by a snake, and was in a terrible way about it. Luckily, however, the "snake" turned out to be nothing but a long black stick!

At Maryborough, where our next match was to take place, there was a great crowd to see us arrive, and they gave us a most hearty reception. Here again we obtained an innings victory. The local twenty-two scored 72 and 74, while we succeeded in totalling 223, Dr Grace hitting up a fine 44 and myself coming next with 32. A ball was given in our honour on the evening of the first day's play. After our match was concluded we went on to Castlemaine the same night, and proceeded to Melbourne the next day. We were pleased to find our captain recovered from his indisposition, and he was delighted likewise that we had returned to Melbourne, and able to give such a good account of our doings with bat and ball.

Our next move was to New Zealand, we being due to play against twenty-two of Otago at Dunedin on February 2. We started on our voyage on the 25th of January in a small steamer called the Alhambra. Several of our team began to be ill as soon as we were out of smooth water, poor George Anderson as usual being one of the first to succumb to sea-sickness. My berth was just below his, and I had my head out inquiring how he was getting on, when, to my alarm, he came tumbling out of his berth, bringing a large basin with him, which fell on my head, cutting me over the top of my forehead (where I bear the mark to this day). Poor "George" too was rather badly hurt by his fall, knocking a large piece of skin off one of his legs and hurting his shoulder.

On the 31st of January we arrived at Port Chalmers, and anchored close to the town. We landed in order to take the opportunity of inspecting a Maori settlement of about forty or fifty natives. We had some rare fun here with George Parr, whom we presented to the Maori chief as "our king." The natives were delighted with our captain's appearance, the chief taking a special fancy to him. He kept following George about wherever he went. "Don't leave me, for goodness' sake!" "George" said in a low voice to several of us. "I don't half like the look of this fellow!" "George" was presented with a piece of matting, which was the highest honour the Maories could confer upon him, and constituted him a "chief." Our captain in return presented the native chieftain with his travelling rug. "George" then had to go through the ceremony of kissing the women. He seemed glad when this was over, thinking, as he said afterwards, that some of the native gentlemen might "turn awkward" about it! We returned to the Alhambra in a small boat, and the sea being rather rough, some of us did not feel at all comfortable. Poor George Parr was terribly nervous, I remember. "Once let me get on board the steamer," he kept saying, "and nothing shall induce me to leave it again on such fool's errands as we've been on to-day!" However, we all got safely on board, and slept comfortably all night.

The next day we again went on shore at Port Chalmers. The sea was much smoother than on

the previous night, or I am quite sure our captain
would have kept his word and never have left the
steamer.   We formed one of a procession of boats,
which had been arranged, we bringing up the rear
in a boat decked out with flags.   Guns were fired,
bands were playing, and altogether a great demonstration was made.   We went to the chief hotel,
where an address was presented to us, and a splendid
luncheon provided, to which we did ample justice.
Afterwards we started for Dunedin in a coach-and-
six, driven by a famous coachman called "Cabbage-
Tree Ned," accompanied by a large number of
carriages and horsemen by way of escort.   The
road was across the mountains, and had been newly
made.   The scenery was grand.   We had a tremendous reception when we arrived.   The people
seemed to have fairly gone mad with excitement.
We commenced our match on the following day.
The wicket was a very rough one.   The twenty-two
scored 71 and 83.   We made 99 and 58 for one
wicket, thus obtaining a victory by 9 wickets.   Tom
Hayward secured 15 wickets in the first innings of
the twenty-two and 9 in the second.   A second
match was got up at the conclusion of the first
one against a combined twenty-two of Canterbury
and Otago.   This was drawn, the twenty-two scoring 91 and 66 and the English Eleven 73 in their
only innings, Dr Grace making 42 and Tom Lockyer
being the only other double-figure scorer with 10.

We left by steamer that evening for Canterbury. We reached Port Lyttelton the next night, and went ashore to sleep. The next day being Sunday, we spent it on shore. A most pleasant day we had too, the scenery being very lovely. On the following morning we drove over to Christchurch, where we were due to play the same day. We were made very welcome on our arrival, and were entertained at a grand luncheon in the Town Hall before proceeding to the ground to begin the match. We once again obtained a one-innings victory, scoring 137 ourselves, and getting the twenty-two out for 30 in the first innings and 105 in the second. They were quite at sea with Cris Tinley's lobs. When the match was over, two sides were chosen by George Parr and George Anderson. Tarrant, Clarke, Hayward, Tinley, and myself were on Parr's side, while Dr Grace, Carpenter, Cæsar, Lockyer, and Jackson played for Anderson, the sides being completed from the local players. The scoring was very small in all four innings, Parr's side eventually winning by 7 runs only. A Mr Tennant, who had played a good innings of 28 against us for the twenty-two, scored well in both innings of the scratch match for Parr's side, making 21 and 33 run out. On the evening after this game was concluded we were all invited to a large dinner at the Town Hall.

On the following morning we left for Port Lyttelton, most of us deciding to walk across the hills there. It was only a distance of a few miles, but we found it very hard "going." We went by boat to Dunedin the next day, and arrived there on the 14th of February. Once more we added a single-innings victory to our list. In this match, against twenty-two of Otago, Jackson and Tinley bowled throughout, disposing of the twenty-two for 98 and 49. The Eleven scored 198, of which I was top scorer with 43 and Tom Hayward next with 40. Here at Dunedin Dr Grace and Tarrant played an eleven composed of local players at single wicket. The two English players scored 8 and 16. The eleven only had one innings, in which they made 7 runs, Tarrant bowling them all out. Some sports were got up at the conclusion of the cricket, in which we all took part. I happen to have a programme of this entertainment, and insert it in this place :—

Jackson v. Tinley	100 yards	Jackson won by a yard.
Caffyn v. Cæsar	100 yards	Cæsar won easily.
Grace v. Holmes	¼ mile	Holmes won as he liked.
Hayward v. Wills	100 yards	Hayward won by a yard.
Grace v. Tarrant	600 yards	Tarrant won by 6 yards.
Anderson v. Jones	100 yards	Two dead heats.
English Eleven handicap	120 yards	Caffyn won (9 yards start).
Caffyn v. Jackson	100 yards	Caffyn won.
Hurdle race	600 yards	Tarrant won.

On the second day of the cricket-match the ceremony of laying the foundation - stone of the Ex-

o

hibition buildings took place. A large procession was formed on the cricket-ground, and marched from there to the site of the building. Before leaving Dunedin we each planted a memorial tree on the cricket-ground, as in the case of the first English team at Melbourne two years before.

We left Dunedin on the 20th of February in a small river steamer, which took us to Port Chalmers, where we went on board a vessel which was to take us to Melbourne. A good number of gentlemen had come down from Dunedin to see us off. When we entered Banks' Straits a few days later we encountered an immense number of sea-birds, which completely covered the surface of the sea for a great distance. We reached Melbourne on the last day of February, having had a very pleasant passage, although one or two of our men had not been able to escape from sea-sickness. The next day we proceeded to Castlemaine, where we easily defeated another twenty-two by an innings and 37 runs. The twenty-two scored 54 and 46 and we made 137. A scarf-pin was presented to each member of our team as a memento of our visit. Another single-wicket match was played here. Mr Grace this time had Jackson for his partner. One innings each was got through. The English pair scored 14, and Jackson disposed of the eleven for 2 runs only.

Our next match was at Melbourne—George Parr's

eleven against George Anderson's. Cæsar, Tinley, Tarrant, Carpenter, and I played for Parr, while Dr Grace, Hayward, Lockyer, Clarke, and Jackson were with Anderson. The two elevens were made up with Australian players, as at Christchurch. Anderson's side were victorious this time, defeating us by 4 wickets. I was the highest scorer in both innings on our side with 34 and 40. Against us Tom Lockyer played two fine innings of 44 and 40 not out. During our stay in Melbourne this time we attended the theatre, where Mr and Mrs Kean were performing. A photograph was taken of the English team here, from which a large picture was produced by an artist. Whether this afterwards came to England or remained in Australia I cannot now recollect. The same artist also painted a portrait of each one of us separately. They were all good likenesses except that of Tom Hayward's, the artist never being able to obtain a satisfactory portrait of him, although he made many attempts to do so. My own picture I have still by me.

On the 11th of March we set out for Sydney in the Alexandra, and arrived there on the 14th. The next day was Sunday, and we passed it in driving about the surrounding country. On the next day we had an address presented to us at our hotel. The day before our first match at Sydney was excessively hot, and made some of us feel quite ill. Rain fell at night, however, and cooled the air a

good deal. Our match was against twenty-two of
New South Wales. There was a huge crowd to
witness it, fully 20,000 people being present. The
twenty-two made a good show against us in their
first innings. My old friend and fellow - county
player Charley Lawrence played for them, having,
as I have mentioned elsewhere, been engaged as
coach for a Sydney club two years before. The
twenty - two totalled 137 in their first venture,
Lawrence being second scorer with 25. In our
first innings we compiled 128, thus being 9 runs
behind. I was the highest run-getter with 25, Tom
Lockyer coming next with 24. The spectators
were very delighted at the success of the twenty-
two, and there was a feeling that they might be
successful in lowering the colours for the first time
of Parr's renowned eleven. A heavy rain coming
on, however, altered the condition of things, and
they only managed to knock up 50 against us in
their second innings. This left us 60 to get to win,
but we lost 6 wickets in obtaining them. Parr
was again attacked by erysipelas during the match.
Rain greatly interfered with the game throughout,
there being two days on which no play took place
at all. The match was concluded on the day before
Good Friday. The return match was begun on
the Saturday before Easter, the ground being in a
very wet state. The game ended in an even draw.
The twenty-two scored 102 and the Eleven 114.

·George Parr was still unwell, and went in to bat last but one.

On the following Saturday a third match, once more against twenty - two of New South Wales, was commenced, the ground being very wet still. Great excitement was felt as to what would be the result of this third contest, which was witnessed by a large number of people. The twenty-two batted first. The weather had rendered the wicket a bowler's one, and the consequence was the twenty-two were only able to reach the small total of 68. Nor did we show to much better advantage when it came to our turn to bat, as we only beat our opponents' score by 7 runs. In the second innings the New South Wales men put on 83, thus leaving us 77 to win. Two or three of our wickets fell for very few runs, and the excitement became intense. Tom Hayward and I then made a stand, each scoring 17. After this several more wickets went down, and again the hopes of the Australians rose high. Tom Lockyer (who had only made one or two when he was joined by Cris Tinley, our last man) had the honour of making the winning hit amidst a scene of indescribable excitement, thus securing us a victory by one wicket. Charley Lawrence bowled splendidly against us in our second innings, taking six of our wickets for very few runs.

On the evening of the 7th of April we went on board the steamer Wonga Wonga, bound for

Melbourne, after partaking of a farewell luncheon in Sydney. There was a great concourse of people on the wharf to see us off. When we had got a few miles outside the "Heads" we came into collision with a small sailing vessel called the Viceroy. We were most of us at tea when this occurred, and were all much alarmed when we felt the shock of the collision. The little Viceroy was sunk almost immediately. A boat was lowered, and we succeeded in saving the crew. Poor George Parr was utterly dazed and paralysed with alarm. Tarrant quite lost his head. The first thing he did was to rush down below to get together a collection of curios which had been given to him at different times during our visit. Then when the boat was lowered he endeavoured to get into it, and was told by the sailors to keep out of the way in no very choice language. Julius Cæsar, on the other hand, behaved in a manner worthy of his name, keeping very cool and collected, and doing all he could to assist the crew. It being quite dark, our situation for a time was no enviable one, and it was some time before we were able to make out the extent of the injury which had occurred to our own vessel. We had a considerable number of ladies on board, most of whom were naturally very excited and nervous. We afterwards had a good laugh at old Jackson over this affair. He had done himself extra well at the farewell luncheon, and

went fast asleep as soon as we got on board the
steamer; and we found him sleeping peacefully
after the excitement of the collision was over and
we were on our way back to Sydney, not having
the least idea that anything had happened! Our
vessel was a good deal injured in the forward part,
so much so that there was nothing for it but to put
back to Sydney for repairs, where our arrival caused
the greatest astonishment. We were not able to
start again until two days later. The mosquitoes
were so troublesome on our voyage to Melbourne
that we were obliged to sleep on deck, and a few
of us caught bad colds in consequence. Some
part of the machinery of our vessel gave way when
we were within a few miles of our destination, which
caused a delay of several hours. Eventually we
arrived at Melbourne about two in the morning
of April 11.

On the following day we went by train to Geelong, where we had to encounter twenty-two of
that district. Our match here was drawn. The
twenty-two scored 103 and 64 for 9 wickets. We
made 135 in our only innings. The next two days
we played at Maryborough—"Tarrant's Eleven v.
Parr's Eleven." This match was won by Tarrant's
side by 50 odd runs. We were without George
Anderson on this occasion, as he had gone back
to Melbourne to see about his luggage, and was
taken ill there and confined to his bed for several

days. At Maryborough E. M. Grace challenged any six local players to play him at single wicket. They accepted the challenge, and the Doctor went in to bat. He made 106 runs, and was not out at the close of the day, nor do I think he would have been at the close of the *year*, had his opponents been contented to have bowled at him for so long !

Our next match was at Ballarat. Here we made the largest score of the tour—310. Bob Carpenter delighted the spectators with a fine three-figure innings of 121. Our captain, too, played splendidly for 65. The game was drawn, the twenty-two scoring 127 and 48 for 15 wickets.

We commenced our last match against twenty-two of Victoria at Melbourne on April 21. The ground, owing to the heavy rains we had recently experienced, was very soft. Heavy showers interfered with the game throughout, and the attendance was small in consequence. The match ended in a draw. The twenty-two scored 150 (which was the highest total that had been made against us during the tour) and 83 for 17 wickets. The Eleven only batted once, and scored 131. Thus ended this memorable and successful tour of the second English team in Australia.

Of the sixteen matches played (all against twenty-twos), ten had been won by us and six drawn. Carpenter came out at the head of the batting averages with 22, his large innings in the last match but one having pulled him up a good deal. He also totalled the highest number of runs (396), and had the honour of scoring the only century made during the tour. I came next to him, having made 348 runs for an average of 18. Tom Hayward also averaged 18, but scored 22 runs less than I did. We each cleared about £250 from the trip, after paying all expenses. Ten of the English team set sail in the Bombay on the 26th of April. Dr Grace stayed behind for some little time in order to visit friends. I myself also remained, having accepted an engagement with the Melbourne club, and I did not again see my native land till seven years later—viz., in 1871.

CHAPTER XXI.

MY RESIDENCE IN AUSTRALIA.

WHEN I left England with Parr's team nothing was further from my thoughts than that I should stay in Australia. While I was at Melbourne an offer was made to me by the executive of the Melbourne Club that I should remain with them for two years —with the option of an extra twelve months—at a salary of £300 a-year, as coach and general instructor of cricket to the members. After some little natural hesitation, I closed with them on the terms stated. I did a good deal of bowling at the club members, and soon succeeded in improving the play of many of them. The system I worked on was never to try and make all bat alike. If a man was a hitter, I tried to make him hit with as great safety as was possible; and if, on the other hand, another player was naturally a "stone-wall" batter, I encouraged him in this style of play. Of course I was careful not to induce either batsman to carry out his particular style of play too far. After a

time, at the suggestion of some of the members
themselves, I myself would take the bat and give
an exhibition of batting at the net.   There were
no side nets in those days, so we were obliged to
have several fielders.   I used to bat for an hour at
a time with three bowlers at me, and found it very
hard work under the intensely hot sun, especially
when there was a hot wind blowing at the same
time.   A great crowd of people would stand and
look on while I was batting, and they would cheer
me lustily whenever I made a good hit.   I never
saw such painstaking cricketers as the Australians
were in those days, and it was most interesting
work teaching them when one could see the way
they improved.   The progress they had made at
cricket was very noticeable to me when I visited
the Antipodes with the second English team after
a lapse of a couple of years, and this improvement
became still more apparent two years later still.
Some of the younger players used, I could see,
to try and copy my own style of batting to the
letter, and I had to caution them against doing
this in *every* particular.   For instance, in playing
back I never used to move my right foot, and all
my pupils endeavoured to play back in the same
way, some of them tucking themselves up and
becoming very helpless in consequence.   I could
soon perceive that some of them were able to
be much more effective in their back play by

stepping nearer the wicket in making the stroke; and whenever I found this to be the case I used to advise their adopting the custom, always taking care to check the fault of drawing away wide of the stumps. There was a fixed belief in Australia in those days that it was bad form to move the right foot at all when defending the wicket; and when I had proved to many of them that it was often advantageous for some batsmen to do so when playing back, they, perhaps not unnaturally, asked me if the same foot might not also be moved when playing *forward*. This idea, of course, I had to negative very strongly. The chief difficulty I had at first in teaching them batting was to keep the ball down in cutting, and for a long time they were at a loss to understand how I was able to do this so successfully myself. I endeavoured to impress it on them that one of the chief essentials to successful cutting was the *timing* of the ball accurately. I used to get the bowlers to bowl ball after ball to me to cut, in order to show them how the stroke should be made. I was able to cut very close to the stumps in those days, and in imitating me in this particular several batsmen used often to try and cut a ball which was dead on the wicket— an attempt which generally resulted in disaster. As a rule, they learnt to do the forward cut, with the left leg advanced, much more quickly than they were able to master the late cut. Although they were aware that the right foot must necessarily be moved in order to make this latter stroke, still they had become so imbued with the idea that the right foot should never be moved for *defensive* purposes that they were often thinking of this rule when an off-ball came which required cutting late, and were not able to move the foot quick enough to make a late cut. Many of them at the early period of which I write had seen comparatively little first-class cricket, and as was only natural, through binding themselves by hard-and-fast rules, they became somewhat automatic in their style of batting—a fault which no one could possibly charge them with in after-years.

They were delightful pupils for one to have to teach, even as far back as " the sixties "—always willing to be shown a new stroke and quick to do their best to retrieve an error, never taking offence at having their faults pointed out, and never jealous of one another. When I remember all this, it is not so much a matter of surprise to me to see what Australian cricket has become to-day as perhaps may be the case with some people. Their bowlers of nearly forty years ago were undoubtedly in front of the batters. Even at that time there were some of them very tricky as regards variety of pace and break, although most of them seemed not to have the confidence to attempt this "head work" when engaged in a match, at which time

they usually were content to try to bowl straight
and to keep a good length: still even at that time
one was able to perceive the germs from which
the present perfect Australian bowling has sprung.
A great impression had been caused by the brilliant
fielding of the two English teams, and young Australian cricketers very wisely undertook to perfect
themselves in this department of the game. The
Melbourne Club played some good matches while
I was with them against Richmond, St Kilda,
Ballarat, and other clubs. It was against Richmond that I made my highest score in Australia
—viz., 121.

I had been engaged to be married some time before
I left England, and soon after I settled in Australia
my wife who was to be came out to me there, and
we were married at Melbourne.

The intercolonial matches, Victoria v. New South
Wales, were played once a-year while I was there.
I never played for Victoria, however. The principal
players of Victoria were Messrs Wardill, Marshall,
Huddlestone, Kelly, Hewett, Conway, Wills, Allen,
and Bryant, the four last-named being bowlers.
Marshall I have alluded to elsewhere as being
one of the best bats in Australia. He was also
an excellent wicket-keeper. He had been in Australia about ten years at this time. He was, I
believe, a Nottingham man by birth. Conway
was the manager of the first team which went to

England, and Wardill was a brother of Major Wardill, who acted as manager of the Australian team which visited England in 1886. Allen, too, will be remembered by English people as forming one of the 1878 team. There were also Sam Cosstick (whom I mentioned in another part of this book), who hailed from Croydon in Surrey, and many others besides.

After I had been at Melbourne twelve months, I happened to hear of a good opening at Sydney for a hairdressing business, and believing that this might be the means of a livelihood for me after I should be past playing cricket, I induced the Melbourne Club to cancel my engagement with them in order that I might remove to Sydney. I felt leaving Melbourne very much indeed, as I had become to feel quite at home there, and had been so kindly treated by all with whom I had come in contact. I started business at my old trade of hairdressing in George Street, Sydney. This was the principal street of the city, and was nearly two miles long. My wife, like myself, had been brought up to the business, and was very clever at dressing ladies' hair, and between us we made a good deal of money. Unfortunately the climate of Australia never seemed to suit my wife, who was very delicate, and for a long period we never had the doctor out of the house.

At Sydney I once more renewed my acquaintance

with my old friend Charles Lawrence, who had now
been about three years engaged with the Albert Club
in that city, to whom he had been of invaluable
assistance in improving the cricket. I became engaged with the Warwick Club at Sydney, at a less
salary than I had been receiving at Melbourne, but
a handsome one nevertheless. I coached the members of the Sydney Warwick Club in the same
manner as I had taught the Melbourne players,
giving an exhibition of batting at the net most
days. Sometimes, however, we dispensed with
the net, and had the field set out as in a match,
in order to improve the fielding of the members.
This fact shows how keen the Australian cricketers
of that day were to perfect themselves in every
department of the game. The fielding of the
Australian team who visited England in 1878 was
a matter of surprise and admiration to the English
spectators, and I can assure my readers that their
excellence in fielding had not been arrived at without a great amount of practice and perseverance.
After I had been one year with the Warwick Club
I requested the executive to allow Edward Gregory
to divide the work with me, and to this they as-
sented, so we each took three days a-week coaching.
Gregory was one of three brothers, one of whom in
later years captained the first Australian team in
England. I remained four years with the Warwick
Club at Sydney, and during that time played in all

the matches, and continued to do so during the rest of my residence in Australia.

I also took part in the New South Wales and Victoria matches, in which contests I was of course opposed to some of my old Melbourne pupils. These matches were looked on as being the most important that were played in Australia, were always largely attended, and were fought out with the keenest rivalry on both sides. We also had some very interesting contests between the two Sydney clubs—the Albert and the Warwick. The former possessed the larger number of members, but the elevens which each were able to place in the field were about of equal merit.

The best bat I ever coached or saw in Australia was undoubtedly Charles Bannerman, nor do I think his superior has yet appeared in that country. Messrs Spofforth and Murdoch—two mighty names indeed—came to the front after my time. That fine English player Mr B. B. Cooper came out to Australia while I was there, and represented Victoria against New South Wales. I can well remember being greatly impressed by his beautiful batting. He was also a very useful bowler. Mr E. S. (now Canon) Carter of Yorkshire likewise paid a visit to the Antipodes while I was there, and was very successful with the bat during the short time he was amongst us. He too played for Victoria. In 1868 Charles Lawrence came over to

P

England with a team of aboriginal cricketers, with which he toured through the country. I played against them once in a match at Sydney, and was matched to play their eleven myself (having three fielders) at single wicket, but the match fell through.

I left Australia in May 1871. The cricket out there during the ten years that had elapsed between the first visit of an English eleven and my leaving the country had made phenomenal improvement, as was proved when a third English team went out from the old country two years after my return to England. It is a source of the greatest satisfaction to me to think that I have in some measure contributed to this successful state of things. I must, however, take this opportunity to speak of the good work done towards the development of Australian cricket by Charles Lawrence, who by his perseverance, energy, and ability did a great deal towards the raising of the game to its present high standard. Altogether, it is very pleasant for me as a Surrey man to remember that my native county has been so closely connected with Australian cricket in its infancy. It was owing in a great measure to Mr. Burrup's energy that the first English visit out there did not fall through, and it fell to the lot of two Surrey players to be the first instructors of the game in the colony.

Four of my children were born in Australia —

three boys and one girl.   Two of the boys died there.

The later history of Australian cricket is well known to most people.   Two English teams visited Australia between my return to England and the arrival of Gregory's team here in 1878, and since that time visits have been exchanged very frequently. I consider that at the present time the colonists are in every respect the equal in cricketing ability of their English contemporaries.   There is no type, however high, of batsman, bowler, fielder, or wicket-keeper, which cannot be found in the list of the great Australian cricketers of the past five-and-twenty years.

I cannot close this chapter without expressing a few words of gratitude to all who are still living with whom I came in contact during my life in Australia; and I thank them from the bottom of my heart for all the kindness, sympathy, and hospitality shown to me during the time I was amongst them, and can assure them that at the present time no one can possibly feel prouder of our colonial cricketers than myself.   Advance, Australia!

CHAPTER XXII.

THE CLOSE OF MY CAREER, TOGETHER WITH A FEW REMARKS ON MODERN CRICKET.

I LEFT Australia for England in the spring of 1871 and arrived early in November, once more taking up my abode at Reigate. Great alterations had taken place in the cricket world in the old country during my absence. The All England Eleven had become practically played out. The great George Parr had retired from first-class cricket, which in his case meant the laying aside of the willow for good and all. A few "All England" matches were still played under the management of Richard Daft or William Oscroft, but they were now few and far between. The United may be said to have shared the same fate as its famous old rival. Cambridgeshire had disappeared from the scene altogether. Her two great batsmen, Hayward and Carpenter, had passed the zenith of their fame, while her equally great bowler Tarrant had "joined the majority." Daft was now the premier batsman

of the North and W. G. Grace of the South. Fortune had at last grown tired of always favouring the
Players when opposed to the Gentlemen, and the
tables were now turned. Of the counties, Nottinghamshire was undoubtedly the strongest. Young
cricketers of to - day, who have only known this
county in her day of weakness, can scarcely imagine the feeling of respect — nay, even of fear —
which she inspired in 1871. Notwithstanding the
loss of such men as Jackson, Parr, Tinley, Grundy,
and Wootton, others had arisen to supply their
places in the persons of Alfred Shaw, J. C. Shaw,
the two M'Intyres, Bignall, Selby, Wild, Oscroft,
and others. Some players, too, of undoubted
merit, the great midland shire had no room for
in her ranks. The resources of Nottinghamshire
appeared then to be inexhaustible. The county
which to - day seems quite unable to produce a
new bowler of ability might in those times have
produced a score. Yorkshire, too, were now very
strong, possessing some of the finest talent in
the cricket world. Another power—Lancashire—
had arisen in the North, and was rapidly coming
to the front; while Gloucestershire, thanks to
the three Graces, was becoming a formidable
antagonist to any county who might oppose her.
Surrey, though not the Surrey of old, possessed
some of the best known names in England, such
as Jupp, Humphrey, Pooley, and Southerton.

In the season following my return to England I took part in only three matches of importance—viz., for Surrey *v.* the Colts, Surrey *v.* Middlesex, and Surrey *v.* Gloucestershire. This last was the last match in first-class cricket I ever took part in. I now took to coaching again, my first engagement being at Clifton College for one season. Afterwards I was engaged at Wellington College, and next at a private school at Tottenham. This was followed up by three seasons at Brighton College, and an engagement of five years at Haileybury College completed my cricketing career. It was owing to my being engaged at Haileybury that I came to live at Hertford, in which quiet and secluded old town I still reside, following my occupation of hairdressing. By my staying so long in Australia I naturally forfeited my claim to a benefit from Surrey, but my county very generously allows me a pension in my declining years. Five of my children were born after I returned to England — two boys and three girls. As my sons did not—to my thinking—show any marked ability for cricket, I never encouraged them to take it up as a means of livelihood.

If after my term of residence in Australia I found an alteration in our great national game on my return here, what have been the alterations that I have lived to see since? Many indeed, and some not, in my opinion, for the better. Now there is of course far more first-class cricket played than formerly, but owing to the great number of drawn matches which occur, I, for my part, certainly consider that the game has for this reason become far less interesting than of yore. The wickets having been brought to such an almost unnatural state of perfection is the chief cause of this. It is difficult to see how this evil—for evil it undoubtedly is—can be remedied. It has been suggested that the wickets should not be brought to such an artificial state of perfection; but this seems to me to be going back to the old remote days of the Hambledon Club, when bowlers prepared their own wickets to suit their own peculiarities. To increase the height and width of the stumps has been another proposal made to solve the difficulty, but I fear if this were carried out it would in a great measure do away with scientific batting. One gentleman I once heard suggest that every county ground should be boarded round about 3 feet high, and all hits should be run out except those hit *over* this barricade. I really think there is something in this last suggestion. It would, I am sure, be the means of reducing the enormous scores which are made at the present time. Having to run our hits all out in the old days was, I know from experience, often the cause of losing our wickets. It was no easy matter to stop a shooter on the middle stump after running a six for the previous ball.

This sort of thing was bad enough for a strong man in good condition; what, then, must it have been to the weaklings? The alteration of the leg-before-wicket law, making a batsman out if the ball hit his leg when in front of the wicket, no matter where it pitched, would no doubt lessen the huge scores which are made. We should then have bowlers bowling round the wicket as well as over, which would also be the means of causing more attractive batting. There would then be more balls bowled outside and on the leg-stump than at present, which would cause a development of really scientific on-side play. There would be more bowling at the wicket and less on the off-side. Batting, from a spectator's point of view, would no doubt become more varied and attractive; but the alteration would not be an unmixed blessing. There are undoubtedly difficulties in the way, chiefly that of putting greater responsibility on the umpires. There would in many cases be no difficulty in deciding whether a man was out leg before or not; but what if a breaking ball hit a batsman's left leg while in the act of playing forward? His leg would be so far down the wicket that it would be impossible to say for certain that the ball, by the time it would have reached the stumps, would still have been straight. The umpire would in such case, if in doubt (as in doubt he must be), have to give the batsman the benefit of it, and would in all probability be roundly grumbled at by the bowler and many of the fielders in consequence. But even if this and the other alterations mentioned were carried out, I greatly doubt whether the large scoring and drawn matches would be done away with. The wickets are so good that batsmen like Mr MacLaren, Abel, Hayward, Gunn, and many others would in time score almost as heavily as at present. The only thing would be that they would have to play more cautiously than they do now, and this might lead to slow and tedious batting, which is not to be desired, and instead of the games being got through more quickly, it might be the means of prolonging them.

The problem of doing away with drawn matches is indeed difficult to solve, as it is of course impossible in England to devote more than three days to a match. I may be wrong, but I believe the day will come when matches will have to be decided on the *first innings*. This alteration would of course enable nearly all cricket-matches to be brought to a conclusion, and cause them to become much more interesting in consequence. As things now stand, when we go to see a contest between counties like Surrey, Yorkshire, or Lancashire played on a billiard - table wicket, in beautiful weather perhaps, it seems too much to expect that we are going to see one county defeat the other. We rather go instead to see an exhibition of fine batting, bowling, and fielding. We know, at any rate, that we shall have a treat from this point of view. We shall see and admire Hayward, Abel, Tunnicliffe, or Brown bat, Richardson and Lockwood bowl, and witness some splendid fielding. But much as we enjoy all this, we would far sooner see our side gain a victory, even with the play of an inferior character, than we would see all this fine exhibition of cricket put forth, as it were, to no purpose. Who amongst us is not eagerly longing for the Test Matches against the Australians which are arranged shortly to come off? But given fine weather and good wickets, how many of the five can we hope to see won or lost? Drawn matches are hateful to the English mind, and if there is not something done to abolish them, there will, I am sure, soon be a large nail knocked in the coffin of the noblest and best of games.

The present conditions under which cricket is played have inevitably caused a different style of batting to that seen in former years. The high over-hand, over-the-wicket bowling, by which means the ball is almost invariably kept either straight or on the off-side, has entirely done away with genuine leg-hitting. From a spectator's point of view this is to be deplored, as he is thus deprived of seeing one of the most exhilarating hits that it is possible for a batsman to make. With what delight can we old men recall the fine leg-hits of George Parr, Mr Mitchell, William Oscroft, and Bob Carpenter, and cannot but regret that we shall never see such again. There is now, too, more fast-footed play than formerly. This is somewhat difficult to account for. There are, it is true, now some very quick-footed batters, but not the percentage one might reasonably be led to expect. I myself fancy that the easy boundaries of to-day are to a certain extent responsible for this. The batsman knows well that that nice off-boundary is waiting for him, and he prefers to wait until he gets a ball *right up* to him, and then without moving his right leg he lunges out with the left, and away goes the ball between cover and extra-cover, and four is registered on the telegraph board without the batsman having had to leave his crease. In years gone by a batsman knew that the harder he made his hit the more runs he would make by it, and he would often risk a "jump in" to a ball even from a fast bowler like Jackson or Tarrant. I wish there were more of this now. A batsman *must* risk a little if he wants to make runs, and he would be running far less risk in jumping in for a drive with a straight bat than in attempting to turn a good-length straight ball on the on-side. It is surprising to me that some batsmen cannot see this, especially as the risk for the drive successfully made is rewarded by 4 runs, and the other stroke in all probability by only 1 or 2. The straight drive is the safest of all hits to make, provided the batsman is a good judge of length, for the simple reason that it can be made with a perfectly straight bat. If one does make a mistake, it is entirely through misjudging the length of the ball and not getting to the pitch. Against very fast bowling driving should be brought into use as much as possible. Cutting is all very well, but the off-side is now so closely packed that when in cutting a mistake is made by the batsman, it is nearly always fatal. The practice of standing outside the crease when batting against fast bowling is to be commended, always provided that the wicket-keeper is standing back. If this is done, a batsman receives many more balls which he can drive with safety than he would have done had he been standing in his ground. It is all very well to say that the bowler can bowl so much shorter in order to counteract this. That is all nonsense. A fast bowler takes a certain run, and has a certain swing, and if he tries to alter this his bowling will, in my opinion, be a good deal upset. Of course he will naturally try to bowl a little shorter, and will in all probability send one down now and then a good deal *too* short, and give the batsman an easy chance of hooking him round to leg.

I must confess that I am sorry for the modern bowler. Since the time the bowler was allowed the privilege of bowling above the shoulder little or nothing has been done for him. The batsman and fielders have been catered for for many years past. The wickets and grounds are prepared for their benefit. The boundaries have been made easier; and when the light becomes at all bad, and when the bowler might reasonably expect a " nibble," an appeal is made to the umpire by the batsman as to whether an adjournment should not be made to the pavilion. The poor bowler is indeed to be pitied. But I am bound to confess that I see no way of helping him except by altering the boundaries as before mentioned, and by bringing in the new leg-before-wicket law. There are two things which I have often wondered that our modern bowlers do not at times take up. The first is to bowl round the wicket more often by way of a change, and the other is that they do not use rather more variety in the elevation of the arm. This variety would be sure to puzzle a batsman, as it would naturally cause a difference in the flight of the ball. This variety of flight is, to my mind, really more fatal, and more difficult to judge, than is the break of a ball after it has pitched. Let a bowler really deceive a batsman in the "length," and he has him in difficulties at once. It is that misjudging of the length of a ball which does the mischief. Let a batsman once make *sure, absolutely sure,* of the length of almost any ball that ever was bowled, and the odds are 20 to 1 that he will kill it, however much break there may be on it. The

length of a ball is to my mind easier to judge
when the bowler is over the wicket than when
round. We have only to see a bowler bowl lobs
round the wicket to a third-rate player to see
what an exhibition of batting will be given! The
"third-rater" is fairly nonplussed by the length,
and the length only. It is not the break, because
he makes either a blind swipe or rushes wildly down
the wicket before the ball has pitched at all. Try
the same batsman to the same lobs *over* the wicket,
and his mistakes will most likely be far less glaring.
There is one ball which is denied to the modern
bowler, which was a terror to all us old batters—
the shooter. Oh, those shooters at Lord's! One
or two balls as high as your head, then perhaps one
in the ribs, and then a shooter! No wonder that
when we used to stop one of these we were greeted
with a round of applause.

I have already said that allowing that a batsman
makes no mistake as regards length, he can stop
almost any ball which can be bowled; but an exception must be made with regard to the old-
fashioned shooter. The judging of the length had
little to do with stopping these. It was done more
by instinct than anything—that, and by being down
on it in time. There were, of course, some shooters
which had to be stopped by forward and others by
back play, and a batsman might in the old times be
quite correct as to which stroke he should play and

yet be too late for the unexpected shooting of the ball. When contending with this dreadful ball, for so I cannot help describing it, the batsman was dealing with a ball which the *wicket* gave him to play, for the bowler had practically nothing to do with it. The wickets of to-day produce no such balls. So much the better for the batsman, and so much the worse once more for the poor bowler !

If asked to compare ancient with modern bowling, I would say that the bowling of to-day is straighter, but of not such accurate length as formerly.   A high, over - hand delivery *must* cause the ball to drop straight; but whether it will be of a decent length or not is quite another matter.   Modern fast bowling has been a good deal criticised because of its want of accuracy of length; but it must be remembered, in justice to modern fast bowlers, that the bowling of short-length balls is often done purposely and with an object.   In the same way critics of to-day are apt to speak of the number of leg-balls old bowlers used to send, and quite forget that many of them were sent for the purpose of catches to be made in that direction.[1]

There are so many first - class cricketers of the present day that one almost shrinks from mention-

[1] When the reader bears in mind the number of wickets Dr W. G. Grace obtained with this kind of bowling in comparatively recent times, he will not be prone to deride this system of attack persisted in by so many of the old bowlers.—EDITOR.

ing them by name. It is quite impossible in any one volume to mention and do justice to all. Of the counties, the most remarkable improvement in recent years has been shown by Essex. Their rise and success has been almost as sudden and remark-able as was the rise of Cambridgeshire nearly forty years ago. A fine team, indeed, have Essex, from their captain downwards. They have in Mr Kort-right a very fast bowler worthy to rank amongst the greatest, and two other excellent bowlers in Mr F. G. Bull and Mead. In batting they are very strong. Messrs Perrin and M'Gahey are particularly fine; and Carpenter, although now thirty years of age, still continues to improve. It is pleasant for us old cricketers to see the name of Carpenter still in the front rank of English batsmen. That Herbert Car-penter may leave behind him a record as great and honourable as that of his father is the wish of all of us. Young Carpenter little resembles his father in style of play, as far as I can see; but the elder Carpenter never played quite the same as any other player, even of his own period.

Yorkshire, Lancashire, and Surrey are particularly strong in every department of the game. The first named has two magnificent batsmen in Brown and Tunnicliffe, who now hold the record partnership for the first wicket. It would be hard to find in any one county a pair of batsmen more deserving of that honour. Then what a fine all-round player Mr F. S.

Jackson is! what a combination of fine clean hitting coupled with splendid defence! He deserves to be placed alongside any of the great all-round players who have come forward since the game of cricket began.

Yorkshire has been extremely fortunate in having a captain like Lord Hawke, who, besides being so useful a bat himself, has so thrown himself heart and soul into the task of managing the team, that their occupying the proud position they do at the present time is in no small measure due to him. Haigh is a fine fast bowler, and Rhodes last year proved himself worthy to wear the armour of Bobby Peel.

Lancashire can now boast of having a batsman who holds the record of the highest individual score ever made in first-class cricket. Mr MacLaren is a batsman of the very highest type, whose equal it would be difficult, and whose superior impossible, to find. His defence is superb, his back-play almost unequalled, and his aggressive strokes are grand in the extreme. Alas! like so many more of the very best batsmen, we seem fated to see little of him. Like the Hon. Alfred Lyttelton, Canon M'Cormick, Mr R. A. H. Mitchell, and others, he is able only to devote part of the summer to cricket. For a model for young players of the present day to copy, I can think of no one more suitable than Mr MacLaren. Tyldesly last year scored with a con-

Q

sistency which I should say was almost a record
for so young a player, and in the ordinary course
of things there is a great future before him.   Albert
Ward is a batsman with a particularly strong defence, and as a fast bowler Arthur Mold ranks
amongst the very best.   The name of Mr A. N.
Hornby, beloved of all cricketers, has virtually disappeared from the ranks of the county he served
so faithfully and so long.

Surrey have a lot of talent in their midst, and still
occupy a leading position amongst the other great
elevens of the country.   Abel, that most wonderful
of all little players, is still well to the fore.   During
his career his performances with the bat have been
indeed almost superhuman.   The two great secrets
of his success have been undoubtedly a straight bat
and patience.   His defence is as strong as a brick
wall.   It used to be said that he did not play with
quite a straight bat.   I once asked a cricketer if this
really were the case.   "*It is quite straight enough!*"
I was curtly informed; "and so you'd find out
after you'd bowled at him for three or four hours!"
Brockwell has, perhaps, hardly come on so much
as one might once have expected.   He has, however, played some exceptionally fine innings in a
style well worth looking at.   There is something
bright, bold, and manly about his play which is
very refreshing to behold.   Holland, too, has a very
taking style, his on-side hitting being particularly

fine, reminding me somewhat of William Oscroft. Surrey has an excellent captain in Mr Key, who, though now getting past his best as a batsman, still at times shows all his old brilliant form. He has ever been a batsman of the courageous order, and could often turn the tide in favour of his side when it appeared to be going dead against them. Lockwood, taking his splendid bowling and batting together, would in himself form the nucleus of a very fair team. His coming back to form last year caused delight to all lovers of cricket. Tom Richardson I have always considered to have been one of the finest fast bowlers that has ever been seen. When we take into consideration the great pace he bowls, with such accuracy of pitch, which he is able to keep up for so great a length of time, it causes us to wonder. Tom Hayward has proved himself a worthy namesake of his famous uncle. Like him, he possesses a fine free style, though little resembling the old Cambridge batsman. The difference in their respective physique is sufficient to account for this. The uncle was slight and delicate, the nephew is big and strong.

Middlesex has now an excellent team—stronger, perhaps, than they have ever had before. Mr A. J. Webbe has at last retired, leaving behind him the record of a career of exceptional brilliancy. In Mr MacGregor they have a wicket-keeper who, in my humble opinion, has only been surpassed by Tom

Lockyer and Blackham. I have always, from the fact of his having been so closely associated with Australian cricket, taken a peculiar interest in the career of Mr Stoddart. Though now past his prime, he is still one of the best bats and finest hitters we possess. His hitting is almost peculiar to himself, and is of a different order to that of Mr C. I. Thornton, the late George Ulyett, and others. I always think that Mr Stoddart drives more with the arms and less with the whole body than any other hitter of note that I have seen. For so powerful a driver, too, he holds the bat lower down the handle than any one else I can call to mind. His defence is equal to his hitting powers, and his name will be handed down to posterity as one of the greatest batsmen that has ever been. When speaking of hard hitting, the name of another celebrated Middlesex player naturally occurs to the mind — Mr F. G. J. Ford. He is a terror to all bowlers, and his being a left-handed bat does not make matters more pleasant for them. Mr Ford is one of the hardest hitters and the quickest of run-getters, and the spectators may always feel confident of being kept interested during the time he is at the wickets. Sir T. C. O'Brien is a fine free bat with a beautiful style; and Mr P. F. Warner will, if I am any judge, soon become one of the very best bats in the kingdom. "In my opinion the coming bat is Warner," were the words used last summer by an old fellow-cricketer of mine, now one of the county umpires. Middlesex used at one time to be noted for its strength of batting only, but now it is much noted for its first-class bowlers as well. J. T. Hearne is of course one of the leading bowlers of the world, and on Lord's ground in particular his achievements with the ball have been very wonderful. Albert Trott, too, is very destructive, possessing great command over the ball, with a big break and a great variety of pace.

Cricket still flourishes in the time-honoured old counties of Kent and Sussex. The county of the White Horse can still hold its own in the cricket-field, as was shown by the brilliant victory obtained over the champion county last year. Mr J. R. Mason is a beautiful bat, whose forward play is exceptionally fine. The Rev. W. Rashleigh, too, is still a splendid bat on all kinds of wickets, as are likewise Mr W. H. Patterson and Mr C. J. Burnup. Alec Hearne keeps up the old family name with both bat and ball.

Sussex has of late years become very prominent, chiefly from the fact of those world-famed players Prince Ranjitsinhji and Mr W. L. Murdoch having become qualified for the team. It is impossible to speak too highly of the play of Prince Ranjitsinhji, and to attempt to praise a batsman who has so recently established so great a reputation seems

almost a superfluity. His career is without a
parallel. Probably no other batsman has made
such a careful study of the science of batting as
has the young Indian Prince, whose deserving
efforts have been crowned with such splendid
success. He has, as we have been told by Mr
Fry and others, made a careful study of certain
strokes of certain players, and has never rested
until he has not only mastered them but improved them almost beyond recognition. The
wickets are so good nowadays that many strokes
may be taught and learned successfully which
would have been waste of time to have attempted
forty years ago. One might just as well then have
tried to practise elaborate billiard strokes on an old
wooden bagatelle-table. But let the wickets be never
so perfect, I question whether there is another batsman alive who could have brought to such perfection
some of the strokes adopted by Prince Ranjitsinhji.
He seems to possess a quickness of eye, a suppleness
of wrist, and a freedom of limb which places him
apart from all other players. He is "a law unto
himself," and however much we may admire his
play, I would caution the young player to be very
careful not to try to imitate him. The Indian
Prince has endeared himself to all Englishmen,
and has for ever dispelled the old-fashioned idea
that only Englishmen can succeed on the cricket-
field. It is gratifying to know that in 1899 we

may welcome him once more in our midst. Mr
W. L. Murdoch, " the prince of Australian batsmen," as he has been aptly styled, was so successful
last season as to cause us almost to believe that he
was as good as when he used to delight us with
those superb innings played in the early "eighties."
Any one who desires to see a better innings than one
of Mr Murdoch's best is indeed hard to please. For
neatness of style combined with sound correct cricket,
Australia never produced a batsman to equal him.
Mr C. B. Fry was last year one of the heroes of
the English cricket season. His success with the
bat was phenomenal, and I sincerely hope he may
be found to be equally fortunate in the season now
at hand. He has improved in his batting immensely during the past few years, and there is no reason
why he should not find himself in the ranks of the
English Eleven when the test matches against our
friends the Australians take place.

As Prince Ranjitsinhji has returned to Sussex,
the position of the county will in all probability
be much higher than it has been for many years.
With such players as Prince Ranjitsinhji, Messrs
Newham, Brann, Fry, Murdoch, Latham, and
others, there can never be any doubt about Sussex
not being a difficult side to dispose of.

For elegance of style Mr Lionel Palairet has very
few equals as a batsman. Perhaps he resembles
Fuller Pilch in his graceful style of forward play

and forward hitting more closely than any other
batsman now living. His brother, Mr R. C. N.
Palairet, is likewise a fine correct player. The
name of Mr S. M. J. Woods conjures up before
our minds all the great all-round players we have
ever heard of, and takes a place amongst them.
Great with the bat as well as with the ball, he
also has ever been noticeable for his indomitable
pluck and untiring energy, and many a match has
he been the means of saving for his side. He has
been of inestimable service to his county and to
the Gentlemen of England, and it is doubtful if
the latter ever possessed his superior as a fast
bowler alone, to say nothing about his batting
abilities.

Hampshire has been styled " the cradle of cricket,"
and it seems only right and proper that this county
should once more figure in the leading contests of
the day. Though Hants does not at present occupy
a very high position, it has of late years possessed
some very fine cricketers in the persons of Captain
Wynyard, Captain Quinton, Major Poore, Mr A. J.
L. Hill, and a good many more.

Cricket does not flourish in the Midlands quite to
the extent that one would expect. Nottinghamshire,
once so famous, appears to have almost exhausted
her stock of useful talent, a matter of as great regret
to the country at large as to the county itself.
Shrewsbury against medium pace or slow bowling

appears to be as safe and reliable as ever; but the
great batsman must soon, in the natural order of
things, be on the wane. An extraordinary career,
indeed, has been his. His magnificent defence has
of course always been the chief feature of his play,
and it must be remembered that his defence has
been equally pre-eminent on either fast or slow
wickets. Shrewsbury has always been master of the
grand secret of playing a totally different game
when on a hard wicket to when on a soft or sticky
one. For a batsman to be really great, he must,
to my mind, realise the necessity of this and carry
it out. How many batsmen do we see who can bat
beautifully on a fast, good wicket, who, by persisting
in playing a similar game on a slow one, become
utterly helpless? Such batsmen may in a dry season
come out high in the averages, but where would they
be in a wet one? I used to think that Richard
Daft and Tom Hayward, good as they were under
all conditions, were seen at their best on fiery,
bumpy wickets. It was then that their extraordinary
ability to keep down rising balls shone forth, and,
on the other hand, the superb defence of Arthur
Shrewsbury appears to me to become most noticeable when on a difficult sticky wicket. There is,
I have always thought, something different in the
defence of Shrewsbury to that of other batsmen
of these or of former times. When playing either
forward or back, his whole body, together with the

bat, seems to advance or recede as though worked by a spring. He always gives me the impression that when well set it is quite impossible to *bowl* him out. His colleague William Gunn, though also a batsman of the defensive type, is of quite a different style. With Gunn it seems to be his great powerful arms and shoulders that do all the work. With one swing he plays forward, the bat coming straight as a line down the wicket,—so straight, indeed, as almost to appear to hide the three stumps from view. Gunn can hit exceedingly hard when so minded, and had he always gone in for that style of play he would most likely have been classed amongst the gigantic hitters of the day, but whether in such case he would have ranked as high as a batsman as he now does is very doubtful. Attewell, after being nearly twenty years before the public, is still doing good work with the ball. Never probably in the history of county cricket has the bowling rested so much on the shoulders of one man as has been of late years the case with Attewell when playing for his county. He has been a worthy successor of Alfred Shaw, who at one time was described as the most accurate bowler in the world. Mr Dixon, the captain of Notts, is quite as good with the bat as ever, and it is earnestly to be hoped that before he retires he may see his county in a position more nearly resembling that which it used to occupy. The best and almost the only " find " Notts have made of late years is Mr A. O. Jones, who is a fine free punishing bat, and who ought to rise to a very high level.

In W. G. Quaife Warwickshire can boast of owning one of the finest little batters in the world. He did so well last year that it almost inclines us to the belief that to be small in stature must really be an advantage to a batsman rather than not. Mr Bainbridge is an excellent captain; and this county has in Lilley a player who is as good with the bat as he is with the gloves.

The mention of Lilley naturally causes one to speak of Storer, the Derbyshire player. To find a parallel of this great cricketer we must turn from modern players to those of ancient times—to Tom Lockyer and H. H. Stephenson. Storer is a grand wicket-keeper, and though by no means a pretty bat, is a very effective one. When we add to these that he is, besides, an extremely useful bowler, I think we may safely say we have described what is truly an "all-round" cricketer. Old Clarke used to declare that in the selection of a team the wicket-keeper ought always to be the first man chosen. Whether he could bat or not was only a secondary consideration. With this I entirely agree. If, however, a wicket-keeper can combine such batting with first-rate wicket-keeping as that shown by Lilley and Storer, their side is immensely strengthened accordingly. Indeed there is no reason why a wicket-

keeper should not be a first-rate bat.   Many of them
have been, and worth playing for their batting
alone.   There were the Hon. A. Lyttelton, Tom
Lockyer, Tom Box, H. H. Stephenson, Ted Pooley,
in times past; while to-day we have two striking
examples in the wicket-keepers of Warwickshire and
Derbyshire.   Derbyshire, we hear, is about to lose
its captain, Mr S. H. Evershed.   This is much to
be regretted, as he is now playing quite as well as
ever he did, if not better, and his office of captain
will be difficult to fill.

Leicestershire seem down on their luck at present.
The captain, Mr C. E. de Trafford, has not been
so successful with the willow as of old.   Coe proved
himself' a good all-round man last season, and the
county has a fine rising bat in Mr H. H. Marriott.
It is to be hoped that this midland shire, so emin-
ently a sporting one, will soon rise higher in the
list of first-class counties at cricket.

Worcestershire has done so well amongst the
"minors" during the past few years that she has
deservedly been promoted, and her career in the
higher sphere in which she now finds herself will
be watched with the greatest interest.

In Mr C. L. Townsend Gloucestershire has one of
the best amateur bowlers and all-round players of
the day.   Very tall, with a long arm, his high delivery must be puzzling to those opposed to him ;
and he is, I have been told by those who have

W. G. GRACE.

From Photo by E. Hawkins & Co., Brighton.

played against him, able to vary his pace, pitch, and break in a more deceptive manner than almost any other bowler. Mr Gilbert Jessop is one of the hardest hitters and pluckiest batsmen of modern times, and when once set going appears able to hit to the boundary almost any ball sent down to him. Mr Troup's strong defence was last season of the greatest assistance to his county, as was the fine batting of Mr C. O. H. Sewell.

No book written either now or in remote ages to come would be complete without containing a few words about the greatest of all cricketers, Dr W. G. Grace. My own experiences of his great performances have been chiefly from a spectator's point of view, and I have often felt pleased that I witnessed some of those great innings of his from the cool shelter of the pavilion rather than from "third man," "long-off," or any other position in the field! Some of the great feats I have seen Dr Grace achieve with the bat have left a lasting impression on my memory. His like will in all probability never be seen again. At the same time, while cheerfully acknowledging him to have been the greatest of all batsmen, one cannot help but smile when reading some of the articles which have been written concerning him of late years. We have been told that he invented modern batting; that no cricketer before his time left any permanent impression on the game; that before Dr Grace appeared the old cricketers used to hit the ball along the ground, and that the great Gloucester- shire batsman was the first to show how it should be hit in the air! I wish some of the gentlemen who write in this strain had had to bowl against Alfred Mynn, Fuller Pilch, or Mr Hankey. As a matter of fact, Dr Grace more closely resembles some of the old players than most of those of modern times resemble *him*. No batsman has more strictly adhered to some of the old rules than has "W. G.," such as playing with a straight bat, not moving the right foot, and not allowing an off ball to go past without dealing with it. If it were possible to see Dr Grace and Mr Hankey at the wickets together, each well set, and each unknown to the spectators, they would in all probability pro- nounce Mr Hankey the finer batsman of the pair. There was, in my opinion, no hit on the board which Mr Hankey was unable to make equally as well as Dr Grace or any one else; and so it was with many others of the old players. So, indeed, is it with some of the present day. What, then, has been the cause of Dr Grace's phenomenal suc- cess? What has caused him to be greater than all others? In my opinion it has been from the fact of his making fewer mistakes than any other player. Dr Grace would go to the wickets accompanied by another famous batsman, and each would make perhaps 50 runs, Dr Grace's partner appearing

perhaps to play the more brilliantly of the two.
But Dr Grace would continue to occupy the wickets
long after his companion had been compelled to retire to the pavilion, and instead of having 50 attached to his name, 100, 200, or perhaps 300 would
appear there instead. When the famous old prize-
fighter Deaf Burke had been defeated by Bendigo
for the English belt, he was asked by his patron,
the Marquis of Waterford, whether there was anything of special peculiarity about the fighting of his
redoubtable antagonist. "Well, my Lord," replied
the old pugilist, "he hits d——d hard, and the
worst of it is he keeps on a-doing of it !" That has
been the grand secret of Dr Grace's success—"*he
keeps on a-doing of it.*" His has been no "flash-in-
the-pan" success. He has been more consistent
than any other player, past or present. He is not
so liable to be caught in two minds as other batsmen, and this, combined with his great science and
splendid physique, practically allow him to have,
so to speak, three innings to another batsman's
one. He possesses every essential necessary to the
making of a great batsman : first, the natural gift,
without which no man can, I think, ever become
really great ; and next, the greatest coolness while
at the wickets, playing with as great an amount
of head work as of physical power. For one
fully to appreciate Dr Grace's play as it deserves,
we must not judge him by one fine innings or by

one brilliant season,—we must judge him by the whole of his career; and when we come to consider the length of that career, equally successful under all sorts of conditions and under all sorts of difficulties, we shall then, and not till then, fully understand *how* great a cricketer he has been.

I am often asked whether I consider the cricket of to-day superior to what it was when I was a young man. A friend of mine lately sent me an eleven on paper, composed of old players, which he declared would equal any eleven of the present generation. In this opinion I entirely concur. The old eleven, as given by my friend, is as follows:—

Hon. C. G. Lyttelton.	Parr.
R. A. H. Mitchell.	Caffyn.
V. E. Walker.	Willsher.
Hayward.	Lockyer.
Carpenter.	Jackson.
Daft.	

And now I must draw to a close. It is a long way for me to look back to the time I first played cricket on the old Reigate ground. I have seen many ups and downs since then, and have lived out most of my old comrades. Of Clarke's famous Eleven only Anderson and myself remain.[1] All the rest have been "bowled out." On the 2nd of Feb-

---

[1] The celebrated umpire of nearly fifty years' standing, "Bob" Thoms, can scarcely be termed a member of the old All England Eleven.—EDITOR.

ruary last I completed my seventy-first year, and so the title of 'Seventy-One Not Out' has been given to this book. As, I am thankful to say, I am blessed with exceptionally good health, I hope I shall be able to "continue my innings" for some time to come, and perhaps even may be permitted to "complete my century."

INDEX.

THE END.

Catalogue

of

Messrs Blackwood & Sons'

Publications

PERIODS OF EUROPEAN LITERATURE. Edited by
PROFESSOR SAINTSBURY.

> THE FLOURISHING OF ROMANCE AND THE RISE OF ALLE-
> GORY. (12TH AND 13TH CENTURIES.) By GEORGE SAINTSBURY, M.A.,
> Professor of Rhetoric and English Literature in Edinburgh University.
> Crown 8vo, 5s. net.

> THE LATER RENAISSANCE. By DAVID HANNAY. Crown 8vo,
> 5s. net.

> THE FOURTEENTH CENTURY. By F. J. SNELL. Crown 8vo,
> 5s. net.

> THE AUGUSTAN AGES. By OLIVER ELTON. Crown 8vo.
> [In the press.

The other Volumes are:—

THE DARK AGES . . . Prof. W. P. Kerr.	THE MID-EIGHTEENTH
THE TRANSITION	CENTURY . . . . J. Hepburn Millar.
PERIOD . . . . . G. Gregory Smith.	THE ROMANTIC REVOLT Prof. C. E. Vaughan.
THE EARLIER RENAISSANCE. The Editor.	THE ROMANTIC TRIUMPH . T. S. Omond.
THE FIRST HALF OF THE SEVENTEENTH	THE LATER NINETEENTH
CENTURY . . Prof. H. J. C. Grierson.	CENTURY . . . . The Editor.

PHILOSOPHICAL CLASSICS FOR ENGLISH READERS.
Edited by WILLIAM KNIGHT, LL.D., Professor of Moral Philosophy
in the University of St Andrews. In crown 8vo Volumes, with Portraits,
price 3s. 6d.

Contents of the Series.—DESCARTES, by Professor Mahaffy, Dublin. — Rev. W. Lucas Collins, M.A.—BERKELEY, by Professor Campbell Fraser. — FICHTE, by Professor Adamson, Glasgow. — KANT, by Professor Wallace, Oxford.—HAMILTON, by Professor Veitch, Glasgow.—HEGEL, by the Master of Balliol.—LEIBNIZ, by J. Theo- dore Merz.—VICO, by Professor Flint, Edin- burgh. — HOBBES, by Professor Croom Robertson.— HUME, by the Editor. — SPINOZA, by the Very Rev. Principal Caird, Glasgow. — BACON: Part I. The Life, by Professor Nichol.—BACON: Part II. Philo- sophy, by the same Author. — LOCKE, by Professor Campbell Fraser.

FOREIGN CLASSICS FOR ENGLISH READERS. Edited by
Mrs OLIPHANT. CHEAP RE-ISSUE. In limp cloth, fcap. 8vo, price 1s.
each.

DANTE, by the Editor. — VOLTAIRE, by General Sir E. B. Hamley, K.C.B. — PASCAL, by Principal Tulloch. — PE- TRARCH, by Henry Reeve, C.B.—GOETHE, by A. Hayward, Q.C.—MOLIÈRE, by the Editor and F. Tarver, M.A.—MONTAIGNE, by Rev. W. L. Collins.—RABELAIS, by Sir Walter Besant. — CALDERON, by E. J. Hasell.—SAINT SIMON, by C. W. Collins. CERVANTES, by the Editor.—CORNEILLE AND RACINE, by Henry M. Trollope.— MADAME DE SÉVIGNÉ, by Miss Thackeray. — LA FONTAINE, AND OTHER FRENCH FABULISTS, by Rev. W. Lucas Collins, M.A. — SCHILLER, by James Sime, M.A. — TASSO, by E. J. Hasell. — ROUSSEAU, by Henry Grey Graham. — ALFRED DE MUSSET, by C. F. Oliphant.

ANCIENT CLASSICS FOR ENGLISH READERS. Edited by
the REV. W. LUCAS COLLINS, M.A. CHEAP RE-ISSUE. In limp cloth,
fcap. 8vo, price 1s. each.

Contents of the Series.—HOMER: ILIAD, by the Editor.—HOMER: ODYSSEY, by the Editor.—HERODOTUS, by G. C. Swayne.— CÆSAR, by Anthony Trollope.—VIRGIL, by the Editor. — HORACE, by Sir Theodore Martin.—ÆSCHYLUS, by Bishop Copleston. —XENOPHON, by Sir Alex. Grant.—CICERO, by the Editor.—SOPHOCLES, by C. W. Col- lins.—PLINY, by Rev. A. Church and W. J. Brodribb.—EURIPIDES, by W. B. Donne.— JUVENAL, by E. Walford. — ARISTOPHANES, by the Editor.—HESIOD AND THEOGNIS, by J. Davies.—PLAUTUS AND TERENCE, by the Editor. — TACITUS, by W. B. Donne.— LUCIAN, by the Editor.—PLATO, by C. W. Collins. — GREEK ANTHOLOGY, by Lord Neaves.—LIVY, by the Editor.—OVID, by Rev. A. Church. — CATULLUS, TIBULLUS, AND PROPERTIUS, by J. Davies.—DEMOS- THENES, by W. J. Brodribb.—ARISTOTLE, by Sir Alex. Grant.—THUCYDIDES, by the Editor.—LUCRETIUS, by W. H. Mallock.— PINDAR, by Rev. F. D. Morice.

CATALOGUE

OF

MESSRS BLACKWOOD & SONS'

PUBLICATIONS.

———————

ALISON.
History of Europe. By Sir ARCHIBALD ALISON, Bart., D.C.L.
1. From the Commencement of the French Revolution to the Battle of Waterloo.
LIBRARY EDITION, 14 vols., with Portraits. Demy 8vo, £10, 10s.
ANOTHER EDITION, in 20 vols. crown 8vo, £6.
PEOPLE'S EDITION, 13 vols. crown 8vo, £2, 11s.

2. Continuation to the Accession of Louis Napoleon.
LIBRARY EDITION, 8 vols. 8vo, £6, 7s. 6d.
PEOPLE'S EDITION, 8 vols. crown 8vo. 34s.

Epitome of Alison's History of Europe. Thirtieth Thousand, 7s. 6d.
Atlas to Alison's History of Europe. By A. Keith Johnston.
LIBRARY EDITION, demy 4to, £3, 3s.
PEOPLE'S EDITION, 31s. 6d.
Life of John Duke of Marlborough. With some Account of his Contemporaries, and of the War of the Succession. Third Edition. 2 vols. 8vo. Portraits and Maps, 30s.
Essays: Historical, Political, and Miscellaneous. 3 vols. demy 8vo, 45s.

ACROSS FRANCE IN A CARAVAN: BEING SOME ACCOUNT OF A JOURNEY FROM BORDEAUX TO GENOA IN THE "ESCARGOT," taken in the Winter 1889-90. By the Author of 'A Day of my Life at Eton.' With fifty Illustrations by John Wallace, after Sketches by the Author, and a Map. Cheap Edition, demy 8vo, 7s. 6d.

ACTA SANCTORUM HIBERNIÆ; Ex Codice Salmanticensi. Nunc primum integre edita opera CAROLI DE SMEDT et JOSEPHI DE BACKER, e Soc. Jesu, Hagiographorum Bollandianorum; Auctore et Sumptus Largiente JOANNE PATRICIO MARCHIONE BOTHAR. In One handsome 4to Volume, bound in half roxburghe, £2, 2s.; in paper cover, 31s. 6d.

ADOLPHUS. Some Memories of Paris. By F. ADOLPHUS. Crown 8vo, 6s.

AFLALO. A Sketch of the Natural History (Vertebrates) of the British Islands. By F. G. AFLALO, F.R.G.S., F.Z.S., Author of 'A Sketch of the Natural History of Australia,' &c. With numerous Illustrations by Lodge and Bennett. Crown 8vo, 6s. net.

AIKMAN.
Manures and the Principles of Manuring. By C. M. AIKMAN,
D.Sc., F.R.S.E., &c., Professor of Chemistry, Glasgow Veterinary College;
Examiner in Chemistry, University of Glasgow, &c. Crown 8vo, 6s. 6d.
Farmyard Manure: Its Nature, Composition, and Treatment.
Crown 8vo, 1s. 6d.

ALLARDYCE.
The City of Sunshine. By ALEXANDER ALLARDYCE, Author of
'Earlscourt,' &c. New Edition. Crown 8vo, 6s.
Balmoral: A Romance of the Queen's Country. New Edition.
Crown 8vo, 6s.

ANCIENT CLASSICS FOR ENGLISH READERS. Edited
by Rev. W. LUCAS COLLINS, M.A. Price 1s. each. *For List of Vols. see p. 2.*

ANDERSON. Daniel in the Critics' Den. A Reply to Dean
Farrar's 'Book of Daniel.' By ROBERT ANDERSON, LL.D., Barrister-at-Law,
Assistant Commissioner of Police of the Metropolis; Author of 'The Coming
Prince,' 'Human Destiny,' &c. Post 8vo, 4s. 6d.

AYTOUN.
Lays of the Scottish Cavaliers, and other Poems. By W.
EDMONDSTOUNE AYTOUN, D.C.L., Professor of Rhetoric and Belles-Lettres in the
University of Edinburgh. New Edition. Fcap. 8vo, 3s. 6d.
ANOTHER EDITION. Fcap. 8vo, 7s. 6d.
CHEAP EDITION. 1s. Cloth, 1s. 3d.

An Illustrated Edition of the Lays of the Scottish Cavaliers.
From designs by Sir NOEL PATON. Cheaper Edition. Small 4to, 10s. 6d.

Bothwell: a Poem. Third Edition. Fcap., 7s. 6d.

Poems and Ballads of Goethe. Translated by Professor
AYTOUN and Sir THEODORE MARTIN, K.C.B. Third Edition. Fcap., 6s.

Memoir of William E. Aytoun, D.C.L. By Sir THEODORE
MARTIN, K.C.B. With Portrait. Post 8vo, 12s.

BADEN-POWELL. The Saving of Ireland. Conditions and
Remedies: Industrial, Financial, and Political. By Sir GEORGE BADEN-POWELL,
K.C.M.G., M.P. Demy 8vo, 7s. 6d.

BEDFORD & COLLINS. Annals of the Free Foresters, from
1856 to the Present Day. By W. K. R. BEDFORD, W. E. W. COLLINS, and other
Contributors. With 55 Portraits and 59 other Illustrations. Demy 8vo, 21s. net.

BELLAIRS. Gossips with Girls and Maidens, Betrothed and
Free. By LADY BELLAIRS. New Edition. Crown 8vo, 3s. 6d. Cloth, extra
gilt edges, 5s.

BELLESHEIM. History of the Catholic Church of Scotland.
From the Introduction of Christianity to the Present Day. By ALPHONS BEL-
LESHEIM, D.D., Canon of Aix-la-Chapelle. Translated, with Notes and Additions,
by D. OSWALD HUNTER BLAIR, O.S.B., Monk of Fort Augustus. Cheap Edition.
Complete in 4 vols. demy 8vo, with Maps. Price 21s. net.

BENTINCK. Racing Life of Lord George Cavendish Bentinck,
M.P., and other Reminiscences. By JOHN KENT, Private Trainer to the Good-
wood Stable. Edited by the Hon. FRANCIS LAWLEY. With Twenty-three full-
page Plates, and Facsimile Letter. Third Edition. Demy 8vo, 25s.

BICKERDYKE. A Banished Beauty. By JOHN BICKERDYKE,
Author of 'Days in Thule, with Rod, Gun, and Camera,' 'The Book of the All-
Round Angler,' 'Curiosities of Ale and Beer,' &c. With Illustrations. Cheap
Edition. Crown 8vo, 2s.

BINDLOSS. In the Niger Country. By HAROLD BINDLOSS.
With 2 Maps. Demy 8vo, 12s. 6d.

BIRCH.

Examples of Stables, Hunting-Boxes, Kennels, Racing Establ-
ishments, &c. By JOHN BIRCH, Architect, Author of 'Country Architecture,
&c. With 30 Plates. Royal 8vo, 7s.

Examples of Labourers' Cottages, &c. With Plans for Im-
proving the Dwellings of the Poor in Large Towns. With 34 Plates. Royal 8vo, 7s.

Picturesque Lodges. A Series of Designs for Gate Lodges,
Park Entrances, Keepers', Gardeners', Bailiffs', Grooms', Upper and Under Servants' Lodges, and other Rural Residences. With 16 Plates. 4to, 12s. 6d.

BLACKIE.

The Wisdom of Goethe. By JOHN STUART BLACKIE, Emeritus
Professor of Greek in the University of Edinburgh. Fcap. 8vo. Cloth, extra
gilt, 6s.

John Stuart Blackie : A Biography. By ANNA M. STODDART.
With 3 Plates. Third Edition. 2 vols. demy 8vo, 21s.
POPULAR EDITION. With Portrait. Crown 8vo 6s.

BLACKMORE.

The Maid of Sker. By R. D. BLACKMORE, Author of 'Lorna
Doone,' &c. New Edition. Crown 8vo, 6s. Cheaper Edition. Crown 8vo,
3s. 6d.

Dariel : A Romance of Surrey. With 14 Illustrations by
Chris. Hammond. Crown 8vo. 6s.

BLACKWOOD.

Annals of a Publishing House. William Blackwood and his
Sons; Their Magazine and Friends. By Mrs OLIPHANT. With Four Portraits.
Third Edition. Demy 8vo. Vols. I. and II. £2, 2s.

—— **Vol. III. John Blackwood. By his Daughter, Mrs**
GERALD PORTER. With 2 Portraits and View of Strathtyrum. Demy 8vo, 21s.

Blackwood's Magazine, from Commencement in 1817 to De-
cember 1898. Nos. 1 to 998, forming 164 Volumes.

Index to Blackwood's Magazine. Vols. 1 to 50. 8vo, 15s.

Tales from Blackwood. First Series. Price One Shilling each,
in Paper Cover. Sold separately at all Railway Bookstalls.
They may also be had bound in 12 vols., cloth, 18s. Half calf, richly gilt, 30s
Or the 12 vols. in 6, roxburghe, 21s. Half red morocco, 28s.

Tales from Blackwood. Second Series. Complete in Twenty-
four Shilling Parts. Handsomely bound in 12 vols., cloth, 30s. In leather back,
roxburghe style, 37s. 6d. Half calf, gilt, 52s. 6d. Half morocco, 55s.

Tales from Blackwood. Third Series. Complete in Twelve
Shilling Parts. Handsomely bound in 6 vols., cloth, 15s.; and in 12 vols. cloth,
18s. The 6 vols. in roxburghe, 21s. Half calf, 25s. Half morocco, 28s.

Travel, Adventure, and Sport. From 'Blackwood's Magazine.
Uniform with 'Tales from Blackwood.' In Twelve Parts, each price 1s. Handsomely bound in 6 vols., cloth, 15s. And in half calf, 25s.

New Educational Series. *See separate Catalogue.*

BLACKWOOD.
New Uniform Series of Novels (Copyright).
Crown 8vo, cloth. Price 3s. 6d. each. Now ready:—

THE MAID OF SKER. By R. D. Blackmore.
WENDERHOLME. By P. G. Hamerton.
THE STORY OF MARGRÉDEL. By D. Storrar Meldrum.
MISS MARJORIBANKS. By Mrs Oliphant.
THE PERPETUAL CURATE, and THE RECTOR. By the Same.
SALEM CHAPEL, and THE DOCTOR'S FAMILY. By the Same.
A SENSITIVE PLANT. By E. D. Gerard.
LADY LEE'S WIDOWHOOD. By General Sir E. B. Hamley.
KATIE STEWART, and other Stories. By Mrs Oliphant.
VALENTINE AND HIS BROTHER. By the Same.
SONS AND DAUGHTERS. By the Same.
MARMORNE. By P. G. Hamerton.

BEATA. By E. D. Gerard.
BEGGAR MY NEIGHBOUR. By the Same.
THE WATERS OF HERCULES. By the Same.
FAIR TO SEE. By L. W. M. Lockhart.
MINE IS THINE. By the Same.
DOUBLES AND QUITS. By the Same.
ALTIORA PETO. By Laurence Oliphant
PICCADILLY. By the Same. With Illustrations.
LADY BABY. By D. Gerard.
THE BLACKSMITH OF VOE. By Paul Cushing.
THE DILEMMA. By the Author of 'The Battle of Dorking.'
MY TRIVIAL LIFE AND MISFORTUNE. By A Plain Woman.
POOR NELLIE. By the Same.

Standard Novels. Uniform in size and binding. Each complete in one Volume.

FLORIN SERIES, Illustrated Boards. Bound in Cloth, 2s. 6d.
TOM CRINGLE'S LOG. By Michael Scott.
THE CRUISE OF THE MIDGE. By the Same.
CYRIL THORNTON. By Captain Hamilton.
ANNALS OF THE PARISH. By John Galt.
THE PROVOST, &c. By the Same.
SIR ANDREW WYLIE. By the Same.
THE ENTAIL. By the Same.
MISS MOLLY. By Beatrice May Butt.
REGINALD DALTON. By J. G. Lockhart.

PEN OWEN. By Dean Hook.
ADAM BLAIR. By J. G. Lockhart.
LADY LEE'S WIDOWHOOD. By General Sir E. B. Hamley.
SALEM CHAPEL. By Mrs Oliphant.
THE PERPETUAL CURATE. By the Same.
MISS MARJORIBANKS. By the Same.
JOHN : A Love Story. By the Same.

SHILLING SERIES, Illustrated Cover. Bound in Cloth, 1s. 6d.
THE RECTOR, and THE DOCTOR'S FAMILY. By Mrs Oliphant.
THE LIFE OF MANSIE WAUCH. By D. M. Moir.
PENINSULAR SCENES AND SKETCHES. By F. Hardman.

SIR FRIZZLE PUMPKIN, NIGHTS AT MESS, &c.
THE SUBALTERN.
LIFE IN THE FAR WEST. By G. F. Buxton.
VALERIUS : A Roman Story. By J. G. Lockhart.

BON GAULTIER'S BOOK OF BALLADS. Fifteenth Edition. With Illustrations by Doyle, Leech, and Crowquill. Fcap. 8vo, 5s.

BOWHILL. Questions and Answers in the Theory and Practice of Military Topography. By Major J. H. Bowhill. Crown 8vo, 4s. 6d. net. Portfolio containing 34 working plans and diagrams, 3s. 6d. net.

BRADDON. Thirty Years of Shikar. By Sir EDWARD BRADDON, K.C.M.G. With Illustrations by G. D. Giles, and Map of Oudh Forest Tracts and Nepal Terai. Demy 8vo, 18s.

BROUGHAM. Memoirs of the Life and Times of Henry Lord Brougham. Written by HIMSELF. 3 vols. 8vo, £2, 8s. The Volumes are sold separately, price 16s. each.

BROWN. The Forester : A Practical Treatise on the Planting and Tending of Forest-trees and the General Management of Woodlands. By JAMES BROWN, LL.D. Sixth Edition, Enlarged. Edited by JOHN NISBET, D.Œc., Author of 'British Forest Trees,' &c. In 2 vols. royal 8vo, with 350 Illustrations, 42s. net.

BROWN. A Manual of Botany, Anatomical and Physiological. For the Use of Students. By ROBERT BROWN, M.A., Ph.D. Crown 8vo, with numerous Illustrations, 12s. 6d.

BRUCE. In Clover and Heather. Poems by WALLACE BRUCE. New and Enlarged Edition. Crown 8vo, 3s. 6d.
A limited number of Copies of the First Edition, on large hand-made paper, 12s. 6d.

BRUCE.
> Here's a Hand. Addresses and Poems. Crown 8vo, 5s.
> Large Paper Edition, limited to 100 copies, price 21s.

BUCHAN. Introductory Text-Book of Meteorology. By ALEX-
ANDER BUCHAN, LL.D., F.R.S.E., Secretary of the Scottish Meteorological
Society, &c. New Edition. Crown 8vo, with Coloured Charts and Engravings.
[*In preparation.*]

BURBIDGE.
> Domestic Floriculture, Window Gardening, and Floral Decora-
> tions. Being Practical Directions for the Propagation, Culture, and Arrangement
> of Plants and Flowers as Domestic Ornaments. By F. W. BURBIDGE. Second
> Edition. Crown 8vo, with numerous Illustrations, 7s. 6d.
> Cultivated Plants: Their Propagation and Improvement.
> Including Natural and Artificial Hybridisation, Raising from Seed, Cuttings,
> and Layers, Grafting and Budding, as applied to the Families and Genera in
> Cultivation. Crown 8vo, with numerous Illustrations, 12s. 6d.

BURKE. The Flowering of the Almond Tree, and other Poems.
By CHRISTIAN BURKE. Fott 4to, 5s.

BURROWS.
> Commentaries on the History of England, from the Earliest
> Times to 1865. By MONTAGU BURROWS, Chichele Professor of Modern History
> in the University of Oxford; Captain R.N.; F.S.A., &c.; "Officier de l'In-
> struction Publique," France. Crown 8vo. 7s. 6d.
> The History of the Foreign Policy of Great Britain. New
> Edition, revised. Crown 8vo, 6s.

BURTON.
> The History of Scotland: From Agricola's Invasion to the
> Extinction of the last Jacobite Insurrection. By JOHN HILL BURTON, D.C.L.,
> Historiographer-Royal for Scotland. Cheaper Edition. In 8 vols. Crown 8vo,
> 3s. 6d. each.
> History of the British Empire during the Reign of Queen
> Anne. In 3 vols. 8vo. 36s.
> The Scot Abroad. Cheap Edition. Crown 8vo, 3s. 6d.
> The Book-Hunter. Cheap Edition. Crown 8vo, 3s. 6d.

BUTCHER. Armenosa of Egypt. A Romance of the Arab
Conquest. By the Very Rev. Dean BUTCHER, D.D., F.S.A., Chaplain at Cairo.
Crown 8vo, 6s.

BUTE. The Altus of St Columba. With a Prose Paraphrase
and Notes. By JOHN, MARQUESS OF BUTE, K.T. In paper cover, 2s. 6d.

BUTE, MACPHAIL, AND LONSDALE. The Arms of the
Royal and Parliamentary Burghs of Scotland. By JOHN, MARQUESS OF BUTE,
K.T., J. R. N. MACPHAIL, and H. W. LONSDALE. With 131 Engravings on
wood, and 11 other Illustrations. Crown 4to. £2, 2s. net.

BUTLER.
> The Ancient Church and Parish of Abernethy, Perthshire.
> An Historical Study. By Rev. D. BUTLER, M.A., Minister of the Parish. With
> 13 Collotype Plates and a Map. Crown 4to, 25s. net.
> John Wesley and George Whitefield in Scotland; or, The
> Influence of the Oxford Methodists on Scottish Religion. Crown 8vo, 5s.

BUTT.
> Theatricals: An Interlude. By BEATRICE MAY BUTT. Crown
> 8vo, 6s.
> Miss Molly. Cheap Edition, 2s.
> Eugenie. Crown 8vo, 6s. 6d.
> Elizabeth, and other Sketches. Crown 8vo, 6s.
> Delicia. New Edition. Crown 8vo, 2s. 6d.

CADELL. Sir John Cope and the Rebellion of 1745. By the
late General Sir ROBERT CADELL, K.C.B., Royal (Madras) Artillery. With 2
Maps. Crown 4to, 12s. 6d. net.

CAIRD. Sermons. By JOHN CAIRD, D.D., Principal of the
University of Glasgow. Seventeenth Thousand. Fcap. 8vo, 5s.

CALDWELL. Schopenhauer's System in its Philosophical Significance (the Shaw Fellowship Lectures, 1893). By WILLIAM CALDWELL, M.A.,
D.Sc., Professor of Moral and Social Philosophy, Northwestern University,
U.S.A.; formerly Assistant to the Professor of Logic and Metaphysics, Edin.,
and Examiner in Philosophy in the University of St Andrews. Demy 8vo,
10s. 6d. net.

CALLWELL. The Effect of Maritime Command on Land
Campaigns since Waterloo. By Major C. E. CALLWELL, R.A. With Plans.
Post 8vo, 6s. net.

CAPES. The Adventures of the Comte de la Muette during the
Reign of Terror. By BERNARD CAPES, Author of 'The Lake of Wine,' 'The Mill
of Silence,' &c. Crown 8vo, 6s.

CARSTAIRS.
Human Nature in Rural India. By R. CARSTAIRS. Crown
8vo, 6s.

British Work in India. Crown 8vo, 6s.

CAUVIN. A Treasury of the English and German Languages.
Compiled from the best Authors and Lexicographers in both Languages. By
JOSEPH CAUVIN, LL.D. and Ph.D., of the University of Göttingen, &c. Crown
8vo, 7s. 6d.

CHARTERIS. Canonicity; or, Early Testimonies to the Exist-
ence and Use of the Books of the New Testament. Based on Kirchhoffer's
'Quellensammlung.' Edited by A. H. CHARTERIS, D.D., Professor of Biblical
Criticism in the University of Edinburgh. 8vo, 18s.

CHENNELLS. Recollections of an Egyptian Princess. By
her English Governess (Miss E. CHENNELLS). Being a Record of Five Years'
Residence at the Court of Ismael Pasha, Khédive. Second Edition. With Three
Portraits. Post 8vo, 7s. 6d.

CHRISTISON. Early Fortifications in Scotland: Motes, Camps,
and Forts. Being the Rhind Lectures in Archæology for 1894. By DAVID
CHRISTISON, M.D., F.R.C.P.E., Secretary of the Society of Antiquaries of Scotland. With 379 Plans and Illustrations and 3 Maps. Fcap 4to, 21s. net.

CHRISTISON. Life of Sir Robert Christison, Bart., M.D.,
D.C.L. Oxon., Professor of Medical Jurisprudence in the University of Edin-
burgh. Edited by his Sons. In 2 vols. 8vo. Vol. I.—Autobiography. 16s.
Vol. II.—Memoirs. 16s.

CHURCH. Chapters in an Adventurous Life. Sir Richard
Church in Italy and Greece. By E. M. CHURCH. With Photogravure
Portrait. Demy 8vo, 10s. 6d.

CHURCH SERVICE SOCIETY.
A Book of Common Order: being Forms of Worship issued
by the Church Service Society. Seventh Edition, carefully revised. In 1 vol.
crown 8vo, cloth, 3s. 6d.; French morocco, 5s. Also in 2 vols. crown 8vo,
cloth, 4s.; French morocco, 6s. 6d.

Daily Offices for Morning and Evening Prayer throughout
the Week. Crown 8vo, 3s. 6d.

Order of Divine Service for Children. Issued by the Church
Service Society. With Scottish Hymnal. Cloth, 3d.

COCHRAN. A Handy Text-Book of Military Law. Compiled
chiefly to assist Officers preparing for Examination; also for all Officers of the
Regular and Auxiliary Forces. Comprising also a Synopsis of part of the Army
Act. By Major F. COCHRAN, Hampshire Regiment Garrison Instructor, North
British District. Crown 8vo, 7s. 6d.

COLQUHOUN. The Moor and the Loch. Containing Minute Instructions in all Highland Sports, with Wanderings over Crag and Corrie, Flood and Fell. By JOHN COLQUHOUN. Cheap Edition. With Illustrations. Demy 8vo, 10s. 6d.

COLVILE. Round the Black Man's Garden. By Lady Z. COLVILE, F.R.G.S. With 2 Maps and 50 Illustrations from Drawings by the Author and from Photographs. Demy 8vo, 16s.

CONDER.

The Bible and the East. By Lieut.-Col. C. R. CONDER, R.E., LL.D., D.C.L., M.R.A.S., Author of 'Tent Work in Palestine,' &c. With Illustrations and a Map. Crown 8vo, 5s.

The Hittites and their Language. With Illustrations and Map. Post 8vo, 7s. 6d.

CONSTITUTION AND LAW OF THE CHURCH OF SCOTLAND. With an Introductory Note by the late Principal Tulloch. New Edition, Revised and Enlarged. Crown 8vo, 3s. 6d.

COUNTY HISTORIES OF SCOTLAND. In demy 8vo volumes of about 350 pp. each. With Maps. Price 7s. 6d. net.

Fife and Kinross. By ÆNEAS J. G. MACKAY, LL.D., Sheriff of these Counties.

Dumfries and Galloway. By Sir HERBERT MAXWELL, Bart. M.P.

Moray and Nairn. By CHARLES RAMPINI, LL.D., Sheriff-Substitute of these Counties.

Inverness. By J. CAMERON LEES, D.D.

Roxburgh, Peebles, and Selkirk. By Sir GEORGE DOUGLAS, Bart. [In the press.

CRAWFORD. Saracinesca. By F. MARION CRAWFORD, Author of 'Mr Isaacs,' &c., &c. Cheap Edition. Crown 8vo, 3s. 6d.

CRAWFORD.

The Doctrine of Holy Scripture respecting the Atonement. By the late THOMAS J. CRAWFORD, D.D., Professor of Divinity in the University of Edinburgh. Fifth Edition. 8vo, 12s.

The Fatherhood of God, Considered in its General and Special Aspects. Third Edition, Revised and Enlarged. 8vo, 9s.

The Preaching of the Cross, and other Sermons. 8vo, 7s. 6d.

The Mysteries of Christianity. Crown 8vo, 7s. 6d.

CROSS. Impressions of Dante, and of the New World; with a Few Words on Bimetallism. By J. W. CROSS, Editor of 'George Eliot's Life, as related in her Letters and Journals.' Post 8vo, 6s.

CUMBERLAND. Sport on the Pamirs and Turkistan Steppes. By Major C. S. CUMBERLAND. With Map and Frontispiece. Demy 8vo, 10s. 6d.

CURSE OF INTELLECT. Third Edition. Fcap. 8vo, 2s. 6d. net.

CUSHING. The Blacksmith of Voe. By PAUL CUSHING, Author of 'The Bull i' th' Thorn,' 'Cut with his own Diamond.' Cheap Edition. Crown 8vo, 3s. 6d.

DARBISHIRE. Physical Maps for the use of History Students. By BERNARD V. DARBISHIRE, M.A., Trinity College, Oxford. Two Series:— Ancient History (9 maps); Modern History (12 maps). [In the press.

DAVIES. Norfolk Broads and Rivers; or, The Waterways, Lagoons, and Decoys of East Anglia. By G. CHRISTOPHER DAVIES. Illustrated with Seven full-page Plates. New and Cheaper Edition. Crown 8vo, 6s.

DE LA WARR. An Eastern Cruise in the 'Edeline.' By the Countess DE LA WARR. In Illustrated Cover. 2s.

DESCARTES. The Method, Meditations, and Principles of Philosophy of Descartes. Translated from the Original French and Latin. With a New Introductory Essay, Historical and Critical, on the Cartesian Philosophy. By Professor VEITCH, LL.D., Glasgow University. Eleventh Edition. 6s. 6d.

DOGS, OUR DOMESTICATED : Their Treatment in reference to Food, Diseases, Habits, Punishment, Accomplishments. By 'MAGENTA.' Crown 8vo, 2s. 6d.

DOUGLAS.

The Ethics of John Stuart Mill. By CHARLES DOUGLAS, M.A., D.Sc., Lecturer in Moral Philosophy, and Assistant to the Professor of Moral Philosophy in the University of Edinburgh. Post 8vo, 6s. net.

John Stuart Mill: A Study of his Philosophy. Crown 8vo, 4s. 6d. net.

DOUGLAS. Chinese Stories. By ROBERT K. DOUGLAS. With numerous Illustrations by Parkinson, Forestier, and others. New and Cheaper Edition. Small demy 8vo, 5s.

DOUGLAS. Iras: A Mystery. By THEO. DOUGLAS, Author of 'A Bride Elect.' Cheaper Edition, in Paper Cover specially designed by Womrath. Crown 8vo, 1s. 6d.

DU CANE. The Odyssey of Homer, Books I.-XII. Translated into English Verse. By Sir CHARLES DU CANE, K.C.M.G. 8vo, 10s. 6d.

DUNSMORE. Manual of the Law of Scotland as to the Relations between Agricultural Tenants and the Landlords, Servants, Merchants, and Bowers. By W. DUNSMORE. 8vo, 7s. 6d.

DZIEWICKI. Entombed in Flesh. By M. H. DZIEWICKI. Crown 8vo, 3s. 6d.

ELIOT.

George Eliot's Life, Related in Her Letters and Journals. Arranged and Edited by her husband, J. W. CROSS. With Portrait and other Illustrations. Third Edition. 3 vols. post 8vo, 42s.

George Eliot's Life. With Portrait and other Illustrations. New Edition, in one volume. Crown 8vo, 7s. 6d.

Works of George Eliot (Standard Edition). 21 volumes, crown 8vo. In buckram cloth, gilt top, 2s. 6d. per vol.; or in roxburghe binding, 3s. 6d. per vol.

    ADAM BEDE. 2 vols.—THE MILL ON THE FLOSS. 2 vols.—FELIX HOLT, THE RADICAL. 2 vols.—ROMOLA. 2 vols.—SCENES OF CLERICAL LIFE. 2 vols.—MIDDLEMARCH. 3 vols.—DANIEL DERONDA. 3 vols.—SILAS MARNER. 1 vol.—JUBAL. 1 vol.—THE SPANISH GIPSY. 1 vol.—ESSAYS. 1 vol.—THEOPHRASTUS SUCH. 1 vol.

Life and Works of George Eliot (Cabinet Edition). 24 volumes, crown 8vo, price £6. Also to be had handsomely bound in half and full calf. The Volumes are sold separately, bound in cloth, price 5s. each.

Novels by George Eliot. New Cheap Edition. Printed on fine laid paper, and uniformly bound.

    Adam Bede. 3s. 6d.—The Mill on the Floss. 3s. 6d.—Scenes of Clerical Life. 3s.—Silas Marner: the Weaver of Raveloe. 2s. 6d.—Felix Holt, the Radical. 3s. 6d.—Romola. 3s. 6d.—Middlemarch. 7s. 6d.—Daniel Deronda. 7s. 6d.

Essays. New Edition. Crown 8vo, 5s.

Impressions of Theophrastus Such. New Edition. Crown 8vo, 5s.

The Spanish Gypsy. New Edition. Crown 8vo, 5s.

The Legend of Jubal, and other Poems, Old and New. New Edition. Crown 8vo, 5s.

ELIOT.
Scenes of Clerical Life. Pocket Edition, 3 vols. pott 8vo, 1s. net each ; bound in leather, 1s. 6d. net each. Popular Edition. Royal 8vo, in paper cover, price 6d.
Adam Bede. Pocket Edition. In 3 vols. pott 8vo, 3s. net ; bound in leather, 4s. 6d. net.
Wise, Witty, and Tender Sayings, in Prose and Verse. Selected from the Works of GEORGE ELIOT. New Edition. Fcap. 8vo, 3s. 6d.

ELTON. The Augustan Ages. 'Periods of European Literature.' By OLIVER ELTON, B.A., Lecturer in English Literature, Owen's College, Manchester. In 1 vol. crown 8vo. [*In the press.*

ESSAYS ON SOCIAL SUBJECTS. Originally published in the 'Saturday Review.' New Edition. First and Second Series. 2 vols. crown 8vo, 6s. each.

FAITHS OF THE WORLD, The. A Concise History of the Great Religious Systems of the World. By various Authors. Crown 8vo, 5s.

FALKNER. The Lost Stradivarius. By J. MEADE FALKNER. Second Edition. Crown 8vo, 6s.

FENNELL AND O'CALLAGHAN. A Prince of Tyrone. By CHARLOTTE FENNELL and J. P. O'CALLAGHAN. Crown 8vo, 6s.

FERGUSON. Sir Samuel Ferguson in the Ireland of his Day. By LADY FERGUSON, Author of 'The Irish before the Conquest,' 'Life of William Reeves, D.D., Lord Bishop of Down, Connor, and Dromore,' &c., &c. With Two Portraits. 2 vols. post 8vo, 21s.

FERGUSSON. Scots Poems. By ROBERT FERGUSSON. With Photogravure Portrait. Pott 8vo, gilt top, bound in cloth, 1s. net.

FERRIER.
Philosophical Works of the late James F. Ferrier, B.A. Oxon., Professor of Moral Philosophy and Political Economy, St Andrews. New Edition. Edited by Sir ALEXANDER GRANT, Bart., D.C.L., and Professor LUSHINGTON. 3 vols. crown 8vo, 34s. 6d.
Institutes of Metaphysic. Third Edition. 10s. 6d.
Lectures on the Early Greek Philosophy. 4th Edition. 10s. 6d.
Philosophical Remains, including the Lectures on Early Greek Philosophy. New Edition. 2 vols. 24s.

FLINT.
Historical Philosophy in France and French Belgium and Switzerland. By ROBERT FLINT, Corresponding Member of the Institute of France, Hon. Member of the Royal Society of Palermo, Professor in the University of Edinburgh, &c. 8vo, 21s.
Agnosticism. Being the Croall Lecture for 1887-88. [*In the press.*
Theism. Being the Baird Lecture for 1876. Ninth Edition, Revised. Crown 8vo, 7s. 6d.
Anti-Theistic Theories. Being the Baird Lecture for 1877. Fifth Edition. Crown 8vo, 10s. 6d.
Sermons and Addresses. In 1 vol. Demy 8vo. [*In the press.*

FOREIGN CLASSICS FOR ENGLISH READERS. Edited by Mrs OLIPHANT. Price 1s. each. *For List of Volumes, see page 2.*

FOSTER. The Fallen City, and other Poems. By WILL FOSTER. Crown 8vo, 6s.

FRANCILLON. Gods and Heroes ; or, The Kingdom of Jupiter. By R. E. FRANCILLON. With 8 Illustrations. Crown 8vo, 5s.

FRANCIS. Among the Untrodden Ways. By M. E. FRANCIS (Mrs Francis Blundell), Author of 'In a North Country Village,' 'A Daughter of the Soil,' 'Frieze and Fustian,' &c. Crown 8vo, 3s. 6d.

FRASER.

Philosophy of Theism. Being the Gifford Lectures delivered
before the University of Edinburgh in 1894-95. By ALEXANDER CAMPBELL
FRASER, D.C.L. Oxford; Emeritus Professor of Logic and Metaphysics in
the University of Edinburgh. Second Edition, Revised. In 1 vol. Post 8vo.
[*In the press.*]

GALT.

Novels by JOHN GALT. With General Introduction and
Prefatory Notes by S. R. CROCKETT. The Text Revised and Edited by D.
STORRAR MELDRUM, Author of 'The Story of Margrédel.' With Photogravure
Illustrations from Drawings by John Wallace. Fcap. 8vo, 3s. net each vol.
ANNALS OF THE PARISH, and THE AYRSHIRE LEGATEES. 2 vols.—SIR ANDREW
WYLIE. 2 vols.—THE ENTAIL; or, The Lairds of Grippy. 2 vols.—THE PRO-
VOST, and THE LAST OF THE LAIRDS. 2 vols.
See also STANDARD NOVELS, p. 6.

GENERAL ASSEMBLY OF THE CHURCH OF SCOTLAND.

Scottish Hymnal, With Appendix Incorporated. Published
for use in Churches by Authority of the General Assembly. 1. Large type,
cloth, red edges, 2s. 6d.; French morocco, 4s. 2. Bourgeois type, limp cloth, 1s.;
French morocco, 2s. 3. Nonpareil type, cloth, red edges, 6d.; French morocco,
1s. 4d. 4. Paper covers, 2d. 5. Sunday-School Edition, paper covers, 1d.;
cloth, 2d. No. 1, bound with the Psalms and Paraphrases, French morocco, 8s.
No. 2, bound with the Psalms and Paraphrases, cloth, 2s.; French morocco, 3s.

Prayers for Social and Family Worship. Prepared by a
Special Committee of the General Assembly of the Church of Scotland. Entirely
New Edition, Revised and Enlarged. Fcap. 8vo, red edges, 2s.

Prayers for Family Worship. A Selection of Four Weeks
Prayers. New Edition. Authorised by the General Assembly of the Church of
Scotland. Fcap. 8vo, red edges, 1s. 6d.

One Hundred Prayers. Prepared by the Committee on Aids
to Devotion. 16mo, cloth limp, 6d.

Morning and Evening Prayers for Affixing to Bibles. Prepared
by the Committee on Aids to Devotion. 1d. for 6, or 1s. per 100.

Prayers for Soldiers and Sailors. Prepared by the Committee
on Aids to Devotion. Thirtieth Thousand. 16mo, cloth limp. 2d. net.

GERARD.

Reata: What's in a Name. By E. D. GERARD. Cheap
Edition. Crown 8vo, 3s. 6d.

Beggar my Neighbour. Cheap Edition. Crown 8vo, 3s. 6d.

The Waters of Hercules. Cheap Edition. Crown 8vo, 3s. 6d.

A Sensitive Plant. Crown 8vo, 3s. 6d.

GERARD.

A Foreigner. An Anglo-German Study. By E. GERARD.
Crown 8vo, 6s.

The Land beyond the Forest. Facts, Figures, and Fancies
from Transylvania. With Maps and Illustrations 2 vols. post 8vo, 25s.

Bis: Some Tales Retold. Crown 8vo, 6s.

A Secret Mission. 2 vols. crown 8vo, 17s.

An Electric Shock, and other Stories. Crown 8vo, 6s.

GERARD.

The Impediment. By DOROTHEA GERARD. Crown 8vo, 6s.

A Forgotten Sin. Crown 8vo, 6s.

A Spotless Reputation. Third Edition. Crown 8vo, 6s.

GERARD.
    The Wrong Man. Second Edition. Crown 8vo, 6s.
    Lady Baby. Cheap Edition. Crown 8vo, 3s. 6d.
    Recha. Second Edition. Crown 8vo, 6s.
    The Rich Miss Riddell. Second Edition. Crown 8vo, 6s.

GERARD. Stonyhurst Latin Grammar. By Rev. JOHN GERARD.
    Second Edition. Fcap. 8vo, 3s.

GOODALL. Association Football. By JOHN GOODALL. Edited
    by S. ARCHIBALD DE BEAR. With Diagrams. Fcap. 8vo, 1s.

GORDON CUMMING.
    At Home in Fiji. By C. F. GORDON CUMMING. Fourth
        Edition, post 8vo. With Illustrations and Map. 7s. 6d.
    A Lady's Cruise in a French Man-of-War. New and Cheaper
        Edition. 8vo. With Illustrations and Map. 12s. 6d.
    Fire-Fountains. The Kingdom of Hawaii: Its Volcanoes,
        and the History of its Missions. With Map and Illustrations. 2 vols. 8vo, 25s.
    Wanderings in China. New and Cheaper Edition. 8vo, with
        Illustrations, 10s.
    Granite Crags: The Yô-semité Region of California. Illus-
        trated with 8 Engravings. New and Cheaper Edition. 8vo, 8s. 6d.

GRAHAM. Manual of the Elections (Scot.) (Corrupt and Illegal
    Practices) Act, 1890. With Analysis, Relative Act of Sederunt, Appendix con-
    taining the Corrupt Practices Acts of 1883 and 1885, and Copious Index. By J.
    EDWARD GRAHAM, Advocate. 8vo, 4s. 6d.

GRAND.
    A Domestic Experiment. By SARAH GRAND, Author of
        'The Heavenly Twins,' 'Ideala: A Study from Life.' Crown 8vo, 6s.
    Singularly Deluded. Crown 8vo, 6s.

GRANT. Bush-Life in Queensland. By A. C. GRANT. New
    Edition. Crown 8vo, 6s.

GREGG. The Decian Persecution. Being the Hulsean Prize
    Essay for 1896. By JOHN A. F. GREGG, B.A., late Scholar of Christ's College,
    Cambridge. Crown 8vo, 6s.

GRIER.
    In Furthest Ind. The Narrative of Mr EDWARD CARLYON of
        Ellswether, in the County of Northampton, and late of the Honourable East India
        Company's Service, Gentleman. Wrote by his own hand in the year of grace 1697.
        Edited, with a few Explanatory Notes, by SYDNEY C. GRIER. Post 8vo, 6s.
    His Excellency's English Governess. Second Edition. Crown
        8vo, 6s.
    An Uncrowned King: A Romance of High Politics. Second
        Edition. Crown 8vo, 6s.
    Peace with Honour. Second Edition. Crown 8vo, 6s.
    A Crowned Queen: The Romance of a Minister of State.
        Crown 8vo, 6s.

GROOT. A Lotus Flower. By J. MORGAN DE GROOT. Crown
    8vo, 6s.

GUTHRIE - SMITH. Crispus: A Drama. By H. GUTHRIE-
    SMITH. Fcap. 4to, 5s.

HAGGARD. Under Crescent and Star. By Lieut.-Col. ANDREW
    HAGGARD, D.S.O., Author of 'Dodo and I,' 'Tempest Torn,' &c. With a
    Portrait. Second Edition. Crown 8vo, 6s.

HALDANE. Subtropical Cultivations and Climates. A Handy
    Book for Planters, Colonists, and Settlers. By R. C. HALDANE. Post 8vo, 9s.

HAMERTON.

Wenderholme: A Story of Lancashire and Yorkshire Life. By P. G. HAMERTON, Author of 'A Painter's Camp.' New Edition. Crown 8vo, 3s. 6d.

Marmorne. New Edition. Crown 8vo, 3s. 6d.

HAMILTON.

Lectures on Metaphysics. By Sir WILLIAM HAMILTON, Bart., Professor of Logic and Metaphysics in the University of Edinburgh. Edited by the Rev. H. L. MANSEL, B.D., LL.D., Dean of St Paul's; and JOHN VEITCH, M.A., LL.D., Professor of Logic and Rhetoric, Glasgow. Seventh Edition. 2 vols. 8vo, 24s.

Lectures on Logic. Edited by the SAME. Third Edition, Revised. 2 vols., 24s.

Discussions on Philosophy and Literature, Education and University Reform. Third Edition. 8vo, 21s.

Memoir of Sir William Hamilton, Bart., Professor of Logic and Metaphysics in the University of Edinburgh. By Professor VEITCH, of the University of Glasgow. 8vo, with Portrait, 18s.

Sir William Hamilton: The Man and his Philosophy. Two Lectures delivered before the Edinburgh Philosophical Institution, January and February 1883. By Professor VEITCH. Crown 8vo, 2s.

HAMLEY.

The Operations of War Explained and Illustrated. By General Sir EDWARD BRUCE HAMLEY, K.C.B., K.C.M.G. Fifth Edition, Revised throughout. 4to, with numerous Illustrations, 30s.

National Defence; Articles and Speeches. Post 8vo, 6s.

Shakespeare's Funeral, and other Papers. Post 8vo, 7s. 6d.

Thomas Carlyle: An Essay. Second Edition. Crown 8vo, 2s. 6d.

On Outposts. Second Edition. 8vo, 2s.

Wellington's Career; A Military and Political Summary. Crown 8vo, 2s.

Lady Lee's Widowhood. New Edition. Crown 8vo, 3s. 6d. Cheaper Edition, 2s. 6d.

Our Poor Relations. A Philozoic Essay. With Illustrations, chiefly by Ernest Griset. Crown 8vo, cloth gilt, 3s. 6d.

The Life of General Sir Edward Bruce Hamley, K.C.B., K.C.M.G. By ALEXANDER INNES SHAND. With two Photogravure Portraits and other Illustrations. Cheaper Edition. With a Statement by Mr EDWARD HAMLEY. 2 vols. demy 8vo, 10s. 6d.

HANNAY. The Later Renaissance. 'Periods of European Literature.' By DAVID HANNAY. Crown 8vo, 5s. net.

HARE. Down the Village Street: Scenes in a West Country Hamlet. By CHRISTOPHER HARE. Second Edition. Crown 8vo, 6s.

HARRADEN.

In Varying Moods: Short Stories. By BEATRICE HARRADEN, Author of 'Ships that Pass in the Night.' Thirteenth Edition. Crown 8vo, 3s. 6d.

Hilda Strafford, and The Remittance Man. Two Californian Stories. Eleventh Edition. Crown 8vo, 3s. 6d.

Untold Tales of the Past. With 40 Illustrations by H. R. Millar. Square crown 8vo, gilt top, 6s.

HARRIS.

From Batum to Baghdad, *via* Tiflis, Tabriz, and Persian Kurdistan. By WALTER B. HARRIS, F.R.G.S., Author of 'The Land of an African Sultan; Travels in Morocco,' &c. With numerous Illustrations and 2 Maps. Demy 8vo, 12s.

HARRIS.

Tafilet. The Narrative of a Journey of Exploration to the
Atlas Mountains and the Oases of the North-West Sahara. With Illustrations
by Maurice Romberg from Sketches and Photographs by the Author, and Two
Maps. Demy 8vo, 12s.

A Journey through the Yemen, and some General Remarks
upon that Country. With 8 Maps and numerous Illustrations by Forestier and
Wallace from Sketches and Photographs taken by the Author. Demy 8vo, 16s.

Danovitch, and other Stories. Crown 8vo, 6s.

HAY. The Works of the Right Rev. Dr George Hay, Bishop of
Edinburgh. Edited under the Supervision of the Right Rev. Bishop STRAIN.
With Memoir and Portrait of the Author. 5 vols. crown 8vo, bound in extra
cloth, £1, 1s. The following Volumes may be had separately—viz. :
The Devout Christian Instructed in the Law of Christ from the Written
Word. 2 vols., 8s.—The Pious Christian Instructed in the Nature and Practice
of the Principal Exercises of Piety. 1 vol., 3s.

HEATLEY.

The Horse-Owner's Safeguard. A Handy Medical Guide for
every Man who owns a Horse. By G. S. HEATLEY, M.R.C.V.S. Crown 8vo, 5s.

The Stock-Owner's Guide. A Handy Medical Treatise for
every Man who owns an Ox or a Cow. Crown 8vo, 4s. 6d.

HEMANS.

The Poetical Works of Mrs Hemans. Copyright Edition.
Royal 8vo, with Engravings, cloth, gilt edges, 7s. 6d.

Select Poems of Mrs Hemans. Fcap., cloth, gilt edges, 3s.

HENDERSON. The Young Estate Manager's Guide. By
RICHARD HENDERSON, Member (by Examination) of the Royal Agricultural
Society of England, the Highland and Agricultural Society of Scotland, and
the Surveyors' Institution. With an Introduction by R. Patrick Wright,
F.R.S.E., Professor of Agriculture, Glasgow and West of Scotland Technical
College. With Plans and Diagrams. Crown 8vo, 5s.

HERKLESS. Cardinal Beaton : Priest and Politician. By
JOHN HERKLESS, Professor of Church History, St Andrews. With a Portrait.
Post 8vo, 7s. 6d.

HEWISON. The Isle of Bute in the Olden Time. With Illus-
trations, Maps, and Plans. By JAMES KING HEWISON, M.A., F.S.A. (Scot.),
Minister of Rothesay. Vol. I., Celtic Saints and Heroes. Crown 4to, 15s. net.
Vol. II., The Royal Stewards and the Brandanes. Crown 4to, 15s. net.

HIBBEN. Inductive Logic. By JOHN GRIER HIBBEN, Ph.D.,
Assistant Professor of Logic in Princeton University, U.S.A. Cr. 8vo, 3s. 6d. net.

HOME PRAYERS. By Ministers of the Church of Scotland
and Members of the Church Service Society. Second Edition. Fcap. 8vo, 3s.

HORNBY. Admiral of the Fleet Sir Geoffrey Phipps Hornby,
G.C.B. A Biography. By Mrs FRED. EGERTON. With Three Portraits. Demy
8vo, 16s.

HUTCHINSON. Hints on the Game of Golf. By HORACE G
HUTCHINSON. Ninth Edition, Enlarged. Fcap. 8vo, cloth, 1s.

HYSLOP. The Elements of Ethics. By JAMES H. HYSLOP,
Ph.D., Instructor in Ethics, Columbia College, New York, Author of 'The
Elements of Logic.' Post 8vo, 7s. 6d. net.

IDDESLEIGH. Life, Letters, and Diaries of Sir Stafford North-
cote, First Earl of Iddesleigh. By ANDREW LANG. With Three Portraits and a
View of Pynes. Third Edition. 2 vols. post 8vo, 31s. 6d.
POPULAR EDITION. With Portrait and View of Pynes. Post 8vo, 7s. 6d.

JEAN JAMBON. Our Trip to Blunderland ; or, Grand Ex-
cursion to Blundertown and Back. By JEAN JAMBON. With Sixty Illustrations
designed by CHARLES DOYLE, engraved by DALZIEL. Fourth Thousand. Cloth,
gilt edges, 6s. 6d. Cheap Edition, cloth, 3s. 6d. Boards, 2s. 6d.

JEBB.
A Strange Career. The Life and Adventures of JOHN
GLADWYN JEBB. By his Widow. With an Introduction by H. RIDER HAGGARD,
and an Electrogravure Portrait of Mr Jebb. Third Edition. Demy 8vo, 10s. 6d.
CHEAP EDITION. With Illustrations by John Wallace. Crown 8vo, 3s. 6d.
Some Unconventional People. By Mrs GLADWYN JEBB,
Author of 'Life and Adventures of J. G. Jebb.' With Illustrations. Cheap
Edition. Paper covers, 1s.

JERNINGHAM.
Reminiscences of an Attaché. By HUBERT E. H. JERNINGHAM.
Second Edition. Crown 8vo, 5s
Diane de Breteuille. A Love Story. Crown 8vo, 2s. 6d.

JOHNSTON.
The Chemistry of Common Life. By Professor J. F. W.
JOHNSTON. New Edition, Revised. By ARTHUR HERBERT CHURCH, M.A. Oxon.;
Author of 'Food: its Sources, Constituents, and Uses,' &c. With Maps and 102
Engravings. Crown 8vo, 7s. 6d.
Elements of Agricultural Chemistry. An entirely New
Edition from the Edition by Sir CHARLES A. CAMERON, M.D., F.R.C.S.I., &c.
Revised and brought down to date by C. M. AIKMAN, M.A., B.Sc., F.R.S.E.,
Professor of Chemistry, Glasgow Veterinary College. 17th Edition. Crown 8vo,
6s. 6d.
Catechism of Agricultural Chemistry. An entirely New
Edition from the Edition by Sir CHARLES A. CAMERON. Revised and Enlarged
by C. M. AIKMAN, M.A., &c. 95th Thousand. With numerous Illustrations.
Crown 8vo, 1s.

JOHNSTON. Agricultural Holdings (Scotland) Acts, 1883 and
1889; and the Ground Game Act, 1880. With Notes, and Summary of Procedure,
&c. By CHRISTOPHER N. JOHNSTON, M.A., Advocate. Demy 8vo, 5s.

JOKAI. Timar's Two Worlds. By MAURUS JOKAI. Authorised
Translation by Mrs HEGAN KENNARD. Cheap Edition. Crown 8vo, 6s.

KEBBEL. The Old and the New: English Country Life. By
T. E. KEBBEL, M.A., Author of 'The Agricultural Labourers,' 'Essays in History
and Politics,' 'Life of Lord Beaconsfield.' Crown 8vo, 5s.

KERR. St Andrews in 1645-46. By D. R. KERR. Crown
8vo, 2s. 6d.

KINGLAKE.
History of the Invasion of the Crimea. By A. W. KINGLAKE.
Cabinet Edition, Revised. With an Index to the Complete Work. Illustrated
with Maps and Plans. Complete in 9 vols., crown 8vo, at 6s. each.
—— Abridged Edition for Military Students. Revised by
Lieut.-Col. Sir GEORGE SYDENHAM CLARKE, K.C.M.G., R.E. In 1 vol. demy 8vo.
[In the press.
History of the Invasion of the Crimea. Demy 8vo. Vol. VI.
Winter Troubles. With a Map, 16s. Vols. VII. and VIII. From the Morrow of
Inkerman to the Death of Lord Raglan. With an Index to the Whole Work.
With Maps and Plans. 28s
Eothen. A New Edition, uniform with the Cabinet Edition
of the 'History of the Invasion of the Crimea.' 6s.
CHEAPER EDITION. With Portrait and Biographical Sketch of the Author.
Crown 8vo, 3s. 6d. Popular Edition, in paper cover, 1s net.

KIRBY. In Haunts of Wild Game: A Hunter-Naturalist's
Wanderings from Kahlamba to Libombo. By FREDERICK VAUGHAN KIRBY,
F.Z.S. (Maqaqamba). With numerous Illustrations by Charles Whymper, and a
Map. Large demy 8vo, 25s.

KNEIPP. My Water-Cure. As Tested through more than Thirty Years, and Described for the Healing of Diseases and the Preservation of Health. By SEBASTIAN KNEIPP, Parish Priest of Wörishofen (Bavaria). With a Portrait and other Illustrations. Authorised English Translation from the Thirtieth German Edition, by A. de F. Cheap Edition. With an Appendix, containing the Latest Developments of Pfarrer Kneipp's System, and a Preface by E. Gerard. Crown 8vo, 3s. 6d.

KNOLLYS. The Elements of Field-Artillery. Designed for the Use of Infantry and Cavalry Officers. By HENRY KNOLLYS, Colonel Royal Artillery; Author of 'From Sedan to Saarbrück,' Editor of 'Incidents in the Sepoy War,' &c. With Engravings. Crown 8vo, 7s. 6d.

LANG.
Life, Letters, and Diaries of Sir Stafford Northcote, First Earl of Iddesleigh. By ANDREW LANG. With Three Portraits and a View of Pynes. Third Edition. 2 vols. post 8vo, 31s. 6d.
POPULAR EDITION. With Portrait and View of Pynes. Post 8vo, 7s. 6d.
The Highlands of Scotland in 1750. From Manuscript 104 in the King's Library, British Museum. With an Introduction by ANDREW LANG. Crown 8vo, 5s. net.

LANG. The Expansion of the Christian Life. The Duff Lec- ture for 1897. By the Rev. J. MARSHALL LANG, D.D. Crown 8vo, 5s.

LAPWORTH. Intermediate Text-Book of Geology. By Pro- fessor LAPWORTH, LL.D., F.R.S., &c. Founded on Dr Page's 'Introductory Text-Book of Geology.' With Illustrations. Crown 8vo, 5s.

LEES. A Handbook of the Sheriff and Justice of Peace Small Debt Courts. With Notes, References, and Forms. By J. M. LEES, Advocate, Sheriff of Stirling, Dumbarton, and Clackmannan. 8vo, 7s. 6d.

LENNOX AND STURROCK. The Elements of Physical Educa- tion : A Teacher's Manual. By DAVID LENNOX, M.D., late R.N., Medical Director of Dundee Public Gymnasium, and ALEXANDER STURROCK, Superintendent of Dundee Public Gymnasium, Instructor to the University of St Andrews and Dundee High School. With Original Musical Accompaniments to the Drill by HARRY EVERITT LOSEBY. With 130 Illustrations. Crown 8vo, 4s.

LEWES. Dr Southwood Smith : A Retrospect. By his Grand- daughter, Mrs C. L. LEWES. With Portraits and other Illustrations. Post 8vo, 6s.

LINDSAY.
Recent Advances in Theistic Philosophy of Religion. By Rev. JAMES LINDSAY, M.A., B.D., B.Sc., F.R.S.E., F.G.S., Minister of the Parish of St Andrew's, Kilmarnock. Demy 8vo, 12s. 6d. net.
The Progressiveness of Modern Christian Thought. Crown 8vo, 6s.
Essays, Literary and Philosophical. Crown 8vo, 3s. 6d.
The Significance of the Old Testament for Modern Theology. Crown 8vo, 1s. net.
The Teaching Function of the Modern Pulpit. Crown 8vo, 1s. net.

LOCKHART.
Doubles and Quits. By LAURENCE W. M. LOCKHART. New Edition. Crown 8vo, 3s. 6d.
Fair to See. New Edition. Crown 8vo, 3s. 6d.
Mine is Thine. New Edition. Crown 8vo, 3s. 6d.

LOCKHART.
The Church of Scotland in the Thirteenth Century. The Life and Times of David de Bernham of St Andrews (Bishop), A.D. 1239 to 1253. With List of Churches dedicated by him, and Dates. By WILLIAM LOCKHART, A.M., D.D., F.S.A. Scot., Minister of Colinton Parish. 2d Edition. 8vo, 6s.

LOCKHART.
   Dies Tristes : Sermons for Seasons of Sorrow.   Crown 8vo, 6s.
LORIMER.
   The Institutes of Law : A Treatise of the Principles of Juris-
      prudence as determined by Nature. By the late JAMES LORIMER, Professor of
      Public Law and of the Law of Nature and Nations in the University of Edin-
      burgh. New Edition, Revised and much Enlarged. 8vo, 18s.
   The Institutes of the Law of Nations. A Treatise of the
      Jural Relation of Separate Political Communities. In 2 vols. 8vo. Volume I.,
      price 16s. Volume II., price 20s.
LUGARD.   The Rise of our East African Empire : Early Efforts
      in Uganda and Nyasaland. By F. D. LUGARD, Captain Norfolk Regiment.
      With 130 Illustrations from Drawings and Photographs under the personal
      superintendence of the Author, and 14 specially prepared Maps. In 2 vols. large
      demy 8vo, 42s.

MABIE.
   Essays on Nature and Culture. By HAMILTON WRIGHT MABIE.
      With Portrait. Fcap. 8vo, 3s. 6d.
   Books and Culture. Fcap. 8vo, 3s. 6d.
MᶜCHESNEY.
   Miriam Cromwell, Royalist : A Romance of the Great Rebel-
      lion. By DORA GREENWELL MᶜCHESNEY. Crown 8vo, 6s.
   Kathleen Clare : Her Book, 1637-41. With Frontispiece, and
      five full-page Illustrations by James A. Shearman. Crown 8vo, 6s.
MᶜCOMBIE. Cattle and Cattle-Breeders. By WILLIAM MᶜCOMBIE,
      Tillyfour. New Edition, Enlarged, with Memoir of the Author by JAMES
      MACDONALD, F.R.S.E., Secretary Highland and Agricultural Society of Scotland.
      Crown 8vo, 3s. 6d.
MᶜCRIE.
   Works of the Rev. Thomas MᶜCrie, D.D. Uniform Edition.
      4 vols. crown 8vo, 24s.
   Life of John Knox. Crown 8vo, 6s. Another Edition, 3s. 6d.
   Life of Andrew Melville. Crown 8vo, 6s.
   History of the Progress and Suppression of the Reformation
      in Italy in the Sixteenth Century. Crown 8vo, 4s.
   History of the Progress and Suppression of the Reformation
      in Spain in the Sixteenth Century. Crown 8vo, 3s. 6d.
MᶜCRIE. The Public Worship of Presbyterian Scotland. Histori-
      cally treated. With copious Notes, Appendices, and Index. The Fourteenth
      Series of the Cunningham Lectures. By the Rev. CHARLES G. MᶜCRIE, D.D.
      Demy 8vo, 10s. 6d.
MACDONALD. A Manual of the Criminal Law (Scotland) Pro-
      cedure Act, 1887. By NORMAN DORAN MACDONALD. Revised by the LORD
      JUSTICE-CLERK. 8vo, 10s. 6d.
MACDOUGALL AND DODDS. A Manual of the Local Govern-
      ment (Scotland) Act, 1894. With Introduction, Explanatory Notes, and Copious
      Index. By J. PATTEN MACDOUGALL, Legal Secretary to the Lord Advocate, and
      J. M. DODDS. Tenth Thousand, Revised. Crown 8vo, 2s. 6d. net.
MACINTYRE. Hindu-Koh : Wanderings and Wild Sports on
      and beyond the Himalayas. By Major-General DONALD MACINTYRE, V.C., late
      Prince of Wales' Own Goorkhas, F.R.G.S. *Dedicated to H.R.H. the Prince of
      Wales.* New and Cheaper Edition, Revised, with numerous Illustrations. Post
      8vo, 3s. 6d.
MACKAY.
   Elements of Modern Geography. By the Rev. ALEXANDER
      MACKAY, LL.D., F.R.G.S. 55th Thousand, Revised to the present time. Crown
      8vo, pp. 300, 3s.

MACKAY.

The Intermediate Geography. Intended as an Intermediate
Book between the Author's 'Outlines of Geography' and 'Elements of Geography.' Eighteenth Edition, Revised. Fcap. 8vo, pp. 238, 2s.

Outlines of Modern Geography. 191st Thousand, Revised to
the present time. Fcap. 8vo, pp. 128, 1s.

Elements of Physiography. New Edition. Rewritten and
Enlarged. With numerous Illustrations. Crown 8vo. *(In the press*

MACKENZIE. Studies in Roman Law. With Comparative
Views of the Laws of France, England, and Scotland. By LORD MACKENZIE,
one of the Judges of the Court of Session in Scotland. Seventh Edition, Edited
by JOHN KIRKPATRICK, M.A., LL.B., Advocate, Professor of History in the
University of Edinburgh. 8vo, 21s.

M'PHERSON. Golf and Golfers. Past and Present. By J.
GORDON M'PHERSON, Ph.D., F.R.S.E. With an Introduction by the Right Hon.
A. J. BALFOUR, and a Portrait of the Author. Fcap. 8vo, 1s. 6d.

MACRAE. A Handbook of Deer-Stalking. By ALEXANDER
MACRAE, late Forester to Lord Henry Bentinck. With Introduction by HORATIO
Ross, Esq. Fcap. 8vo, with 2 Photographs from Life. 3s. 6d.

MAIN. Three Hundred English Sonnets. Chosen and Edited
by DAVID M. MAIN. New Edition. Fcap. 8vo, 3s. 6d.

MAIR. A Digest of Laws and Decisions, Ecclesiastical and
Civil, relating to the Constitution, Practice, and Affairs of the Church of Scotland. With Notes and Forms of Procedure. By the Rev. WILLIAM MAIR, D.D.,
Minister of the Parish of Earlston. New Edition, Revised. Crown 8vo, 9s. net.

MARSHMAN. History of India. From the Earliest Period to
the present time. By JOHN CLARK MARSHMAN, C.S.I. Third and Cheaper
Edition. Post 8vo, with Map, 6s.

MARTIN.

The Æneid of Virgil. Books I.-VI. Translated by Sir THEODORE MARTIN, K.C.B. Post 8vo, 7s. 6d.

Goethe's Faust. Part I. Translated into English Verse.
Second Edition, crown 8vo, 6s. Ninth Edition, fcap. 8vo, 3s. 6d.

Goethe's Faust. Part II. Translated into English Verse.
Second Edition, Revised. Fcap. 8vo, 6s.

The Works of Horace. Translated into English Verse, with
Life and Notes. 2 vols. New Edition. Crown 8vo, 21s.

Poems and Ballads of Heinrich Heine. Done into English
Verse. Third Edition. Small crown 8vo, 5s.

The Song of the Bell, and other Translations from Schiller,
Goethe, Uhland, and Others. Crown 8vo, 7s. 6d.

Madonna Pia : A Tragedy ; and Three Other Dramas. Crown
8vo, 7s. 6d.

Catullus. With Life and Notes. Second Edition, Revised
and Corrected. Post 8vo, 7s. 6d.

The 'Vita Nuova' of Dante. Translated, with an Introduction
and Notes. Third Edition. Small crown 8vo, 5s.

Aladdin : A Dramatic Poem. By ADAM OEHLENSCHLAEGER.
Fcap. 8vo, 5s.

Correggio : A Tragedy. By OEHLENSCHLAEGER. With Notes.
Fcap. 8vo, 3s.

MARTIN. On some of Shakespeare's Female Characters. By
HELENA FAUCIT, Lady MARTIN. *Dedicated by permission to Her Most Gracious
Majesty the Queen.* Fifth Edition. With a Portrait by Lehmann. Demy 8vo,
7s. 6d.

MARWICK. Observations on the Law and Practice in regard
to Municipal Elections and the Conduct of the Business of Town Councils and
Commissioners of Police in Scotland. By Sir JAMES D. MARWICK, LL.D.,
Town-Clerk of Glasgow. Royal 8vo, 30s.

MATHESON.

Can the Old Faith Live with the New? or, The Problem of Evolution and Revelation. By the Rev. GEORGE MATHESON, D.D. Third Edition. Crown 8vo, 7s. 6d.

The Psalmist and the Scientist; or, Modern Value of the Religious Sentiment. Third Edition. Crown 8vo, 5s.

Spiritual Development of St Paul. Fourth Edition. Cr. 8vo, 5s.

The Distinctive Messages of the Old Religions. Second Edition. Crown 8vo, 5s.

Sacred Songs. New and Cheaper Edition. Crown 8vo, 2s. 6d.

MATHIESON. The Supremacy and Sufficiency of Jesus Christ our Lord, as set forth in the Epistle to the Hebrews. By J. E. MATHIESON, Superintendent of Mildmay Conference Hall, 1880 to 1890. Second Edition. Crown 8vo, 3s. 6d.

MAURICE. The Balance of Military Power in Europe. An Examination of the War Resources of Great Britain and the Continental States. By Colonel MAURICE, R.A., Professor of Military Art and History at the Royal Staff College. Crown 8vo, with a Map, 6s.

MAXWELL.

The Honourable Sir Charles Murray, K.C.B. A Memoir. By Sir HERBERT MAXWELL, Bart., M.P., F.S.A., &c., Author of 'Passages in the Life of Sir Lucian Elphin.' With Five Portraits. Demy 8vo, 18s.

Life and Times of the Rt. Hon. William Henry Smith, M.P. With Portraits and numerous Illustrations by Herbert Railton, G. L. Seymour, and Others. 2 vols. demy 8vo, 25s.
POPULAR EDITION. With a Portrait and other Illustrations. Crown 8vo, 3s. 6d.

Scottish Land-Names: Their Origin and Meaning. Being the Rhind Lectures in Archæology for 1893. Post 8vo, 6s.

Meridiana: Noontide Essays. Post 8vo, 7s. 6d.

Post Meridiana: Afternoon Essays. Post 8vo, 6s.

A Duke of Britain. A Romance of the Fourth Century. Fourth Edition. Crown 8vo, 5s.

Dumfries and Galloway. Being one of the Volumes of the County Histories of Scotland. With Four Maps. Demy 8vo, 7s. 6d. net.

MELDRUM.

Holland and the Hollanders. By D. STORRAR MELDRUM. With numerous Illustrations in 1 vol. square 8vo.   [In the press.

The Story of Margrédel Being a Fireside History of a Fifeshire Family. Cheap Edition. Crown 8vo, 3s. 6d.

Grey Mantle and Gold Fringe. Crown 8vo, 6s.

MELLONE. Studies in Philosophical Criticism and Construction. By SYDNEY HERBERT MELLONE, M.A. Lond., D.Sc. Edin. Post 8vo. 10s. 6d. net.

MERZ. A History of European Thought in the Nineteenth Century. By JOHN THEODORE MERZ. Vol. I., post 8vo, 10s. 6d. net.

MICHIE.

The Larch: Being a Practical Treatise on its Culture and General Management. By CHRISTOPHER Y. MICHIE, Forester, Cullen House. Crown 8vo, with Illustrations. New and Cheaper Edition, Enlarged, 5s.

The Practice of Forestry. Crown 8vo, with Illustrations. 6s.

MIDDLETON. The Story of Alastair Bhan Comyn; or, The Tragedy of Dunphail. A Tale of Tradition and Romance. By the Lady MIDDLETON. Square 8vo, 10s. Cheaper Edition, 5s.

MIDDLETON. Latin Verse Unseens. By G. MIDDLETON, M.A. Lecturer in Latin, Aberdeen University; late Scholar of Emmanuel College. Cambridge; Joint-Author of 'Student's Companion to Latin Authors.' Crown 8vo, 1s. 6d.

MILLER. The Dream of Mr H——, the Herbalist. By HUGH
MILLER, F.R.S.E., late H.M. Geological Survey, Author of 'Landscape Geology.'
With a Photogravure Frontispiece. Crown 8vo, 3s. 6d.

MILLS. Greek Verse Unseens. By T. R. MILLS, M.A., late
Lecturer in Greek, Aberdeen University; formerly Scholar of Wadham College,
Oxford; Joint-Author of 'Student's Companion to Latin Authors. Crown 8vo,
1s. 6d.

MINTO.
A Manual of English Prose Literature, Biographical and
Critical: designed mainly to show Characteristics of Style. By W. MINTO,
M.A., Hon. LL.D. of St Andrews; Professor of Logic in the University of Aber-
deen. Third Edition, Revised. Crown 8vo, 7s. 6d.

Characteristics of English Poets, from Chaucer to Shirley.
New Edition, Revised. Crown 8vo, 7s. 6d.

Plain Principles of Prose Composition. Crown 8vo, 1s. 6d.

The Literature of the Georgian Era. Edited, with a Biographical Introduction, by Professor KNIGHT, St Andrews. Post 8vo, 6s.

MOIR.
Life of Mansie Wauch, Tailor in Dalkeith. By D. M. MOIR.
With CRUIKSHANK's Illustrations. Cheaper Edition. Crown 8vo, 2s. 6d.
Another Edition, without Illustrations, fcap. 8vo, 1s. 6d.

Domestic Verses. Centenary Edition. With a Portrait. Crown
8vo, 2s. 6d. net.

MOLE. For the Sake of a Slandered Woman. By MARION
MOLE. Fcap. 8vo, 2s. 6d. net.

MOMERIE.
Defects of Modern Christianity, and other Sermons. By Rev.
ALFRED WILLIAMS MOMERIE, M.A., D.Sc., LL.D. Fifth Edition. Crown 8vo, 5s.

The Basis of Religion. Being an Examination of Natural
Religion. Third Edition. Crown 8vo, 2s. 6d.

The Origin of Evil, and other Sermons. Eighth Edition,
Enlarged. Crown 8vo, 5s.

Personality. The Beginning and End of Metaphysics, and a Necessary Assumption in all Positive Philosophy. Fifth Ed., Revised. Cr. 8vo, 3s.

Agnosticism. Fourth Edition, Revised. Crown 8vo, 5s.

Preaching and Hearing; and other Sermons. Fourth Edition,
Enlarged. Crown 8vo, 5s.

Belief in God. Fourth Edition. Crown 8vo, 3s.

Inspiration; and other Sermons. Second Edition, Enlarged.
Crown 8vo, 5s.

Church and Creed. Third Edition. Crown 8vo, 4s. 6d.

The Future of Religion, and other Essays. Second Edition.
Crown 8vo, 3s. 6d.

The English Church and the Romish Schism. Second Edition.
Crown 8vo, 2s. 6d.

MONCREIFF.
The Provost-Marshal. A Romance of the Middle Shires. By
the Hon. FREDERICK MONCREIFF. Crown 8vo, 6s.

The X Jewel. A Romance of the Days of James VI. Cr. 8vo, 6s.

MONTAGUE. Military Topography. Illustrated by Practical
Examples of a Practical Subject. By Major-General W. E. MONTAGUE, C.B.,
P.S.C., late Garrison Instructor Intelligence Department, Author of 'Campaign-
ing in South Africa.' With Forty-one Diagrams. Crown 8vo, 5s.

MONTALEMBERT. Memoir of Count de Montalembert. A
Chapter of Recent French History. By Mrs OLIPHANT, Author of the 'Life of
Edward Irving,' &c. 2 vols. crown 8vo, £1, 4s.

MORISON.
Rifts in the Reek. By JEANIE MORISON. With a Photogravure
Frontispiece. Crown 8vo, 5s. Bound in buckram for presentation, 6s.
Doorside Ditties. With a Frontispiece. Crown 8vo, 3s. 6d.
Æolus. A Romance in Lyrics. Crown 8vo, 3s.
There as Here. Crown 8vo, 3s.
₊ *A limited impression on hand-made paper, bound in vellum, 7s. 6d.*
Selections from Poems. Crown 8vo, 4s. 6d.
Sordello. An Outline Analysis of Mr Browning's Poem.
Crown 8vo, 3s.
Of "Fifine at the Fair," "Christmas Eve and Easter Day,"
and other of Mr Browning's Poems. Crown 8vo, 3s.
The Purpose of the Ages. Crown 8vo, 9s.
Gordon : An Our-day Idyll. Crown 8vo, 3s.
Saint Isadora, and other Poems. Crown 8vo, 1s. 6d.
Snatches of Song. Paper, 1s. 6d. ; cloth, 3s.
Pontius Pilate. Paper, 1s. 6d.; cloth, 3s.
Mill o' Forres. Crown 8vo, 1s.
Ane Booke of Ballades. Fcap. 4to, 1s.

MUNRO.
John Splendid. The Tale of a Poor Gentleman and the Little
Wars of Lorn. By NEIL MUNRO. Fifth Edition. Crown 8vo, 6s.
The Lost Pibroch, and other Sheiling Stories. Second
Edition. Crown 8vo, 3s. 6d.

MUNRO.
Rambles and Studies in Bosnia-Herzegovina and Dalmatia.
With an Account of the proceedings of the Congress of Archæologists and
Anthropologists held at Sarajevo in 1894. By ROBERT MUNRO, M.A., M.D.,
F.R.S.E., Author of the 'Lake Dwellings of Europe,' &c. With numerous illus-
trations. Demy 8vo, 12s. 6d. net.
Prehistoric Problems. With numerous Illustrations. Demy
8vo, 10s. net.

MUNRO. On Valuation of Property. By WILLIAM MUNRO,
M.A., Her Majesty's Assessor of Railways and Canals for Scotland. Second
Edition, Revised and Enlarged. 8vo, 3s. 6d.

MURDOCH. Manual of the Law of Insolvency and Bankruptcy:
Comprehending a Summary of the Law of Insolvency, Notour Bankruptcy.
Composition - Contracts, Trust - Deeds, Cessios, and Sequestrations; and the
Winding-up of Joint-Stock Companies in Scotland : with Annotations on the
various Insolvency and Bankruptcy Statutes ; and with Forms of Procedure
applicable to these Subjects. By JAMES MURDOCH, Member of the Faculty of
Procurators in Glasgow. Fifth Edition, Revised and Enlarged. 8vo, 12s. net.

MYERS. A Manual of Classical Geography. By JOHN L.
MYERS, M.A., Fellow of Magdalene College; Lecturer and Tutor, Christ Church,
Oxford. In 1 vol. crown 8vo. [*In the press.*]

MY TRIVIAL LIFE AND MISFORTUNE: A Gossip with
no Plot in Particular. By A PLAIN WOMAN. Cheap Edition. Crown 8vo, 3s. 6d.
By the SAME AUTHOR.
POOR NELLIE. Cheap Edition. Crown 8vo, 3s. 6d.

NAPIER. The Construction of the Wonderful Canon of Loga-
rithms. By JOHN NAPIER of Merchiston. Translated, with Notes, and a
Catalogue of Napier's Works, by WILLIAM RAE MACDONALD. Small 4to, 15s.
A few large-paper copies on Whatman paper, 30s.

NEAVES. Songs and Verses, Social and Scientific. By An Old
Contributor to 'Maga.' By the Hon. Lord NEAVES. Fifth Edition. Fcap.
8vo, 4s.

NICHOLSON.

A Manual of Zoology, for the Use of Students. With a
General Introduction on the Principles of Zoology. By HENRY ALLEYNE
NICHOLSON, M.D., D.Sc., F.L.S., F.G.S., Regius Professor of Natural History in
the University of Aberdeen. Seventh Edition, Rewritten and Enlarged. Post
8vo, pp. 956, with 555 Engravings on Wood, 18s.

Text-Book of Zoology, for Junior Students. Fifth Edition.
Rewritten and Enlarged. Crown 8vo, with 358 Engravings on Wood, 10s. 6d.

Introductory Text-Book of Zoology. New Edition. Revised
by AUTHOR and ALEXANDER BROWN, M.A., M.B., B.Sc., Lecturer on Zoology in
the University of Aberdeen. [In the press.

A Manual of Palæontology, for the Use of Students. With a
General Introduction on the Principles of Palæontology. By Professor H.
ALLEYNE NICHOLSON and RICHARD LYDEKKER, B.A. Third Edition, entirely
Rewritten and greatly Enlarged. 2 vols. 8vo, £3,18s.

The Ancient Life-History of the Earth. An Outline of the
Principles and Leading Facts of Palæontological Science. Crown 8vo, with 276
Engravings, 10s. 6d.

On the "Tabulate Corals" of the Palæozoic Period, with
Critical Descriptions of Illustrative Species. Illustrated with 15 Lithographed
Plates and numerous Engravings. Super-royal 8vo, 21s.

Synopsis of the Classification of the Animal Kingdom. 8vo,
with 106 Illustrations, 6s.

On the Structure and Affinities of the Genus Monticulipora
and its Sub-Genera, with Critical Descriptions of Illustrative Species. Illustrated
with numerous Engravings on Wood and Lithographed Plates. Super-royal
8vo, 18s.

NICHOLSON.

Thoth. A Romance. By JOSEPH SHIELD NICHOLSON, M.A.,
D.Sc., Professor of Commercial and Political Economy and Mercantile Law in
the University of Edinburgh. Third Edition. Crown 8vo, 4s. 6d.

A Dreamer of Dreams. A Modern Romance. Second Edition. Crown 8vo, 6s.

OLIPHANT.

Masollam : A Problem of the Period. A Novel. By LAURENCE
OLIPHANT. 3 vols. post 8vo, 25s. 6d.

Scientific Religion; or, Higher Possibilities of Life and
Practice through the Operation of Natural Forces. Second Edition. 8vo, 16s.

Altiora Peto. Cheap Edition. Crown 8vo, boards, 2s. 6d.;
cloth, 3s. 6d. Illustrated Edition. Crown 8vo, cloth, 6s.

Piccadilly. With Illustrations by Richard Doyle. New Edition, 3s. 6d. Cheap Edition, boards, 2s. 6d.

Traits and Travesties; Social and Political. Post 8vo, 10s. 6d.

Episodes in a Life of Adventure; or, Moss from a Rolling
Stone. Cheaper Edition. Post 8vo, 3s. 6d.

Haifa : Life in Modern Palestine. Second Edition. 8vo, 7s. 6d.

The Land of Gilead. With Excursions in the Lebanon.
With Illustrations and Maps. Demy 8vo, 21s.

Memoir of the Life of Laurence Oliphant, and of Alice
Oliphant, his Wife. By Mrs M. O. W. OLIPHANT. Seventh Edition. 2 vols.
post 8vo, with Portraits. 21s.
POPULAR EDITION. With a New Preface. Post 8vo, with Portraits. 7s. 6d.

OLIPHANT.

Annals of a Publishing House. William Blackwood and his
Sons; Their Magazine and Friends. By Mrs OLIPHANT. With Four Portraits.
Third Edition. Demy 8vo. Vols. I. and II. £2, 2s.

A Widow's Tale, and other Stories. With an Introductory
Note by J. M. BARRIE. Second Edition. Crown 8vo, 6s.

OLIPHANT.

Who was Lost and is Found. Second Edition. Crown
8vo, 6s.
Miss Marjoribanks. New Edition. Crown 8vo, 3s. 6d.
The Perpetual Curate, and The Rector. New Edition. Crown
8vo, 3s. 6d.
Salem Chapel, and The Doctor's Family. New Edition.
Crown 8vo, 3s. 6d
Chronicles of Carlingford. 3 vols. crown 8vo, in uniform
binding, gilt top, 3s. 6d. each.
Katie Stewart, and other Stories. New Edition. Crown 8vo,
cloth, 3s. 6d.
Katie Stewart. Illustrated boards, 2s. 6d.
Valentine and his Brother. New Edition. Crown 8vo, 3s. 6d.
Sons and Daughters. Crown 8vo, 3s. 6d.
Two Stories of the Seen and the Unseen. The Open Door
—Old Lady Mary. Paper covers, 1s.

OLIPHANT. Notes of a Pilgrimage to Jerusalem and the Holy
Land. By F. R. OLIPHANT. Crown 8vo, 3s. 6d.

PAGE.

Intermediate Text-Book of Geology. Founded on Page's 'In-
troductory Text-Book of Geology.' By Professor LAPWORTH of Mason Science
College, Birmingham. With Illustrations. Crown 8vo, 5s.
Advanced Text-Book of Geology, Descriptive and Industrial.
With Engravings, and Glossary of Scientific Terms. New Edition. Revised by
Professor LAPWORTH.   [In preparation.
Introductory Text-Book of Physical Geography. With Sketch-
Maps and Illustrations. Edited by Professor LAPWORTH, LL.D., F.G.S., &c.,
Mason Science College, Birmingham. Thirteenth Edition, Revised and Enlarged.
2s. 6d.
Advanced Text-Book of Physical Geography. Third Edition.
Revised and Enlarged by Professor LAPWORTH. With Engravings. 5s.

PATERSON. A Manual of Agricultural Botany. From the
German of Dr A. B. FRANK, Professor in the Royal Agricultural College, Berlin.
Translated by JOHN W. PATERSON, B.Sc., Ph.D., Free Life Member of the Highland and Agricultural Society of Scotland, and of the Royal Agricultural Society
of England. With over 100 Illustrations. Crown 8vo, 3s. 6d.

PATON.

Spindrift. By Sir J. NOEL PATON. Fcap., cloth, 5s.
Poems by a Painter. Fcap., cloth, 5s.

PATON. Castlebraes. Drawn from "The Tinlie MSS." By
JAMES PATON, B.A., Editor of 'John G. Paton: an Autobiography,' &c., &c.
Crown 8vo, 6s.

PATRICK. The Apology of Origen in Reply to Celsus. A Chapter in the History of Apologetics. By the Rev. J. PATRICK, D.D., Professor of
Biblical Criticism in the University of Edinburgh. Post 8vo, 7s. 6d.

PAUL. History of the Royal Company of Archers, the Queen's
Body-Guard for Scotland. By JAMES BALFOUR PAUL, Advocate of the Scottish
Bar. Crown 4to, with Portraits and other Illustrations. £2, 2s.

PEARSE. Soldier and Traveller: Being the Memoirs of
Alexander Gardner, Colonel of Artillery in the Service of Maharaja Ranjit
Singh. Edited by Major HUGH PEARSE, 2nd Battalion the East Surrey Regiment.
With an Introduction by the Right Hon. Sir RICHARD TEMPLE, Bart., G.C.S.I.
With Two Portraits and Maps. Demy 8vo, 15s.

PEILE. Lawn Tennis as a Game of Skill. By Lieut.-Col. S. C.
F. PEILE, B.S.C. Revised Edition, with new Scoring Rules. Fcap. 8vo, cloth, 1s.

PERIODS OF EUROPEAN LITERATURE. Edited by Professor SAINTSBURY. *For List of Volumes, see page 2.*

PETTIGREW. The Handy Book of Bees, and their Profitable Management. By A. PETTIGREW. Fifth Edition, Enlarged, with Engravings. Crown 8vo, 3s. 6d.

PFLEIDERER. Philosophy and Development of Religion. Being the Edinburgh Gifford Lectures for 1894. By OTTO PFLEIDERER, D.D., Professor of Theology at Berlin University. In 2 vols. post 8vo, 15s. net.

PHILLIPS. The Knight's Tale. By F. EMILY PHILLIPS, Author of 'The Education of Antonia.' Crown 8vo, 3s. 6d.

PHILOSOPHICAL CLASSICS FOR ENGLISH READERS. Edited by WILLIAM KNIGHT, LL.D., Professor of Moral Philosophy, University of St Andrews. In crown 8vo volumes, with Portraits, price 3s. 6d.
[*For List of Volumes, see page 2.*

POLLARD. A Study in Municipal Government: The Corporation of Berlin. By JAMES POLLARD, C.A., Chairman of the Edinburgh Public Health Committee, and Secretary of the Edinburgh Chamber of Commerce. Second Edition, Revised. Crown 8vo, 3s. 6d.

POLLOK. The Course of Time: A Poem. By ROBERT POLLOK, A.M. New Edition. With Portrait. Fcap. 8vo, gilt top, 2s. 6d.

PORT ROYAL LOGIC. Translated from the French; with Introduction, Notes, and Appendix. By THOMAS SPENCER BAYNES, LL.D., Professor in the University of St Andrews. Tenth Edition, 12mo, 4s.

POTTS AND DARNELL.
    Aditus Faciliores: An Easy Latin Construing Book, with Complete Vocabulary. By A. W. POTTS, M.A., LL.D., and the Rev. C. DARNELL, M.A., Head-Master of Cargilfield Preparatory School Edinburgh. Tenth Edition, fcap. 8vo, 3s. 6d.
    Aditus Faciliores Graeci. An Easy Greek Construing Book, with Complete Vocabulary. Fifth Edition, Revised. Fcap. 8vo, 3s.

POTTS. School Sermons. By the late ALEXANDER WM. POTTS, LL.D., First Head-Master of Fettes College. With a Memoir and Portrait. Crown 8vo, 7s. 6d.

PRINGLE. The Live Stock of the Farm. By ROBERT O. PRINGLE. Third Edition. Revised and Edited by JAMES MACDONALD. Crown 8vo, 7s. 6d.

PUBLIC GENERAL STATUTES AFFECTING SCOTLAND from 1707 to 1847, with Chronological Table and Index. 3 vols. large 8vo, £3, 3s.

PUBLIC GENERAL STATUTES AFFECTING SCOTLAND, COLLECTION OF. Published Annually, with General Index.

RAMSAY. Scotland and Scotsmen in the Eighteenth Century. Edited from the MSS. of JOHN RAMSAY, Esq. of Ochtertyre, by ALEXANDER ALLARDYCE, Author of 'Memoir of Admiral Lord Keith, K.B.,' &c. 2 vols. 8vo, 31s. 6d.

RANJITSINHJI. The Jubilee Book of Cricket. By PRINCE RANJITSINHJI.
    EDITION DE LUXE. Limited to 350 Copies, printed on hand-made paper, and handsomely bound in buckram. Crown 4to, with 22 Photogravures and 85 full-page Plates. Each copy signed by Prince Ranjitsinhji. Price £5, 5s. net.
    FINE PAPER EDITION. Medium 8vo, with Photogravure Frontispiece and 106 full-page Plates on art paper. 25s. net.
    POPULAR EDITION. With 107 full-page Illustrations. Sixth Edition. Large crown 8vo, 6s.

RANKIN.
    Church Ideas in Scripture and Scotland. By JAMES RANKIN, D.D., Minister of Muthill; Author of 'Character Studies in the Old Testament,' &c. Crown 8vo, 6s.
    A Handbook of the Church of Scotland. An entirely New and much Enlarged Edition. Crown 8vo, with 2 Maps 7s. 6d.

RANKIN.

The First Saints. Post 8vo, 7s. 6d.

The Creed in Scotland. An Exposition of the Apostles Creed. With Extracts from Archbishop Hamilton's Catechism of 1552, John Calvin's Catechism of 1556, and a Catena of Ancient Latin and other Hymns. Post 8vo, 7s. 6d.

The Worthy Communicant. A Guide to the Devout Observance of the Lord's Supper. Limp cloth, 1s. 3d.

The Young Churchman. Lessons on the Creed, the Commandments, the Means of Grace, and the Church. Limp cloth, 1s. 3d.

First Communion Lessons. 25th Edition. Paper Cover, 2d.

RANKINE. A Hero of the Dark Continent. Memoir of Rev. Wm. Affleck Scott, M.A., M.B., C.M., Church of Scotland Missionary at Blantyre, British Central Africa. By W. Henry Rankine, B.D., Minister at Titwood. With a Portrait and other Illustrations. Cheap Edition. Crown 8vo, 2s.

ROBERTSON.

The Poetry and the Religion of the Psalms. The Croall Lectures, 1893-94. By James Robertson, D.D., Professor of Oriental Languages in the University of Glasgow. Demy 8vo, 12s.

The Early Religion of Israel. As set forth by Biblical Writers and Modern Critical Historians. Being the Baird Lecture for 1888-89. Fourth Edition. Crown 8vo, 10s. 6d.

ROBERTSON.

Orellana, and other Poems. By J. Logie Robertson, M.A. Fcap. 8vo. Printed on hand-made paper. 6s.

A History of English Literature. For Secondary Schools. With an Introduction by Professor Masson, Edinburgh University. Cr. 8vo, 3s.

English Verse for Junior Classes. In Two Parts. Part I.— Chaucer to Coleridge. Part II.—Nineteenth Century Poets. Crown 8vo, each 1s. 6d. net.

Outlines of English Literature for Young Scholars. With Illustrative Specimens. Crown 8vo, 1s. 6d.

English Prose for Junior and Senior Classes. Part. I.—Malory to Johnson. Part II.—Nineteenth Century Writers. Crown 8vo, each 2s. 6d.

ROBINSON. Wild Traits in Tame Animals. Being some Familiar Studies in Evolution. By Louis Robinson, M.D. With Illustrations by Stephen T. Dadd. Demy 8vo, 10s. 6d. net.

ROSS and SOMERVILLE. Beggars on Horseback : A Riding Tour in North Wales. By Martin Ross and E. Œ. Somerville. With Illustrations by E. Œ. Somerville. Crown 8vo, 3s. 6d.

RUTLAND.

Notes of an Irish Tour in 1846. By the Duke of Rutland, G.C.B. (Lord John Manners). New Edition. Crown 8vo, 2s. 6d.

Correspondence between the Right Honble. William Pitt and Charles Duke of Rutland, Lord-Lieutenant of Ireland, 1781-1787. With Introductory Note by John Duke of Rutland. 8vo, 7s. 6d.

RUTLAND.

Gems of German Poetry. Translated by the Duchess of Rutland (Lady John Manners). [*New Edition in preparation.*

Impressions of Bad-Homburg. Comprising a Short Account of the Women's Associations of Germany under the Red Cross. Crown 8vo, 1s. 6d.

Some Personal Recollections of the Later Years of the Earl of Beaconsfield, K.G. Sixth Edition. 6d.

Employment of Women in the Public Service. 6d.

Some of the Advantages of Easily Accessible Reading and Recreation Rooms and Free Libraries. With Remarks on Starting and Maintaining them. Second Edition. Crown 8vo, 1s.

RUTLAND.
    A Sequel to Rich Men's Dwellings, and other Occasional
Papers. Crown 8vo, 2s. 6d.
    Encouraging Experiences of Reading and Recreation Rooms,
Aims of Guilds, Nottingham Social Guide, Existing Institutions, &c., &c.
Crown 8vo, 1s.

SAINTSBURY. The Flourishing of Romance and the Rise of
Allegory (12th and 13th Centuries). 'Periods of European Literature.' By GEORGE
SAINTSBURY, M.A., Professor of Rhetoric and English Literature in Edinburgh
University. Crown 8vo, 5s. net.

SCHEFFEL. The Trumpeter. A Romance of the Rhine. By
JOSEPH VICTOR VON SCHEFFEL. Translated from the Two Hundredth German
Edition by JESSIE BECK and LOUISA LORIMER. With an Introduction by Sir
THEODORE MARTIN, K.C.B. Long 8vo, 3s. 6d.

SCOTT. Tom Cringle's Log. By MICHAEL SCOTT. New Edition.
With 19 Full-page Illustrations. Crown 8vo, 3s. 6d.

SELKIRK. Poems. By J. B. SELKIRK, Author of 'Ethics and
Æsthetics of Modern Poetry,' 'Bible Truths with Shakespearian Parallels,' &c.
New and Enlarged Edition. Crown 8vo, printed on antique paper, 6s.

SELLAR'S Manual of the Acts relating to Education in Scotland. By J. EDWARD GRAHAM, B.A. Oxon., Advocate. Ninth Edition. Demy
8vo, 12s. 6d.

SETH.
    Scottish Philosophy. A Comparison of the Scottish and
German Answers to Hume. Balfour Philosophical Lectures, University of
Edinburgh. By ANDREW SETH (A. S. Pringle Pattison, LL.D.), Professor of
Logic and Metaphysics in Edinburgh University. Third Edition. Crown
8vo, 5s.
    Hegelianism and Personality. Balfour Philosophical Lectures.
Second Series. Second Edition. Crown 8vo, 5s.
    Man's Place in the Cosmos, and other Essays. Post 8vo,
7s. 6d. net.
    Two Lectures on Theism. Delivered on the occasion of the
Sesquicentennial Celebration of Princeton University. Crown 8vo, 2s. 6d.

SETH. A Study of Ethical Principles. By JAMES SETH, M.A.,
Professor of Moral Philosophy in the University of Edinburgh. Fourth Edition. Revised. Post 8vo, 7s. 6d.

SHARPE. Letters from and to Charles Kirkpatrick Sharpe.
Edited by ALEXANDER ALLARDYCE, Author of 'Memoir of Admiral Lord Keith,
K.B.,' &c. With a Memoir by the Rev. W. K. R. BEDFORD. In 2 vols. 8vo.
Illustrated with Etchings and other Engravings. £2, 12s. 6d.

SIM. Margaret Sim's Cookery. With an Introduction by L. B.
WALFORD, Author of 'Mr Smith: A Part of his Life,' &c. Crown 8vo, 5s.

SIMPSON. The Wild Rabbit in a New Aspect; or, Rabbit-
Warrens that Pay. A book for Landowners, Sportsmen, Land Agents, Farmers,
Gamekeepers, and Allotment Holders. A Record of Recent Experiments con-
ducted on the Estate of the Right Hon. the Earl of Wharncliffe at Wortley Hall.
By J. SIMPSON. Second Edition, Enlarged. Small crown 8vo, 5s.

SIMPSON. Side-Lights on Siberia. Some account of the Great
Siberian Iron Road: The Prisons and Exile System. By J. Y. SIMPSON, M.A.,
B.Sc. With numerous Illustrations and a Map. Demy 8vo, 16s.

SINCLAIR.
    Mr and Mrs Nevill Tyson. By MAY SINCLAIR. Crown 8vo,
3s. 6d.
    Audrey Craven. Second Edition. Crown 8vo, 6s.

SKELTON.
    The Table-Talk of Shirley. By Sir JOHN SKELTON, K.C.B.,
LL.D., Author of 'The Essays of Shirley.' With a Frontispiece. Sixth Edition,
Revised and Enlarged. Post 8vo, 7s. 6d.

SKELTON.

The Table-Talk of Shirley. Second Series. With Illustrations. Two Volumes. Second Edition. Post 8vo, 10s. net.

Maitland of Lethington; and the Scotland of Mary Stuart. A History. Limited Edition, with Portraits. Demy 8vo, 2 vols., 28s. net.

The Handbook of Public Health. A New Edition, Revised by JAMES PATTEN MACDOUGALL, Advocate, Secretary of the Local Government Board for Scotland, Joint-Author of 'The Parish Council Guide for Scotland,' and ABIJAH MURRAY, Chief Clerk of the Local Government Board for Scotland. In Two Parts. Crown 8vo. Part I.—The Public Health (Scotland) Act, 1897, with Notes. 3s. 6d. net.
    Part II.—Circulars of the Local Government Board, &c.   [*In preparation.*

The Local Government (Scotland) Act in Relation to Public Health. A Handy Guide for County and District Councillors, Medical Officers, Sanitary Inspectors, and Members of Parochial Boards. Second Edition. With a new Preface on appointment of Sanitary Officers. Crown 8vo, 2s.

SMITH. The Victory over Sin and Death gained by the Son of God for His people. The Teaching of the Lord Jesus during His Personal Ministry on Earth considered. By GEORGE S. SMITH, M.A., D.D., Minister of the Parish of Cranstoun, Mid-Lothian. Crown 8vo, 5s.

SMITH. Retrievers, and how to Break them. By Lieutenant-Colonel Sir HENRY SMITH, K.C.B. With an Introduction by Mr S. E. SHIRLEY, President of the Kennel Club. Dedicated by special permission to H.R.H. the Duke of York. With Illustrations. Crown 8vo, 5s.

SMITH. Greek Testament Lessons for Colleges, Schools, and Private Students, consisting chiefly of the Sermon on the Mount and the Parables of our Lord. With Notes and Essays. By the Rev. J. HUNTER SMITH, M.A., King Edward's School, Birmingham. Crown 8vo, 6s.

SMITH.

Thorndale; or, The Conflict of Opinions. By WILLIAM SMITH, Author of 'A Discourse on Ethics,' &c. New Edition. Crown 8vo, 10s. 6d.

Gravenhurst; or, Thoughts on Good and Evil. Second Edition. With Memoir and Portrait of the Author. Crown 8vo, 8s.

SNELL. The Fourteenth Century. "Periods of European Literature." By F. J. SNELL. Crown 8vo, 5s. net.

"SON OF THE MARSHES, A."

From Spring to Fall; or, When Life Stirs. By "A SON OF THE MARSHES." Cheap Uniform Edition. Crown 8vo, 3s. 6d.

Within an Hour of London Town: Among Wild Birds and their Haunts. Edited by J. A. OWEN. Cheap Uniform Edition. Cr. 8vo, 3s. 6d.

With the Woodlanders and by the Tide. Cheap Uniform Edition. Crown 8vo, 3s. 6d.

On Surrey Hills. Cheap Uniform Edition. Crown 8vo, 3s. 6d.

Annals of a Fishing Village. Cheap Uniform Edition. Crown 8vo, 3s. 6d.

SORLEY. The Ethics of Naturalism. Being the Shaw Fellowship Lectures, 1884. By W. R. SORLEY, M.A., Fellow of Trinity College, Cambridge, Professor of Moral Philosophy, University of Aberdeen. Crown 8vo, 6s.

SPIELMANN. Millais and his Works. By M. H. SPIELMANN, Author of 'History of Punch.' With 28 Full-page Illustrations. Large crown 8vo. Paper covers, 1s.; in cloth binding, 2s. 6d.

SPROTT. The Worship and Offices of the Church of Scotland. By GEORGE W. SPROTT, D.D., Minister of North Berwick. Crown 8vo, 6s.

STEEVENS.

With Kitchener to Khartum. By G. W. STEEVENS. With 8 Maps and Plans. Eighteenth Edition. Crown 8vo, 6s.

Egypt in 1898. With Illustrations. Crown 8vo, 6s.

STEEVENS.
> The Land of the Dollar. Third Edition. Crown 8vo, 6s.
> With the Conquering Turk. With 4 Maps. Demy 8vo, 10s. 6d.

STEPHENS.
> The Book of the Farm; detailing the Labours of the Farmer,
> Farm-Steward, Ploughman, Shepherd, Hedger, Farm-Labourer, Field-Worker,
> and Cattle-man. Illustrated with numerous Portraits of Animals and Engravings
> of Implements, and Plans of Farm Buildings. Fourth Edition. Revised, and
> in great part Re-written, by JAMES MACDONALD, F.R.S.E., Secretary Highland
> and Agricultural Society of Scotland. Complete in Six Divisional Volumes,
> bound in cloth, each 10s. 6d., or handsomely bound, in 3 volumes, with leather
> back and gilt top, £3, 3s.
> Catechism of Practical Agriculture. 22d Thousand. Revised
> by JAMES MACDONALD, F.R.S.E. With numerous Illustrations. Crown 8vo, 1s.
> The Book of Farm Implements and Machines. By J. SLIGHT
> and R. SCOTT BURN, Engineers. Edited by HENRY STEPHENS. Large 8vo, £2, 2s.

STEVENSON. British Fungi. (Hymenomycetes.) By Rev.
> JOHN STEVENSON, Author of 'Mycologia Scotica,' Hon. Sec. Cryptogamic Society
> of Scotland. Vols. I. and II., post 8vo, with Illustrations, price 12s. 6d. net each.

STEWART. Advice to Purchasers of Horses. By JOHN
> STEWART, V.S. New Edition. 2s. 6d.

STEWART. The Good Regent. A Chronicle Play. By Professor
> Sir T. Grainger Stewart, M.D., LL.D. Crown 8vo, 6s.

STODDART.
> John Stuart Blackie: A Biography. By ANNA M. STODDART.
> With 3 Plates. Third Edition. 2 vols. demy 8vo, 21s.
> POPULAR EDITION, with Portrait. Crown 8vo, 6s.
> Sir Philip Sidney: Servant of God. Illustrated by MARGARET
> L. HUGGINS. With a New Portrait of Sir Philip Sidney. Small 4to, with a
> specially designed Cover. 5s.

STORMONTH.
> Dictionary of the English Language, Pronouncing, Etymo-
> logical, and Explanatory. By the Rev. JAMES STORMONTH. Revised by the
> Rev. P. H. PHELP. Library Edition. New and Cheaper Edition, with Supple-
> ment. Imperial 8vo, handsomely bound in half morocco, 18s. net.
> Etymological and Pronouncing Dictionary of the English
> Language. Including a very Copious Selection of Scientific Terms. For use in
> Schools and Colleges, and as a Book of General Reference. The Pronunciation
> carefully revised by the Rev. P. H. PHELP, M.A. Cantab. Thirteenth Edition,
> with Supplement. Crown 8vo, pp. 800. 7s. 6d.
> The School Dictionary. New Edition, thoroughly Revised.
> By WILLIAM BAYNE. 16mo, 1s.

STORY. The Apostolic Ministry in the Scottish Church (The
> Baird Lecture for 1897). By ROBERT HERBERT STORY, D.D. (Edin.), F.S.A.
> Scot., Principal of the University of Glasgow, Principal Clerk of the General
> Assembly, and Chaplain to the Queen. Crown 8vo, 7s. 6d.

STORY.
> Poems. By W. W. Story, Author of 'Roba di Roma,' &c. 2
> vols. 7s. 6d.
> Fiammetta. A Summer Idyl. Crown 8vo, 7s. 6d.
> Conversations in a Studio. 2 vols. crown 8vo, 12s. 6d.
> Excursions in Art and Letters. Crown 8vo, 7s. 6d.
> A Poet's Portfolio: Later Readings. 18mo, 3s. 6d.

STRACHEY. Talk at a Country House. Fact and Fiction.
> By Sir EDWARD STRACHEY, Bart. With a portrait of the Author. Crown 8vo,
> 4s. 6d. net.

STURGIS. Little Comedies, Old and New. By JULIAN STURGIS.
Crown 8vo, 7s. 6d.

TAYLOR. The Story of my Life. By the late Colonel
MEADOWS TAYLOR, Author of 'The Confessions of a Thug,' &c., &c. Edited by
his Daughter. New and Cheaper Edition, being the Fourth. Crown 8vo, 6s.

THEOBALD. A Text-Book of Agricultural Zoology. By FRED.
V. THEOBALD, M.A. (Cantab.), F.E.S., Foreign Member of the Association of
Official Economic Entomologists, U.S.A., Zoologist to the S.E. Agricultural
College, Wye, &c. With numerous Illustrations. In 1 vol. crown 8vo.
                                                        [*In the press.*

THOMAS. The Woodland Life. By EDWARD THOMAS. With a
Frontispiece. Square 8vo, 6s.

THOMSON.
   The Diversions of a Prime Minister. By Basil Thomson.
   With a Map, numerous Illustrations by J. W. Cawston and others, and Repro-
   ductions of Rare Plates, from Early Voyages of Sixteenth and Seventeenth Cen-
   turies. Small demy 8vo, 15s.
   South Sea Yarns. With 10 Full-page Illustrations. Cheaper
   Edition. Crown 8vo, 3s. 6d.

THOMSON.
   Handy Book of the Flower-Garden : Being Practical Direc-
   tions for the Propagation, Culture, and Arrangement of Plants in Flower-
   Gardens all the year round. With Engraved Plans. By DAVID THOMSON,
   Gardener to his Grace the Duke of Buccleuch, K.T., at Drumlanrig. Fourth
   and Cheaper Edition. Crown 8vo, 5s.
   The Handy Book of Fruit-Culture under Glass : Being a
   series of Elaborate Practical Treatises on the Cultivation and Forcing of Pines,
   Vines, Peaches, Figs, Melons, Strawberries, and Cucumbers. With Engravings
   of Hothouses, &c. Second Edition, Revised and Enlarged. Crown 8vo, 7s. 6d.

THOMSON. A Practical Treatise on the Cultivation of the
Grape Vine. By WILLIAM THOMSON, Tweed Vineyards. Tenth Edition. 8vo, 5s.

THOMSON. Cookery for the Sick and Convalescent. With
Directions for the Preparation of Poultices, Fomentations, &c. By BARBARA
THOMSON. Fcap. 8vo, 1s. 6d.

THORBURN. Asiatic Neighbours. By S. S. THORBURN, Bengal
Civil Service, Author of 'Bannú; or, Our Afghan Frontier,' 'David Leslie :
A Story of the Afghan Frontier,' 'Musalmans and Money-Lenders in the Pan-
jab.' With Two Maps. Demy 8vo, 10s. 6d. net.

THORNTON. Opposites. A Series of Essays on the Unpopular
Sides of Popular Questions. By LEWIS THORNTON. 8vo, 12s. 6d.

TIELE. Elements of the Science of Religion. Part I.—Morpho-
logical. Part II.—Ontological. Being the Gifford Lectures delivered before the
University of Edinburgh in 1896-98. By C. P. TIELE, Theol. D., Litt.D. (Bonon.),
Hon. M.R.A.S., &c., Professor of the Science of Religion, in the University of
Leiden. In 2 vols. post 8vo, 7s. 6d. net. each.

TOKE. French Historical Unseens. For Army Classes. By
N. E. TOKE, B.A. Crown 8vo. 2s.

**TRANSACTIONS OF THE HIGHLAND AND AGRICUL-
TURAL** SOCIETY OF SCOTLAND. Published annually, price 5s.

TRAVERS.
   Windyhaugh. By GRAHAM TRAVERS (Margaret G. Todd,
   M.D.) Third Edition. Crown 8vo, 6s.
   Mona Maclean, Medical Student. A Novel. Thirteenth Edi-
   tion. Crown 8vo, 6s.
   Fellow Travellers. Fourth Edition. Crown 8vo, 6s.

TRYON. Life of Vice-Admiral Sir George Tryon, K.C.B. By
Rear-Admiral C. C. PENROSE FITZGERALD. Cheap Edition. With Portrait and
numerous Illustrations. Demy 8vo, 6s.

TULLOCH.

Rational Theology and Christian Philosophy in England in
the Seventeenth Century. By JOHN TULLOCH, D.D., Principal of St Mary's College in the University of St Andrews, and one of her Majesty's Chaplains in Ordinary in Scotland. Second Edition. 2 vols. 8vo, 16s.

Modern Theories in Philosophy and Religion. 8vo, 15s.

Luther, and other Leaders of the Reformation. Third Edition, Enlarged. Crown 8vo, 3s. 6d.

Memoir of Principal Tulloch, D.D, LL.D. By Mrs OLIPHANT,
Author of 'Life of Edward Irving.' Third and Cheaper Edition. 8vo, with Portrait, 7s. 6d.

TWEEDIE. The Arabian Horse: His Country and People.

By Major-General W. TWEEDIE, C.S.I., Bengal Staff Corps; for many years H.B.M.'s Consul-General, Baghdad, and Political Resident for the Government of India in Turkish Arabia. In one vol. royal 4to, with Seven Coloured Plates and other Illustrations, and a Map of the Country. Price £3, 3s. net.

TYLER. The Whence and the Whither of Man. A Brief History of his Origin and Development through Conformity to Environment. The Morse Lectures of 1895. By JOHN M. TYLER, Professor of Biology, Amherst College, U.S.A. Post 8vo, 6s. net.

VANDERVELL. A Shuttle of an Empire's Loom; or, Five Months before the Mast on a Modern Steam Cargo-Boat. By HARRY VANDERVELL. Crown 8vo, 6s.

VEITCH.

Memoir of John Veitch, LL.D., Professor of Logic and Rhetoric,
University of Glasgow. By MARY R. L. BRYCE. With Portrait and 3 Photogravure Plates. Demy 8vo, 7s. 6d.

Border Essays. By JOHN VEITCH, LL.D., Professor of Logic
and Rhetoric, University of Glasgow. Crown 8vo, 4s. 6d. net.

The History and Poetry of the Scottish Border: their Main
Features and Relations. New and Enlarged Edition. 2 vols. demy 8vo, 16s.

Institutes of Logic. Post 8vo, 12s. 6d. .

Merlin and other Poems. Fcap. 8vo, 4s. 6d.

Knowing and Being. Essays in Philosophy. First Series.
Crown 8vo, 5s.

Dualism and Monism; and other Essays. Essays in Philosophy. Second Series. With an Introduction by R. M. Wenley. Crown 8vo, 4s. 6d. net.

WACE. Christianity and Agnosticism. Reviews of some Recent Attacks on the Christian Faith. By HENRY WACE, D.D., late Principal of King's College, London; Preacher of Lincoln's Inn; Chaplain to the Queen. Second Edition. Post 8vo, 10s. 6d. net.

WADDELL. An Old Kirk Chronicle: Being a History of Auld-
hame, Tyninghame, and Whitekirk, in East Lothian. From Session Records, 1615 to 1850. By Rev. P. HATELY WADDELL, B.D., Minister of the United Parish. Small Paper Edition, 300 Copies. Price £1. Large Paper Edition, 50 Copies. Price, £1, 10s.

WALDO. The Ban of the Gubbe. By CEDRIC DANE WALDO.
Crown 8vo, 2s. 6d.

WALFORD. Four Biographies from 'Blackwood': Jane Taylor,
Hannah More, Elizabeth Fry, Mary Somerville. By L. B. WALFORD. Crown 8vo, 5s.

WARREN'S (SAMUEL) WORKS:—

Diary of a Late Physician. Cloth, 2s. 6d.; boards, 2s.

Ten Thousand A-Year. Cloth, 3s. 6d.; boards, 2s. 6d.

Now and Then. The Lily and the Bee. Intellectual and
Moral Development of the Present Age.' 4s. 6d.

Essays: Critical, Imaginative, and Juridical. 5s.

WENLEY.
Socrates and Christ: A Study in the Philosophy of Religion.
By R. M. WENLEY, M.A., D.Sc. D.Phil., Professor of Philosophy in the University of Michigan, U.S.A. Crown 8vo, 6s.
Aspects of Pessimism.   Crown 8vo, 6s.

WHITE.
The Eighteen Christian Centuries.   By the Rev. JAMES WHITE. Seventh Edition. Post 8vo, with Index, 6s.
History of France, from the Earliest Times.   Sixth Thousand.
Post 8vo, with Index, 6s.

WHITE.
Archæological Sketches in Scotland—Kintyre and Knapdale.
By Colonel T. P. WHITE, R.E., of the Ordnance Survey. With numerous Illustrations. 2 vols. folio, £4, 4s. Vol. I., Kintyre, sold separately, £2, 2s.
The Ordnance Survey of the United Kingdom.   A Popular Account. Crown 8vo, 5s.

WILKES.   Latin Historical Unseens.   For Army Classes.   By L. C. VAUGHAN WILKES, M.A   Crown 8vo, 2s.

WILLIAMSON.   The Horticultural Handbook and Exhibitor's Guide.   By W. WILLIAMSON, Gardener. Revised by MALCOLM DUNN, Gardener to his Grace the Duke of Buccleuch and Queensberry, Dalkeith Park. Cheap Edition. Crown 8vo, paper cover, 1s.

WILLS.   Behind an Eastern Veil.   A Plain Tale of Events occurring in the Experience of a Lady who had a unique opportunity of observing the Inner Life of Ladies of the Upper Class in Persia. By C. J. WILLS, Author of 'In the Land of the Lion and Sun,' 'Persia as it is,' &c., &c. Cheaper Edition. Demy 8vo, 5s.

WILSON.
Works of Professor Wilson.   Edited by his Son-in-Law, Professor FERRIER. 12 vols. crown 8vo, £2, 8s.
Christopher in his Sporting-Jacket.   2 vols., 8s.
Isle of Palms, City of the Plague, and other Poems.   4s.
Lights and Shadows of Scottish Life, and other Tales.   4s.
Essays, Critical and Imaginative.   4 vols., 16s.
The Noctes Ambrosianæ.   4 vols., 16s.
Homer and his Translators, and the Greek Drama.   Crown 8vo, 4s.

WORSLEY.
Homer's Odyssey.   Translated into English Verse in the Spenserian Stanza. By PHILIP STANHOPE WORSLEY, M.A. New and Cheaper Edition. Post 8vo, 7s. 6d. net.
Homer's Iliad.   Translated by P. S. Worsley and Prof. Conington. 2 vols. crown 8vo, 21s.

YATE.   England and Russia Face to Face in Asia.   A Record of Travel with the Afghan Boundary Commission. By Captain A. C. YATE, Bombay Staff Corps. 8vo, with Maps and Illustrations, 21s.

YATE.   Northern Afghanistan; or, Letters from the Afghan Boundary Commission.   By Colonel C. E. YATE, C.S.I., C.M.G., Bombay Staff Corps, F.R.G.S. 8vo, with Maps, 18s.

ZACK.   Life is Life, and other Tales and Episodes.   By ZACK.
Second Edition. Crown 8vo, 6s.

3/99.

www.ingramcontent.com/pod-product-compliance
Lightning Source LLC
Chambersburg PA
CBHW020940030726
47496CB00005B/1284